Lois and Pat -
Happy Chre
from Ange

Denis Green

GH00939443

MORE BY ACCIDENT

by

Denis Greenhill

First published in Great Britain in 1992

by

WILTON 65

Copyright Denis Greenhill

ISBN 0 947828 15 X

Typeset and Published
by
WILTON 65,
Bishop Wilton, York. YO4 1RY.

Printed and bound by Antony Rowe Ltd.,

TO ANGELA

DENIS GREENHILL
Official photograph taken when Head of the Diplomatic Service. It hangs with other pictures of Permanent Under Secretaries in the Foreign and Commonwealth Office.

MORE BY ACCIDENT

PREFACE

For most of our lives we look forward. It is sometimes with apprehension, sometimes with expectation, but more often with a mixture of both. Later in life the balance shifts and we more often look to the lessons of the past. We then encounter the phenomenon of the human memory which retrieves, in an entirely haphazard way, facts and impressions from times gone by. Those who have had the foresight and opportunity to keep records have great advantages. I am not one of those.

This book is therefore not an autobiography, nor is it a profound book involving a critique of foreign policy in which I was for long involved. It recounts many of the incidents in a long career which, if not unique, was not a usual one. As a railway apprentice, a Royal Engineer Officer in several theatres of war and as a British diplomat, I have played a part in the events which fundamentally changed the status of this country. In less than half a century it seemed near to disaster and moved from an empire of unprecedented power to a dependent U.S. ally and a reluctant European partner. During this time I have seen across the conference table, the majority of the statesmen who have made the headlines in the world and formed my own opinion of them. As Head of our Diplomatic Service, I was privy to the management of our international relations by British Government leaders of opposing views, differing styles and varying abilities and consequently was close to some of their successes and failures.

For four years, as an operating apprentice on the London North Eastern Railway, I got to know at the ground level, a large area of industrial Britain and worked with those who manned the industries, which were the core of our economic strength. This experience was dramatically widened by six years of war service in the Middle East, North Africa, Italy and the Far East, always a staff officer and never a battlefield soldier.

After the subsequent twenty seven years in the Diplomatic Service, I was appointed to the boards of several British companies with large international interests. In addition, I joined the Upper House of Parliament. This course of events has given me an unusually broad acquaintance and friendship with persons of all ranks and many nationalities. From them I hope I have learned much and developed a balanced and unprejudiced outlook. In this book I have set down some personal views and memories, sometimes trivial and amusing and occasionally of importance.

It is perhaps natural that my major interest remains with international affairs. It is not possible to forecast the shape of things to come. My great regret is that I cannot know how the events in which I have participated will eventually unfold.

In 1973, when I retired as Head of the British Diplomatic Service, it was still attracting the best students, male and female from our universities. But their responsibilities in the future are likely to be fundamentally different. One has only to compare a photograph of the League of Nations Assembly in 1935 with a picture of the United Nations General Assembly in 1991. The means of conducting foreign affairs have already been revolutionised and may well be unrecognisable in the first quarter of the 21st Century if the opportunities created by recent events are realised. What influence will this country then exercise and who will be the personalities who wield it? What is certain is that the human resources not only of this country but of the world will be taxed in a way which is presently unimaginable.

ACKNOWLEDGEMENTS

I would like to thank the many friends and colleagues, British and foreign, who have helped me remember past events. Mr. Charles E. Courtney of the United States Embassy in London, and Sir Roger Cary of the B.B.C. have been of special help as well as David Jones and his staff of the House of Lords Library and Richard Bone of the Foreign and Commonwealth Office Library. The secretarial work and typing have been admirably managed by Alison Stanistreet. Without the help of Angela's memory I am sure many things might have been missed, and her help in sorting the illustrations has been invaluable. I am deeply indebted to Helga Auberjonois for the Index and to her and her husband Fernand for much wise general advice, and to Marcella Spencer for invaluable assistance in proof reading. I am especially grateful to Richard and Diana Holderness who have put their considerable publishing experience willingly at my disposal. Where possible I have acknowledged the photographer of the illustrations. If I have not done so in every case it is due to my inability to contact them and I would ask their forgiveness for any omission. Very special thanks are due to Roy Still, the artist responsible for the caricature on the dust jacket.

iv

CONTENTS

ILLUSTRATIONS

CHAPTER 1

EARLY DAYS AND FAMILY CONNECTIONS

I have no recollection of the house in which I was born in South Woodford shortly before the outbreak of World War I. My first memories of the outside world are of Southbourne on Sea, Hampshire in 1916/7. My mother had moved there with my elder brother prompted by the certainty that my father, then in army training at Aldershot, would be posted overseas. There were relatives in the district who could be of assistance in the event of the worst happening to him. In any case it was seen as a quiet, safe and inexpensive seaside place for a family to live in the uncertain days of the war.

My father was duly posted to East Africa where the campaign against the enterprising German General von Lettow Vorbeck was drawing to a close. For the next two years we were on our own. Nowadays childhood recollections would be fortified by photographs and often movies. But these are not available and the responsibility is thrown back on personal memory and family legend. Isolated incidents only remain in my mind. I can remember refusing to say goodbye to my father and preferring to shelter under the dining room table. I can recall watching the grooming of army horses at the local depot, crowding to see one of the first tanks, observing a damaged freighter being towed across Bournemouth bay until its back broke and it sank leaving two masts to mark its grave. An excursion to Poole harbour to see the first concrete ship has left a lasting impression. Memorable also was an Australian soldier in traditional hat bending down to speak into the ear of a frightened horse fallen on the tramlines and coaxing it to get up when all others had failed. Finally, slowly pushing as close as we dared to the exuberant Armistice celebration in the Square at nearby Bournemouth on November 11th 1918.

Whilst we were in Southbourne we found lodgings with a family named Clarke who were modest builders and decorators. Mrs. Clarke, a jolly friendly lady, came from Somerset. Her two sons and three daughters were all old enough to be in the Services. The house was full of the comings and goings of young people in uniform. I remember a sudden great sadness when the soldier son died from the effects of poison gas. Money and food were short for all of us but there was much laughter and kindness amongst the problems of the war.

There were other lonely wives and many widows in the neighbourhood.

My mother made a particular friend of a Mrs. Elton, lately returned from India whose husband had earlier been killed in the Middle East. Her small son Charles became our constant companion and a life long friend. He became an officer on Blue Funnel ships and I met up with him in Algiers in 1943 when he was commanding a small Royal Naval vessel. The two mothers cooperated to provide care and amusement for us and give mutual aid in cases of childish illnesses. The local G.P. Dr. Littlejohn, operated his own N.H.S. At no time were we charged for visits and attendance. For us boys our 'exile' in Southbourne was not an unhappy time.

Soon after the Armistice my mother brought us back from Southbourne to live with her parents in Walthamstow until my father could return from Africa to resume his peace time job in the City and re-establish a new home.

My maternal grandfather, Arthur Mathews, was well known in Free Church circles and local government. I never knew precisely how he earned his living at the local Town Hall and that was certainly not his main interest. He was first and foremost a dedicated Free Church man, a Temperance worker, an active lay preacher and a leader in a local community organisation called the 'Men's Own Brotherhood.' This was established in a deprived part of Walthamstow and, over the years, grew into a substantial church known as the Mathews Memorial Church. He had long white hair and a large moustache. He addressed all men with sincerity as "brother" and it was not until I worked for the Labour Foreign Secretary, George Brown, that I heard again this method of address so widely used. For my brother and me my grandfather was an awesome but kindly figure with the Bible always within reach and an embarrassing tendency to pray aloud. Although his house was spacious he had very little money. My mother in years to come, ruefully reminded us that his wedding present to her had been two guineas. From the fourth floor balcony of his house, which commanded a panoramic view of the Lea Valley, my grandparents had watched a German Zeppelin vainly seeking to evade the searchlight beam, until it sank slowly down to a sensational fiery crash at Cuffley. It was a story they loved to relate to their two small grandsons. My mother was one of three sisters and one brother, who always remained close to us. Three times he contested unsuccessfully as a Liberal candidate for Parliament but was an Essex County Alderman for many years.

My mother was a very kindly person but averse to formal entertaining. A more loving mother we could not have wished for. My brother Brian was three years my senior and my sister Barbara came nine years after me. Barbara was not born until after we had returned from Southbourne and were well established in Woodford. We were always a happy family for which our mother was largely responsible. She extended her love and care to our families after our marriages, which have all been successful. It has always been a sadness for me that World War II not only separated us but deprived my mother of much of the comfort, modest luxury and peace of mind which my father's success in the City was enabling her to enjoy in her later years. Nor must their housekeeper for many years, Miss Muriel Bevis be forgotten. She stayed on after my mother's death, until my father died in 1965. My brother and I were able to provide for her until she died many years later.

My brother Brian and I were always good friends. My reliance on him was never misplaced. After the outbreak of war, we were separated for four years, but later were always in close touch. For those outside our family, he had an unusual gift for friendship and secured, without effort, the confidence of all sorts and conditions of people. He was a most adept helper of 'lame dogs over stiles' and his counsel was widely sought. After retirement from the City, he entered local government politics as a Conservative, with considerable success and was a popular chairman of Epping Forest Rural District Council. Some years later I was introduced in the House of Commons to Stan Newens, the left wing M.P. for Harlow with whom my brother had had frequent contact in local government. He recognised my name and greatly pleased me by paying a very warm tribute to him. He concluded his eulogy by saying, "You know, he wasn't really a Conservative."

My sister Barbara, well known locally for her horsemanship. married Ben Symes, a Dorset born wartime naval officer, who became a tenant farmer on one of the Queen's College Oxford farms on the Isle of Wight. She had served in the WAAF during the war and had seen the Luftwaffe from the exacting position of a 'filter plotter' at Fighter Command. At their farm on leave in my Whitehall days, I enjoyed amateur harrowing after their hay harvest.

My father returned to us from Africa late one wet winter evening in 1919. Together with my mother we impatiently watched from our bedroom for him coming up the hill from the railway station towards the house and identified him as he walked into the light of a street lamp. Red letter days were to follow. First, a visit to Hamley's in Regent Street for my brother and me to pick any toy of our choice and second the unpacking of his metal tropical trunks. The latter contained leopard skins, small ivory elephants, wooden carvings and so on. To us they seemed rare and exciting. His discarded uniforms and elaborate solar topees provided dressing up materials for many years to come. His camp bed was called into service for visiting guests.

It did not seem too long before a new home in South Woodford was available. Even on a small salary, which would seem unbelievably derisory today my father was able to secure a Victorian terrace house, gas lit, with two interconnecting sitting rooms, a dining room, four large bedrooms and an attic bedroom. There was also a spacious cellar. The kitchen looked onto a tiled scullery with a large 'copper' separately fired for the weekly wash. The garden contained William pear trees, white heart cherry trees, a conservatory and a dilapidated wooden summer house capped with dense ivy. Adjoining was a sizeable vegetable garden with raspberry and currant bushes and with room for potatoes, beans, peas and marrows. Eggs came from a neighbour. It was all sufficiently rural for a wide variety of butterflies and moths to be found during the summer months. There was ample space to live and play. We could afford a resident maid who came from a private orphanage run by strongly religious friends of my grandfather.

We were very happy in this house and I am grateful to my parents. I would be wrong to say that as children we were not aware of financial restraints. We did not suffer hardships but we lacked many of the amenities that we knew were enjoyed by some of our contemporaries. I can recall my father's insistence on the prompt payment of bills and his refusal to pay for luxuries by instalments. An exception was made when an expensive new edition of Chambers encyclopedia was published from which he wanted us to benefit. The lack of a car was a long disappointment. Just when it appeared likely to be overcome my father paid for a car for one of his brothers whose business had failed and for whom a car was essential for him to start again. When I protested he asked if I would refuse to help my brother.

My father commuted, bowler hatted, each day to the City from the Great Eastern Railway station at George Lane about seven or eight minutes walk from home. This station served the less affluent part of Woodford and by the time the morning rush hour trains reached it from Woodford, Buckhurst Hill, Loughton and Epping the majority of the first class seats were taken by season ticket holders. Two or three shabby horse drawn cabs, the cast offs of a previous generation of gentry, met the returning commuters in the evening and, in an emergency, for two shillings my father could take one. The cabs started with a brief trot but were soon reduced to a walk on the slight incline over the last half mile.

Although South Woodford had a 'London E18' postmark it was not a typical East London suburb and could not be considered as a part of the 'East End' as it is commonly understood. Most men worked in the city or in businesses en route often associated with the huge Port of London. Stratford lay between South Woodford and the City and my mother used its department stores instead of the longer journey to London's West End. The direct road to the City lay through Whitechapel which was still the Jewish quarter of London. All suburbs were beginning to expand and new houses at sometimes substantially less than £500 were common. But Woodford was happily protected from the worst of urban sprawls by the existence of Epping Forest under the effective administration of the City of London Corporation. Woodford Green had all the characteristic of a village green and was the scene of Saturday cricket matches in summer. In 1926 during the General Strike it was used as a distribution point for milk brought up from the Essex and Hertfordshire farms. I remember watching with fascination, the great activity.

My paternal grandfather, Samuel Greenhill was a very different man from Arthur Mathews my mother's father, with whom we had been living in Walthamstow. Samuel Greenhill had married twice. Both his wives had died by the time we returned from Southbourne. My father was one of the youngest of eight children by his first wife and his second wife was the mother of a further six by him. I have no recollection of him and indeed I am not sure I ever saw him. He was a coach builder by trade and was manager of that department at the Army and Navy Stores until he set up his own business in Saffron Walden in Essex. He had the dubious distinction of being involved, in February 1899, in the first fatal motor car accident in England. A Daimler car, on a test drive with the manufacturer's driver overturned on Grove Hill, Harrow, killing two of the occupants. My grandfather, one of them, escaped. I have a photograph of him standing by the wrecked car with its collapsed wooden spoked wheels.

According to an article in Picture Post in the nineteen thirties, my grandfather afterwards explained the cause to the Press in the following terms, "The driver (Sewell) mapped out a splendid course down the hill, scarcely swerving at all from a direct line. We were travelling at about 20 m.p.h. Someone shouted at Sewell not to go so fast but he didn't seem to hear. His face was beaming with confidence. He made a beautiful curve to turn round the bend, when the tyre flew off and the wheel collapsed."
Mr. Sewell, who was one of those killed, could well have served as a model for Mr. Toad.

A coach built by my grandfather is in a museum in Florida, but I failed to go and see it when I lived in the U.S. My father was extremely reticent about his childhood. There was cause of great bitterness in the family, the precise nature of which he could never be persuaded to speak. My grandfather married as his second wife, the girl friend of one of his sons, who emigrated at once to Australia. Another son fled to Canada rather than face his father after having crashed a car belonging to the company to which he was apprenticed.

When his mother was dying, my father was sent away with a brother to stay with friends who treated them with great kindness. However, their hosts refrained from telling them when their mother died. The two little boys returned home only to find that there was no one to whom they could tell of their happy time. An experience my father claimed never to forget.

The net result of this was that my father seemed only to have had a brief education up to the age of fifteen or sixteen, partly in a school in Saffron Walden where my grandfather carried on his craft in a spacious workshop at the back of an inn in the main street. After leaving school, with no help from his father but with encouragement from a former schoolmaster, my father undertook his own education. Back in London he read very widely and whilst working in low paid employment took advantage of every facility for adult education which the capital could offer, including Birkbeck College. He eventually secured a post in Parr's Bank which offered some prospects. When he informed his father with some pride, he was told that, "Banks are good places for fools. " He retired more than forty years later as Deputy Chief General Manager of the Westminster Bank and was Deputy Chairman of the Anglo-Portuguese Bank in the City. There is little doubt in my mind that had he enjoyed a university education he would have excelled. He made it his unspoken ambition that his family would have the best education he could afford. My brother and I both went to Oxford University and he lived long enough to see his grandsons, Nigel and Robin, win scholarships to Westminster School and to Christ Church and New College. He had a passion for clean shoes. When late in life I called on him at his house he quickly relieved me of my shoes and handed them to the gardener for a thoroughly professional shine, or did it himself. Tall, good looking and always well turned out he was nevertheless rather a solitary man and did not seem to feel the need for a wide circle of friends. I still retain the small Bible which he carried with him in Africa with carefully marked passages - evidence of study and reflection.

There was in fact a link between the Greenhill family and Trinity College Oxford and Sidney Sussex Cambridge which, but for the fecklessness of our forefathers could have solved many of our financial problems of education.

There is a monument in the Parish Church of Abbots Langley to the memory of Mrs. Anne Coombe daughter of Thomas Greenhill who died in 1641. It records that the will of Anne Coombe and her husband (they died without issue) gave 'the manor of Abbots Langley and certain lands to Sidney Sussex College Cambridge and Trinity College Oxford for the education in piety and learning of his own and his wife's kindred for ever.' The Greenhill family foolishly took no advantage of this for more than 200 years. In 1913 the two colleges together succeeded in a complicated legal action against the Greenhill family in appropriating for their own purposes, the money involved. A senior member of Trinity College once told me that they might, in spite of the legal action, have given some special consideration to my sons had it been necessary. Whether any member of the family will seek in future a favour from either college remains to be seen.

To prepare for the legal action against the two colleges it was necessary to research for details of the family ancestry. This permitted a family tree to be drawn up which incidentally traced the family connection with the Harrow area back to the 15th Century and possibly earlier. We have farm account books recording transactions as far back as the late 17th Century. These researches revealed certain matters of unusual interest. In 1698 Thomas Greenhill 'chirurgeon' of London petitioned the Earl Marshall, being the thirty-ninth child and seventh son of one father by one mother, 'that he might be allowed a difference in his Arms to be borne by him in commemoration thereof.' This request was granted.

The researches also revealed a family link with John Greenhill (1640/76) portrait painter and pupil of Lely, some of whose portraits are in the Dulwich Picture Gallery. His self portrait bears a striking likeness to my elder son and through the kindness of Lord Shawcross the Gallery loaned it to me to hang in my office when I was Permanent Under Secretary at the Foreign Office. Fortunately no link was shown with Bob Greenhill the notorious Australian convict murderer and cannibal who came significantly from Middlesex, perhaps Harrow. Details of his infamous exploits are set out in *Fatal Shore* by Robert Hughes, which records the history of the early convict settlement of Australia.

CHAPTER 2

EDUCATION, SCHOOL AND OXFORD

We settled very happily in our home in South Woodford. It is only in retrospect that I can appreciate the sacrifices that my parents made. It is true that my father had a safe job and was making good progress but neither he nor my mother had any money behind them. Indeed, it was necessary for both to give subsidies to their parents and some relatives. Our parents were nevertheless able to send us to the best local preparatory school. This was in the hands of two elderly sisters, Fanny and Rhoda Crump - two ladies of gentle birth and strong character. We were sent there as day boys, equipped in slightly bizarre uniforms. Its most noticeable feature was a baggy blue cap reminiscent of Don Bradman's Test headgear. The journey to school on foot involved intersecting a stream of less fortunate children on the way to the local state Board school. This was a hazard as baggy blue caps were a target for a snatch by the underprivileged. We had to time the crossing of our paths to avoid being hopelessly outnumbered. The teaching at the Crump regime was good but the staff was female and no games were available. There was an annual sports day with three-legged races including an egg and spoon race. In one year I came second in the latter having lost first place by turning at the last moment to see how close was my nearest rival. It was a useful lesson never to be forgotten.

The school fortunately was purchased by a retired ex-Colonel W. H. Colley, a bachelor from York. He rapidly and successfully transformed it into a high class prep school capable of preparing boys for competitive common entrance and training them in the traditional games. In the latter, my brother had considerable success. I did not. Colonel Colley assembled a good staff and was himself an excellent teacher using methods derived from his old schools, St. Peters York and Uppingham. He appreciated the value of a good sporting reputation. He helped to start the local Woodford Rugby Club, which soon greatly prospered and whose members were potential parents for future pupils. The academic record of the school was also satisfactory and a steady stream of boys went to Haileybury, Felsted and Uppingham and to lesser known public schools like Chigwell, Forest and Bishop's Stortford. The last named was my father's choice for us. It had developed from 1868 into a public school from a Nonconformist Grammar School. The link continued with the Nonconformist Church of which my parents were regular members. The Colonel had established good relations with these public schools which were comparatively near at hand and our teams played their 'under fourteen sides' at cricket and rugby.

My brother was first to go to Bishop's Stortford. He did well and I followed a few years later. I surprisingly won a modest scholarship. My success was due at least in part to the fortuitous accident that the unseen Latin translation, a 'make or break' paper, happened to be a piece which I had encountered during the period of cramming before the exam.

My five years at Bishop's Stortford were happy. Not for the first time in my life my elder brother made things easier for me at the start. Thanks to him I experienced less of the disturbing novelty which some apprehensive new boarders undergo. I was lucky also as my brother was one of the school's best athletes. The tone of the school was good with none of the abuses so beloved by latter day journalists and novelists. The core of the staff were men of character, sympathy and professional skill. This was in part due to the school's strong links with the Nonconformist church. The headmaster for most of my time was F. S. Young, an athlete, scholar and climber. He remained at the school for many years and on retirement took Holy Orders. Our housemaster F. Sutton and his wife were especially sympathetic. W. J. Strachan the language master became, after retirement, a well known lecturer, translator and art collector. He was still lecturing at the Victoria and Albert Museum and elsewhere at the age of 87. But this link also had some disadvantages. The governing body had narrow horizons and funds for capital expenditure were scarce. There was, for religious reasons, no Officer Training Corps which distinguished us from the majority of other public schools. The school's athletic successes at Oxford and Cambridge were infrequent although the families of Price and Doggart secured wide fame in cricket, rugby and hockey in the mid war years. Our school excelled in the nineteen thirties in the inter-school swimming contests at the Bath Club in London. A professional coach came to Bishop's Stortford weekly and his efforts were reflected in exceptional results for a small school. The design of the war memorial chapel was uncharacteristically entrusted to the controversial architect Clough Williams Ellis and over the years its other buildings were greatly expanded.

Not many Stortford boys then went to Oxbridge. At a singularly fortunate time my father received a dramatic rise in salary and my brother was able to go to Queen's College Oxford, three years ahead of me. When my time came the masters considered it was just worth my trying for a history scholarship and in any case, colleges would more likely accept one for entry in the event of failure to win an award. My best friend Barry Douglas won an Exhibition to St. Catherine's College Cambridge in modern languages. I tried two 'groups' at Oxford without success but Christ Church and another college offered me a place. I opted for Christ Church although it was pointed out to me that it was large and its members often much wealthier than we were. But an admired member of my old school, (Sir) Dick White, later Head of MI5 and MI6 had done well there earlier and was an athletic blue. This reassured me.

During one of the scholarship exams in Keble Hall, the candidates were seated alphabetically at separate tables. At my table for the H's and G's I found myself facing David Hunt from Rugby school and was discouraged by the avidity with which he tackled the papers. Later he was first a don, then a distinguished military intelligence officer and finally a highly valued colleague in the Diplomatic Service. He also gained wide public fame by becoming an early winner of the BBC Mastermind competition. It was clear to me from the time of the exam that he could not fail to have a successful career.

I look back at my time at Oxford with pleasure but with many regrets. I enjoyed myself in an inconspicuous way and made several good friends, whose careers have happily crossed my path most of my later life. Amongst them was Michael Maclagan the distinguished genealogist and herald and vice president of Trinity College. He was also one of the most successful mayors of Oxford City. Others were the late Stormont (Lord) Mancroft at one time the most popular after dinner speaker in London, Alan Campbell-Johnson whose writings on the independence of the Indian subcontinent are invaluable source papers now lodged in Southampton University. Brigadier Michael Gordon-Watson of the Irish Guards was Military Attaché at the Embassy in Washington during the time we were there. I am ashamed that I failed to take advantage of the wide opportunities at the university which foolishly I did not recognise and I did not then appreciate. I did not, for example, ever speak at the Union, but I attended often and was present at the famous 'King and Country' debate and voted in a patriotic way. Some of the then leaders of the Union - John Boyd Carpenter, Max Beloff, Jo Grimond and Christopher Mayhew - I now regularly see in the House of Lords. Their distinguished manner of speaking remains much as it was then and bears the stamp of Union training. I saw Oswald Mosley at his memorable meeting in the Carfax Assembly rooms when in the fracas Frank Pakenham was allegedly converted to socialism by a blow on the head by a chair. Although I was a member of political clubs I refused to join the communist October Club, which was actively seeking members. Also busily recruiting, but for the Christian Union, was Trevor Huddleston a fellow undergraduate at Christ Church, later to become the famous anti-apartheid archbishop. He approached me an hour after my first arrival in College.

Generally speaking I was, it must be admitted, far too diffident. It took my immediately post-university career and a measure of success in the war to give me the confidence which would have been such an asset ten years earlier.

Nor did I use the vacations for language learning, as I should have done, although I spent them in Germany and Italy. I watched Mussolini address a hysterical crowd from the balcony in the Piazza Venezia in Rome and saw at close range the first Nazi marchings. I did so without a full realisation of their sinister possibilities. The well organised youth hostels in Germany were wonderful value. Week after week on a tandem bicycle, a friend, John Hennell from school and Queen's College and I toured for virtually nothing. The tandem seemed to be a novelty to young Germans and it was easy to make friends.

The history dons at Christ Church, Dr. Keith Feiling and J.C. Masterman were both very prominent in Oxford but also influential outside the University. The latter is described in Lord Annan's book *'Our Age* as 'the capo of the Christ Church mafia.' Later in Whitehall I found how often he was consulted by Ministers about public appointments. A much less prominent don was Patrick Gordon-Walker, a comparatively new Student (Fellow) at the college. I was frequently his pupil. His helpful tutorials were conducted usually in a striking dressing gown and in a rather lackadaisical manner. After a year or so I was called to see the Senior Censor. He explained that the extension of Gordon-Walker's appointment was under discussion by the college authorities. Was he, the Censor asked indoctrinating me in his left wing politics? I was affronted to be approached in this way and said that I thought I could be left to look after myself. Frank Pakenham (later Lord Longford) was also a don at Christ Church. I was never his pupil, and came to know him later when he was a Cabinet Minister in Labour Governments and a member of the House of Lords.

Many years later Gordon-Walker and I met again when after the Election of 1964, he was very briefly Foreign Secretary and I was a senior officer in the Department. As in his room at Oxford, at our first meeting in the Foreign Office, we sat for some time on either side of the fireplace in the Foreign Secretary's historic office and he talked to me very much as if I was his pupil again. Later after he had failed to win a seat in Parliament for the second time in three months he was crossing St. James Park in despair, followed by a mob of photographers and newsmen calling for pictures and comment. Suddenly his private detective turned and stopped the group with the words

"Don't you know when to leave a man alone?"

They slunk off. By some horrible chance I arrived at the House of Lords one day in 1980 and saw his body driven away to Westminster mortuary in the taxi in which he had just collapsed and died.

In my time at Oxford it was still expected that undergraduates would attend many lectures. Those of Dr. Feiling were almost too scholarly for me. One week I was hard pressed to finish an essay for him and borrowed a lot of the material from Winston Churchill's Life of Marlborough. When I had finished reading it to him he said,

"You took that from Chapter 6 of Churchill's book".

I admitted the plagiarism.

"I know" he said, "because I wrote it."

Masterman on the other hand was clear, practical and targeted squarely on your final exams. My special subject was by chance colonial history, shared with my close New Zealand friend, Antony Riddiford, whose family had first settled there in 1849. The lectures of Professors Coupland and Harlow at Rhodes House on this subject captured my imagination and eventually had some influence on the choice of my post war career. For recreation I played a certain amount of rugby football and very little cricket. The most memorable part of the latter were the long white trousers worn by Eric Gray an Australian classical scholar who certified them as over a century old. After a distinguished war career in Greece he returned to the University as a don. When the trousers were taken out of service I do not know.

I emerged from Oxford in 1935 with a respectable second class degree but little else to recommend me to potential employers. It is not surprising therefore that few things gave me greater pleasure in my life than being made an Honorary Student (Fellow) of Christ Church in 1977. I often have doubts about the vaunted Oxford tutorial system as practised in my own and indeed in my son's period at Christ Church. All of us would have benefited from closer supervision and more regular guidance but no doubt the fault was ours. It was due in part to the size of the college but in my three years I do not think Dean White addressed a single word to me after our initial introduction.

In the traditional way I went to the Christ Church Commemoration Ball at the end of my last term. I invited as my partner an American, Lucy Young, the daughter of a former Governor of California. I have remained in touch with her and her family ever since. Angela and I have visited them in their house in Pasadena when we were posted in the U.S.

Twice during my time at school and university I was invited to the annual Duke of York's camp at Southwold. It was cleverly organised by the Industrial Society to bring together public school and 'industrial' boys. On the whole it achieved its objective, now outdated. Occasional errors of judgment were made as, for example, when one of the most prominent public school participants, later a Lord Mayor of London, was fetched away on the last day, before the eyes of all, by his parents' chauffeur, in a large open touring Rolls Royce.

CHAPTER 3

CHOICE OF CAREERS

With 'finals' behind me the search for a job began in earnest. The Oxford Appointments Board was an amateurish body but there was no shortage of jobs. Masterman's reference for me said that I was 'more likely to succeed in commerce than in the civil service.' The civil service had no attractions for me, nor had the City where my father's connections might have been of help. I was especially attracted by the graduate recruitment schemes of large companies, particularly Unilever which was an obviously successful company with international ramifications. I applied unsuccessfully. I suspect due in part to my failure to reply sufficiently aggressively to the questions of how much I expected to earn when I was thirty years of age. I was told recently that this question was still put to applicants in the nineteen eighties. A university friend simultaneously applied and cycled from his London home to the interview. He attributed his rejection to his failure to remove his cycle clips before facing the Board of Directors.

We both finally settled for joining the London North Eastern Railway as 'Traffic Apprentices' or graduate trainees. The starting salary was a little below Unilever but the idea of three years moving around the railway system, in parts of the U.K. unknown to me, was attractive. There was also a not negligible 'perk' in the form of reduced fares for private journeys at home and overseas. The medical officer of the company was ready to accept me solely, it appeared, on the basis of my ability to distinguish between a green and a red signal. I was assigned for my first three months instruction to Armley Station near Leeds. At the same time I was handed a copy of the Railway Rule Book. Some of the rules read quaintly for present day commuters. Rule number 164 says 'When a deficiency of room occurs in a train on the journey a Guard must advise the Station Master who must take steps, as may be necessary to have the train strengthened.' Rule number 2 (iii) is equally severe 'When on duty be neat in appearance and, where supplied, wear uniform, number and badge.' It was my introduction to the industrial north of England. It was September 1935 and the country was just beginning to pull out of the worst of the Great Depression. Rusting workshops, deserted textile mills and idle miners crouching at street corners were still a common sight. A vivid picture still remains in my mind of Newcastle station where I saw a poverty stricken couple seeing off their small son to an unknown future at the Fairbridge Schools in Australia. All his wordly possessions were contained in a very small pack on his back. I prayed he would succeed. Another apprentice named Dunman, a son of the manse, had preceded me at Armley. Shortly afterwards he left the company and in later years became one of the chief organisers of the British Communist Party. He had obviously spent a good deal of time arguing with the Armley staff, which included an active communist and an evangelising Christian. The arguments still rumbled on whilst I was there.

The station yard was swept by a former plate layer who had lost his leg whilst working on the many crisscrossing lines near Leeds station. It had been a foggy Saturday morning and he was standing in for a mate who wanted to go to a football match. The injustice of the accident had affected his brain. He carried with him a constantly changing record of the total sum that he had lost in his weekly wage packet over the intervening years since the accident. He was unkindly teased and was always on the look out for someone new, like myself, to whom he could re-tell his melancholy tale.

At the end of the three months the first report on me was made by the station master, Mr. Pedley, to the Headquarters in London. He showed it to me. Its central verdict was, 'He is a good timekeeper.' It seemed unlikely to carry me very far, but I have tried hard to maintain this reputation ever since. The training programme for an apprentice included evening courses in economics and law at Leeds University, Manchester University and the London School of Economics. In addition technical courses including signalling were obligatory. But the main activity was to gain experience by day and night in the work in every aspect of railway operating activity. We lived in digs and worked over the three years in virtually every industrial town in North East England. All these places and their condition were new to me. My family had been entirely protected from the effect of the Industrial Depression by my father's success in the City. Our standard of living had steadily improved. We had moved house twice from South Woodford, first to Buckhurst Hill and then to Ashfields, a handsome and well situated house, much admired by Nikolaus Pevsner, on the edge of Epping Forest at Loughton. Two minutes walk from the front gate carried one deep into the forest where one was immediately alone. On an exceptionally clear day the dome of St. Paul's could be seen from a nearby point of vantage. My father was driven daily to the City in his large Buick saloon. The days of company cars had not yet arrived. Our beautiful garden was maintained by a gardener and his boy assistant. During my railway apprenticeship I was seldom at home, but this house was a most welcome refuge from the north. It was, in later years, much loved by our children who admitted that when they felt homesick at boarding school, it was for my father's house, not for our own.

The England that my railway career revealed was fascinating and disturbing. By the time war came I felt I knew a great deal about my country. The four years spent on the railway were more important to my education than the three years at Oxford. The railwaymen with whom I daily and nightly mixed were friendly people, proud of their industry and their status amongst working people. Moving every few weeks from one digs to another was sometimes amusing but often irksome. I was silenced by the landlady who, when rebuked for serving a cockroach in my breakfast, retorted that considering the number of them I was lucky to get only one. Called to mediate between a tearful middle-aged landlady in Leeds and a commercial traveller from Manchester who had long deceived her, I failed to solve their dispute by assuring them both that there were plenty more fish in the sea. One of my pleasantest memories is of a very old Welsh lady in Penyfford who charged me seventeen shillings a week and served her home made wine with supper.

Long day and night talks in marshalling yards, signal boxes and on goods trains shattered beneficially many of my preconceptions. Although their weekly wage packet seldom exceeded £6 and was often less, I was surprised to find, especially in Scotland, how many railwaymen owned their own houses and whose children by scholastic success were moving into the professional classes. In the North the railway was a 'family' industry. Members of the staff were more often than not related. The 'old boy net' worked powerfully at the lowest and highest levels. To be referred to as a 'railwayman' was a compliment in those circles.

There were inevitably 'no go' areas for graduate apprentices. For example, the appearance of one of us on the dock of the goods depot at Ardwick Manchester was a signal for all to stop work until one's purpose was ascertained. On my arrival in Sheffield I was advised by the local manager to avoid a certain militant goods guard who was clearly described to me. Some weeks later I climbed on to a guards van as a train was slowly leaving a small colliery. On entering the van I found myself face to face with a man who was unmistakably the guard in question. After mutual introductions we travelled slowly together towards Sheffield. He proved to be a friend of Bernard Shaw and carried with him in the van a small portable library in which I noticed inter alia two volumes of Walter Bagehot. I spent an interesting and useful afternoon, not unlike a university tutorial.

There were of course, mixed experiences, but from a distance of fifty years my recollections are, both at work and in lodgings, mainly of kindness.

The training was interesting to me. The management of the LNER was, on the whole, conservative. They seemed more interested in 'playing trains' and in engineering than in making money for the shareholders. Most of the talent went to the operating side of the company and commercial objectives took second place. A Central Timing Office for the system was one of the operating innovations. The introduction in 1935 of 'The Silver Jubilee' express between London and Newcastle (in four hours) drawn by streamlined locos of Sir Nigel Gresley's design was highly successful and widely acclaimed. In 1936 a similar train to Edinburgh accomplished the journey in six hours. The chairman of the LNER was William Whitelaw, the grandfather of the present Viscount Whitelaw, with whom I worked in Whitehall during the Heath Administration and subsequently. But commercial enterprise on the railways began to show more clearly on the rival London Midland and Scottish system where Sir Josiah (later Lord) Stamp had taken control. By instituting revolutionary and simpler rates for parcels and goods he was clearly indicating that the company was determined to make money. It was the time when the impact of road transport was beginning to be felt and the government assisted the railways by restricting the freedom of individual enterprise on the roads by bullying and restrictive licensing legislation. I attended several 'courts' in which road transport licences were granted or withheld by government appointed officials. I watched with dismay the enterprise of the 'little man' mercilessly eliminated.

It was customary during the summer season to send an apprentice to act as relief or assistant Station Master to fill a holiday vacancy. One of my most enjoyable was a spell at Great Ponton on the main London-Edinburgh line just north of the Stoke Tunnel at the top of the gradient which leads down to Grantham station. Not more than four passenger trains per day stopped at Great Ponton. But twenty four hours of the day the great expresses and important freight trains could be seen puffing strongly up the gradient to Stoke Tunnel or accelerating spectacularly down the hill to Grantham. Trains have always attracted the clergy and on my first Monday at Great Ponton the Bishop of Grantham arrived by car with two colleagues to watch the Flying Scotsman heading north. I was required, in consultation with our signalman to report to the Bishop on its progress up the line from Peterborough. The visit to my station was a regular Monday recreation for the bishop before lunch and it clearly gave great satisfaction.

Towards the weekend on our first train in the morning, boxes of racing pigeons had to be off-loaded from time to time at Great Ponton. Each crate contained a polite note to the station master giving feeding and watering instructions for the birds. Most important was the time of release 'away from telegraph wires.' I greatly enjoyed setting free these racing teams which, after a wide circle over the station, disappeared into the distance. I noticed later on one occasion crossing the Channel by sea that racing pigeons returning to this country kept pace with the steamers. However I also saw that a small number of them perched on the vessel throughout most of the crossing and took off refreshed as we neared Dover. How these rides were reflected in the race results I do not know.

Each evening on the last southbound train from Great Ponton to King's Cross I was required to put my takings for the day, seldom more than three shillings, into a steel security box in the guard's van. One day I forgot, but a few minutes after the scheduled time of the train's arrival in King's Cross I received a harsh telephone call from London asking what I had done with the day's takings. I realised then I was not as isolated as I had imagined and even pennies were keenly being counted. On the passage of the Royal Train I was instructed to stand on the platform wearing my uniform cap, having previously inspected the bridge adjoining the station. A longer spell one summer as Assistant Station Master at the crowded resort of Clacton on Sea was full of incidents which mostly beggar description. The excursion trains from London arriving at weekends had no corridors. One of my duties was to keep an eye on the station's ladies lavatory which was supervised by the widow of a former signalman. The door locks soon became jammed with coins. She would wave a towel at the door to summon me to empty them. I soon learned that our takings on a Sunday were often in excess of £100 in pennies. Nowadays this would be a case for privatisation and the idea occurred to me then.

The British rail passengers of that era seemed more often than not to lose their heads when starting a journey. At Clacton when directed to join a train on their left, they almost always mounted a train on their right. No amount of guidance seemed to avert this. Every Sunday evening people left for Manchester who intended to arrive in London.

My apprenticeship finished in September 1938. I hoped then to be given more money and a real job. Nothing, however, transpired except for a brief time as an Inspector of East Coast trains. I decided to tackle Mr. R. Bell, the Deputy General manager, who supervised the apprentice scheme. He was an impressive and likeable Scot. He received me in his office at King's Cross. I had done well enough in the regular exams which we had to undergo, especially in Railway Law, but not so well in economics. Having listened politely to me as I asked for advancement, I was finally dismissed with the sensible advice to "keep pegging away." In later life when I felt I was getting stuck I always reminded myself of Mr. Bell's advice.

But the growing threat of war was becoming disruptive. I was sent on an anti-gas course which could have served as an episode in the 'Dad's Army' T.V. programme. At the time of Munich things became more serious.

I was called to London at very short notice and was told that I would be in charge of Sudbury Hill station on the outskirts of London, which would be an exchange point at which large numbers of evacuees from inner London would be transferred from underground trains to main line steam trains to convey them far from the capital. I knew the situation was really serious when I was authorised by the management to buy a few pounds worth of first aid equipment from the local chemist. The figures for passengers and trains to be involved in the exchange were alarming. It was not hard to imagine what would happen in the anticipated event of enemy bombing. My little store of first aid material would have been useless. For that reason at least, I was considerably relieved when the Prime Minister returned from Bad Godesberg with his famous piece of paper. However it made me turn my mind urgently to consider what to do with myself if war did break out.

CHAPTER 4

WAR

I had read about the role that railwaymen had played in France in World War I and particularly of the careers of Sir Eric Geddes and of Col. Sir Cecil Paget of the Midland Railway. The railways traditionally provided the personnel for a Territorial Supplementary Reserve of Royal Engineer Railway Operating and Dock operating companies. I applied to join one or the other, but found no vacancies. It was clear that these activities had been made the preserve of patriotically minded people drawn largely from the N.E. section of the LNER. They had been training together for some years and did not welcome strangers - especially if they came from another section of the system. Although the amalgamation of the railways forming the LNER had taken place in 1923 the component parts retained a certain clannishness. As I was seen to have joined the company at Armley, a Great Northern station, I was not particularly welcome in a preserve of the North Eastern area.

But I was determined to be involved in the war at the start. It was obvious to me that I had applied my mind too late to this particular problem and something would have to be done quickly to remedy it. I decided to go direct to the Royal Engineers Transportation section at the War Office. I got an appointment and was cordially received by a Major Langley who was a typical intellectual Royal Engineer officer with a gallantry medal from the First War. Later I was to serve with him in Egypt and the Far East. Once again I had to prove that I could distinguish between a green and red lamp. I left my particulars, took their telephone numbers and returned to my railway work. For some time I heard nothing. In mid August 1939 the international outlook was so menacing that I had a sudden impulse to try to see the War Office people again. After a telephone conversation I was told to call and ask for a Capt. de Rhé Phillipe. I later served under him in North Africa and Italy. He came down to the side door of the War Office in Whitehall Place, to speak to me. I repeated my particulars and gave him my whereabouts. He seemed mildly interested and again said they would get in touch if I was required.

When the Prime Minister made his famous announcement on September 3rd I was staying in the Petergate Hotel in York with another apprentice. It was a sunny morning and after listening to the radio we went for a walk on the City Walls. My colleague asked me why I seemed so depressed. I suggested the declaration of war was a serious business and who could foretell our future fate. He dismissed this and said, to my surprise, with great conviction that all had been foretold by the Pyramids and that he was a member of the British Israelites. The Pyramids, he claimed, foretold an eventual massive clash between Good and Evil and this was it. He assured me that there was no need for alarm because Good would prevail and Evil, represented by the Nazis, would be defeated. I could not compete with this and we separated. I returned to London that evening and went to my parents' home. Next morning I remember lying in bed and hearing the air raid siren for the first time - a false alarm. I found it inconceivable that death and destruction could possibly come to the place in my own country in which I had spent many of my youthful years. Wars took place on the Continent not at home. I had to return North that day and was on the way to Newcastle when I was called by loud speaker off the train at Darlington and told on the station master's telephone to report at once to the War Office. Within a few days I was commissioned in the Royal Engineers to serve at once at the War Office and told the railway I was leaving them. It took me more than six months to receive any army pay.

I had to find somewhere to live, preferably in short walking distance from the War Office in Whitehall, not least because of the blackout. By good fortune my friend from Christ Church, Alan Campbell-Johnson had recently moved with his wife into a basement flat in Greycoat Gardens, Westminster. He was working for Sir Archibald Sinclair, a leading Liberal M.P., and was expecting his call up papers. He suggested I should stay temporarily with them. I was delighted to do so. For the next six months I had the benefit of their delightful company. I had the pleasure of walking across St. James Park each day, where for three hundred years, Londoners had amused themselves by feeding the birds on the lake. On this daily walk I passed the spot where my father, as a child, bought milk taken straight from the cow at one penny a glass. The café which now stands in the Park by the lakeside is the direct descendant of that Victorian facility.

Reporting to the War Office on September 7th I had no idea what to expect. The professional army was totally unfamiliar and I knew no member of it. I did not even have the elementary knowledge obtained in a school Officers' Training Corps. I did, however, know a fair amount about British railways. I expected to go to the Royal Engineers Transportation section, who were the people who had originally interviewed me. But I learned that I had been assigned to the Quarter Master General's staff in Movement Control. This took me aback but it was prudent not to argue.

After mutual introductions, I was taken at once deep into the basement of the War Office and into a well lit and decorated room. There were very evident signs of bomb proofing. Later my colleagues enjoyed recounting to me how immediately after the declaration of war on September 3rd, the air raid warning sounded and officers gathered in the rooms as shelter. Soon, bumps and bangs were heard and certain know-alls of those present, readily identified the sounds as this and that type of bomb or ack-ack gunfire. When the all clear sounded later, on a peaceful city, the bumps and bangs continued as the builders in a nearby room carried on their noisy work. In the room to which I was directed were six uniformed officers of recognisably military appearance seated at desks loaded with papers and telephones. My welcome was cordial and it did not take long to find out the object of their concentration. They explained that they were controlling the movement, then in full progress, of men, vehicles and stores to the British Expeditionary Forces urgently assembling on the Continent. These movements had been meticulously planned in advance and there were complicated rail schedules to supervise and to revise as necessary. One could not help being impressed by the completeness of the preparations and reassured by the smoothness of the operation, the competence of the officers involved and the eager cooperation of those at the ports, ordnance depots and assembly points.

Admittedly there was not the slightest sign of enemy interference at ports, depots or railway junctions, but the possibility constantly existed. How adaptable the plans would have been in that case can only be imagined. As far as I was concerned, the railway aspects were fairly plain sailing and I was soon satisfied that my professional knowledge was fully equal to it. There was an immense amount to be learned of the military machine and the organisation of the War Office itself. As always in such situations, it was soon possible to identify, at one's own level, the comparatively few key persons on whom one could rely for information and action. Within our own office, my colleagues were in their early thirties and had come straight from the Staff College to the War Office some few weeks earlier. Outstanding amongst them was John Cowley who had been awarded the Albert Medal for bravery in the 1935 Quetta earthquake and became in time a highly decorated Lt. General and a controversial strategic thinker. The two most senior officers were both Royal Engineers, Lt. Col. Bill Williams and 'Dome' Napier and were both shown during the war to be men of exceptional administrative ability.

The 'phoney war' surprisingly continued. Our staff increased. Another LNER traffic apprentice, my friend Kenneth Harrison, a scholar from Queens College Oxford and a Yorkshireman was recruited. A senior man from the LMS, Sydney Screen and a former Master, Tom Breen from the New Zealand shipping company to help with shipping problems also joined.

Both became Brigadiers before the war's end. Harrison fitted excellently into the War Office organisation and remained with Movement Control throughout the war working with Bill Williams, who in due course became a Major General. One of the reasons for the success of Movement Control was the consistency of its most senior officers. In particular General 'Mickey' Holmes who was Director of Movements at the War Office throughout the war. He was exceptionally not a Royal Engineer like the majority of the others. In addition to the regulars the organisation attracted capable outsiders like Denis Healey, (Sir) Val Duncan later of RTZ and (Lord) Marcus Sieff. Most of the regulars had been trained at the Royal Engineer Depot at Longmoor. Their enthusiasm for transport and railways was great.

Lack of enemy action made it possible to leave the War Office on occasions and visit the loading ports and depots. Most of the ports were on the South Coast and in South Wales but there was a constant search for new facilities. Littlehampton became a major ammunition port and stretches of isolated railway lines had to be found for the storage of naval mines. On Boxing Day 1939, a freezing cloudless morning, I crossed from Harwich to France on the LNER train ferry - a relic of World War I. This ferry was the only 'roll on and roll off' vessel available and was especially useful for heavy constructional machinery needed for the airfields being hastily built on the Continent. All other vehicles going to the BEF had to be loaded slowly on freighters by crane or derrick. There were, when I arrived at Harwich, several heavy duty private lorries with civilian drivers waiting by the ferry. Army vehicles and drivers were expected to pick up their loads of constructional machinery, but none appeared. As the equipment was urgently wanted, I suggested to the civilian drivers that they waited no longer and went themselves with their vehicles to the continent. This idea was received with enthusiasm and onto the ferry they went. The drivers eventually returned but their vehicles were requisitioned on their arrival at the other side. Correspondence between the owners and the RAF was still continuing when I left the U.K. six months later. In France I visited our opposite numbers at GHQ. Life in the towns and villages everywhere seemed entirely normal and it was hard to realise that there was a war on.

After several weeks in the continued absence of air raids, we moved up from our underground office to the ground floor of the War Office overlooking the flats in Whitehall Court. This gave us the weekly treat of watching Bernard Shaw and his wife en route for their country house, at Ayot St. Lawrence, being tucked up with a heavy travelling rug in the back seats of a brown Rolls Royce whose chauffeur wore a matching uniform. So much for the practice of his political views.

But there were some signs that a real war might one day break out. The Russians had attacked Finland at the end of September. I was deputed to receive a distracted Finnish Consul who came almost daily to the War Office to beg for arms. I had the humiliation, which those more directly responsible carefully avoided, of offering him an unlimited number of gas capes when he asked for field guns. In the course of these exchanges I began to learn confidentially from colleagues just how pitifully short the British Army was of modern equipment. Production of the 25 pound field gun was just beginning, designed to replace the weapons which had survived from the First War. This and other scraps of information were disturbing and added to fears of RAF deficiencies which were the subject of current rumour. Nevertheless I had, like so many others, complete confidence, then and later, in a favourable outcome of the war. This irrational confidence which survived the fall of France was shared by almost all of us. It sustained me until the entry of the U.S. and the Soviet Union made it plain, even for the doubters, to see that the balance was tilting our way.

In early April 1940, the Germans invaded Denmark and Norway. There followed a flurry of muddled activity in our department as together with the French, hasty preparations were made for Allied landings in Norway. Their disastrous failure gave a clear demonstration of German superiority which boded ill for the future. Personnel of the Norwegian Air Force began to arrive in the U.K. Some were stationed at an airfield near to my father's home - much to his and my young sister's satisfaction. It was at this point that I learned that I was to go with my colleague John Cowley to join GHQ Middle East which was in the process of being formed in Cairo. This took me entirely by surprise but was welcome not least because it involved promotion. We were to leave with others by flying boat from Poole Harbour on May 9th.

Thus ended the first six months of the war. The work I had done had been to help implement and modify the day to day plans of others at the centre. It had been virtually a peace time exercise but a lesson in comradeship and working together with a clear unity of purpose. I felt I had taken part in an essential but not glamorous operation and that we had together performed pretty well.

CHAPTER 5

THE MIDDLE EAST

Preparations for the journey had to be made at once. Basic tropical equipment had hastily to be purchased at the Army and Navy stores, the traditional suppliers of servicemen eastward bound. I packed a zinc lined trunk to follow me by sea. This piece of luggage took almost a year to arrive in Egypt as the Mediterranean was closed in June; the ship was diverted and finally returned to the U.K. Our party of about half a dozen officers assembled at the Sandbanks Hotel which was well known to me from our early life near Bournemouth. Our party included, in addition to John Cowley my War Office colleague, Brigadier Whiteley who was to be General Wavell's Director of Intelligence in Cairo and Major Bainbridge who later became a senior General Staff Officer. We made our way individually to Sandbanks. My father came to Waterloo to see me off on May 8th. As the train snaked out of the station I could see him standing at the end of the platform with his black homburg hat and rolled umbrella. I remembered that I had failed to say good-bye to him when he had gone to Africa more than twenty years earlier and wondered whether this was going to be a one way journey. I did not return to England for more than four years. Throughout all that time, he wrote me weekly a numbered letter. All eventually reached me.

The first day's flight on May 9th took us to Marseilles via Biscarosse, a French seaplane base on the Atlantic coast. Their huge unsuccessful six engined flying boat was drawn up on a slipway. Next stop on May 10th was the French Tunisian base Bizerta where we were met by the Royal Navy liaison officer wearing a stiff winged collar and carrying a silver topped stick. He had a self important air about him and justified it by announcing that the German attack on France had taken place a few hours earlier.

The news brought relief, regret and some anxiety. Relief that the waiting was over, regret that I was not in England when it happened and anxiety for the family at home. The fear of the German bombing which had not materialised in September last, now returned. But the question of immediate concern to our party was Italy. Their entry into the war, always expected, now seemed inevitable. If it took place, the situation in the Middle East would be completely changed and with it, the work we were being sent to do. In the event their decision did not come for a further month.

We were able to continue our journey from Bizerta at once but were held up for some days in Crete and arrived in Alexandria in the middle of

May. None of us could have imagined that a year later Crete would be in German hands. The port of Alexandria as we flew low over it was an unforgettable sight. It seemed to be entirely filled with warships of all shapes and sizes. A large proportion were easily recognisable as units of the French navy and the overall strength of the combined fleet looked overwhelming. In fact, these significant French units never moved out of the harbour during the darkest days of the war. After the necessary British attack on their comrades in Oran in July they chose to sulk in Alexandria amusing themselves at our expense and apparently careless of the final outcome of the war. I found it hard to forgive them then and do not do so now.

At first in Cairo there seemed to be considerable confusion. The peace time British headquarters British Troops in Egypt (B.T.E.) was in the process of being superseded by General Headquarters Middle East, (GHQ.ME). For this new establishment large apartment blocks had been requisitioned in the wealthy Garden City area. Over the next three years this complex steadily grew into a huge bureaucratic machine. It became an overseas mini Whitehall and after June 1941 housed a Resident War Cabinet Minister and a powerful civil staff charged with the overall coordination of the Allied war effort. Nearby was the British Embassy under Sir Miles Lampson, (Lord Killearn) with the especial brief of keeping a watchful eye on the latent threat of hostile Egyptian nationalism, possibly led by King Farouk or Nahas Pasha. These apparently over-large static organisations attracted the constant hostility of the Government at home and invited the contempt of front line soldiers on leave from the dangers of the Western Desert or from the discomfort and boredom of the Canal area base. Artemis Cooper's book , *Cairo at War* tells of the 'high life' in the city and shows how justified was some of this contempt. However she gives little credit to the achievements of GHQ and ignores many of its problems. The military situation was such that it permitted acts of great daring like the Long Range Desert Group. Between such adventures were periods of recreation. The 'high life' was a justifiable relaxation for those who took exceptionally high risk.

The inevitable recruitment into the Headquarters' offices of wives of servicemen already in Egypt in the pre-war garrison and expatriate businessmen was not without problems. An early casualty was a young lady who, when reprimanded for revealing secret information, burst into tears exclaiming

"I only joined Military Intelligence to be interesting at dinner!"

Many officers were unhappy with their sheltered existence in General Headquarters and sought to escape from it. One such major decided to spend his week's leave visiting some of his more exposed colleagues in the desert. En route he was taken prisoner, put on board an enemy submarine en route for Sicily, bombed to the surface by an RAF plane, rescued from the submarine and was back at his desk within the week. Office hours at General Headquarters were from 8 a.m. to 8 p.m. with a break in the afternoon when the Gezira Sports Club came into its own. This timetable was, of course largely theoretical.

I subsequently worked in several headquarters during the remainder of the war - in Allied Forces Headquarters in Algiers and in Caserta in Italy, in Allied Land Forces, South East Asia in India and Ceylon. They all had the same characteristics of any bureaucracy. A core of overworked and efficient officers, surrounded by many superfluous hangers-on. Repeated attempts to cut down their numbers were almost always frustrated.

As General Headquarters in Cairo grew, the huge base in the Suez canal zone was taking shape with camps, training areas, depots, hospitals, lighter ports, repair shops and airfields. The terrain, for the most part unobstructed desert, was ideal for the purpose. I found my first glimpse of the Suez canal more moving than the first sight of the Pyramids and the Sphinx. The spectacle of a large freighter gliding through its dark waters between the shimmering sands was always irresistible to me. Its very vulnerability added excitement to its contemplation. Only once was it blocked for a short time by a ship mined from the air.

Egypt from 1940-42 was a fascinating place to be. Until Japan entered the war, it was the only land area where the British and Allied land forces were in active physical contact with the enemy and the spotlight was firmly fixed on it. Troops from Australia, New Zealand, India and Africa thronged the streets of Cairo and heightened the sense of drama. Refugees from the Balkans intensified it. Many people who were then famous or were to become famous were there for all to see. I saw a lonely and virtually unknown de Gaulle walking unaccompanied into General Headquarters, saw the legendary Smuts and the then unrecognised Enoch Powell coming and going purposefully to and from his intelligence activities in our office buildings.

The desert west of Alexandria towards enemy territory in Libya, might have been designed for a military conflict between mechanised forces. Its wide sandy wastes contained no centres of population, no possibility of complicated refugee problems and no river barriers. It could be seen as an unobstructed and macabre 'killing field' for two opposing teams. In the west lay the enemy, at the eastern extremity was Alexandria, the Suez Canal, the Nile Delta with Cairo the Allied Headquarters and Palestine beyond. Within a few hours of the battle, Egypt's capital city provided for the Allied Forces not only an ideal military base area, but every amenity that the fighting forces could require.

Those arriving by sea in convoys from the rationed British Isles were dazed to find good food and drink in abundance. In addition some far-seeing speculators had, with impeccable timing, contrived to land from an Egyptian freighter 'SS Zam Zam' an apparently inexhaustible supply of luxuries from the United States. Literally millions of food parcels and nylon stockings were sent home to families in the U.K. from the Cairo shops of Ades, Lappas and others who quickly seized their opportunities.

When we arrived in Cairo in May 1940 much of all this lay in the future. Staff officers posted to the Headquarters were expected to find their own accommodation in Cairo city. This meant in practice Gezira Island in the Nile and its immediate environs. There were a limited number of pension/hotels but plenty of vacant flats. The island included a large sporting club providing every sporting facility from which, in peace time in the imperial tradition, Egyptians had been largely excluded. However great its sins in the past, they were partially redeemed by the welcome the club gave to those on leave from the desert, or convalescing from hospital. But its golf course and race track offered an inviting dropping area for hostile parachutists. In early 1940 New Zealand bren-gunners were temporarily stationed on it as a precaution. From the golf course a chance hooked drive of mine one day landed in one of their gun posts and happily reunited me with my New Zealand friend Riddiford, from Christ Church, now a sergeant whom I had not seen since we came down together in 1935. Later we were able to give some hospitality to him when he came back wounded from the Desert.

My colleague John Cowley quickly found an admirable small flat overlooking the club on one side and the Nile and the City on the other. He invited me to join him and I was delighted to do so. I bought for £35 an elderly Chrysler coupe. He had a more modern Chevrolet. There was a quarrelsome cook and a highly intelligent houseboy, Ibrahim. The latter was fascinated by all aircraft and constantly quizzed me about the Imperial Airways flying boats that landed on the river. More than twenty years later I was waiting at Cairo airport and felt a touch on my shoulder. I turned to see Ibrahim in a smart blue BOAC uniform and peaked cap. Whether he advanced eventually to cabin staff or higher I do not know, but clearly one part of his ambition had been satisfied.

In the new headquarters John Cowley served initially in the planning branch reserved for professional 'flyers.' I continued my Movement Control work closely associated with the Transportation section. In these sections were specialists, like myself, from the U.K. to whom were added locally recruited English from the Egyptian railways, inland water transport and local ports. A few months after the fall of France, we were powerfully reinforced by senior officers and junior officers from home. Brigadier Russell from General headquarters in France and Marcus (Lord) Sieff of Marks and Spencer was amongst them. Marcus showed constantly the initiative which made him such an outstanding businessman and proved himself a first class port commandant in North Africa and Italy. All this he recounts in his autobiography *Don't Ask the Price*.

The Sieff family had a small farm at Tel Mond in Palestine. It was not occupied at the time by any member. A year or two later Marcus generously made it available to some of us for short spells of rest and recreation. Angela and I went there for a week when she was first expecting a baby. Set in the midst of orange groves it was blissful. Adjoining was an army camp of pack mules waiting in vain for possible deployment in the Caucasus. The officer in charge - a Captain Webster - invited us for drinks and, with a warped sense of hospitality, served a home made cocktail of fruit juice laced with alcohol of his own preparation. Mercifully Angela refused but I accepted with disastrous consequences. It was a dangerous practical joke but I suppose one must try to forgive someone who has had to endure the prolonged company of idle mules.

Over the next two and a half years our functions in Egypt, broadly speaking, were divided into two parts. One was to organise the Egyptian and other Middle Eastern ports to receive and discharge rapidly the cargo and personnel ships arriving round the Cape of Good Hope from primarily the U.K., but also from India, South Africa, Australia and ultimately the U.S. We also had responsibilities to the East in Iraq and Iran.

This naturally involved knowing the secret timing and contents of the incoming convoys from their hazardous passages, allocating them to chosen ports and ensuring that the contents were quickly in the hands of the Forces. Since these Forces were desperately short of fighting formations and up-to-date weapons the whole conduct of the war in the Western Desert, offensively and defensively, depended on safe arrival and quick distribution of certain cargoes. Compared to the enemy we were at a disadvantage being at the end of long and vulnerable lines of communication. Italians and Germans in Cyrenaica had a shorter supply line from Italy and Sicily although at certain critical times, thanks in part to Ultra decodes, they suffered damaging losses from the Royal Navy and the RAF. Indeed, such losses of individual cargoes saved Egypt from Rommel's military successes.

The second part of our work was to help arrange the shipment of supplies from our Egyptian base to the ports of Tobruk, Benghazi, Tripoli, (when in our hands) for our forces in the desert. Only small ships could be used. These were ancient coasters already in the Eastern Mediterranean with crews of mixed nationalities and several different flags. Prominent amongst them was the Polish Master of the 'S.S. Sophi' who eventually perished. Their courage was outstanding. The most hazardous cargo was motor and aviation spirit. This was inefficiently canned in the Middle East with imported tinplate. Loss by leakage and the resulting danger was appalling. Ships arrived in Tobruk or Benghazi awash with leaked gasoline. The arrival of the Germans and their faultless jerricans put us to shame.

The shipment of fresh meat, so eminently desirable, was throughout dependent on a single refrigerated trawler, requisitioned under strong protest from its Greek owner and sailed from the Red Sea into the Mediterranean. After long negotiations a British built 'roll on and roll off ferry' en route for the Bosphorus to fulfil a Turkish pre-war order, was taken over and used with great effect on this supply line. No other landing craft of any kind were available to us. Later on when British forces were sent to Greece their supply was our responsibility from the base in Egypt.

The supply of Malta by convoy was a special problem, demanding each time a major naval protective effort and the inevitable loss of numbers of the Allies' fastest and most modern freighters. It was a painful sight to watch the loading of these splendid ships in the knowledge that one or more would perish on the dash to the besieged island. Our staff was involved in the assembly of cargo and the loading of the vessels. On arrival in Cairo in May 1940, I had been handed for comment a large report. It dealt with the future supply situation in the island and gave details of its civil stocks and reserves. To my amazement the terms of reference of the study assumed that Italy would not enter the war. So much for official foresight. In the event the responsibility for the development of a coordinated supply scheme in Malta was entrusted by the Governor General Dobbie to an outspoken young Australian naval officer, Commander Jackson (later Sir Robert). He made an outstanding success of it. His first arrival in Cairo for consultation made an instant impact. He became known in the years to come for his work at the United Nations, where, however, his frank speaking made him many enemies. On one occasion he was flown home from Cairo for brief discussions in London. On his return he remarked that he had met a remarkable young woman economist who was making her name in Whitehall, a certain Barbara Ward. If he remarried, he said, he hoped it would be to someone like her. He indeed achieved this ambition in later years but it did not turn out to be the success we all wished for.

After the entry of Italy into the war, not long after the first convoy was to sail to Malta, I called on the Consul-General in Alexandria, a scholarly if somewhat absent-minded member of the famous Levant Service. Some weeks earlier he had entertained to luncheon in his garden the newly appointed Headmistress of the English girls school in Alexandria together with a fellow passenger of hers, who had just disembarked in Alexandria, a young girl on her way out from England to a post in the Cairo Embassy. He gallantly plucked the latter a rose but completely forgot her request to inform the Cairo Embassy of her arrival. Not having been provided with any address or specific instructions she therefore arrived unmet at Cairo station in a state of mild confusion. That girl, as yet unknown to me, was to become my future wife.

I found the Consul General in his study surrounded by a dozen or more loaves of bread. He explained that the Royal Navy had asked him to bake a new loaf each day with Egyptian flour so that a sample could go on the convoy in order that the Governor of Malta could know the effect when the population were cut off from their customary flour supplies from Australia. As the sailing date and time was a deadly secret some loaves had to be ready at a moment's notice. Supply to Malta was also by submarine. This led to an interesting argument on one occasion. Clergy are by tradition not allowed on these vessels. They are thought to bring bad luck. General Arthur Smith at General Headquarters Cairo was a deeply religious man and wanted a particular lay preacher sent to the besieged island. Did he or did he not count as clergy? After long debate, the Navy allowed him to embark.

From the Italian declaration of war in June until September there was a lull in Cairo. No move was made on Egypt by the numerically superior Italian forces in Libya. On the night of Italy's declaration of war I was a duty officer in Cairo at General Headquarters. A telephone call came from the office of Admiral Cunningham, the Naval Commander in Chief in Alexandria. The caller announced himself as
"Staff Officer, Intelligence."
He then uttered a single word. I cannot now recall it but I believe it was 'Alligator.' It meant nothing to me and I asked him to repeat it. He did so with vehemence and suggested I sought advice from a higher level. I tried in vain and finally got Brigadier Whiteley the army Commander in Chief's Director of Intelligence. He too had no idea. He consulted General Wavell the Commander in Chief himself, without result. I told the officer in Alexandria who rang off petulantly. In fact it was the code word meaning that Admiral Cunningham had put to sea his fleet in a gesture of defiance by which he secured and maintained a domination over the numerically

superior Italian fleet which lasted until their surrender. The survival of our armies in the Middle East was thereby assured.

The news from Europe in June and July was appalling but as I read about Dunkirk and other events on the ticker-tape, I felt strangely detached. There were no uncensored newspapers or broadcasts to elaborate the news or to speculate on its significance. Perhaps as a result confidence of the outcome was unaffected and the majority of us, far from home, did not feel we were heading for defeat or that our families were in mortal danger. The value of censorship in war has been debated in the Falklands and Gulf Wars. It was certainly of value in Cairo in 1940.

The lull had given me an opportunity to familiarise myself with the capacities of Egyptian ports and the depots of the Canal area. My inexperience led to an error of judgement at Port Said. Prominent in the port was a freighter with a large deck cargo of over 30 new Ford ambulances which could be easily identified from the quayside. They were enroute to 'neutral' Romania whose neutrality was obviously going to be short-lived. I made a signal to General Headquarters repeated to the Commander in Chief Mediterranean in Alexandria saying that on no account was the ship to sail. This produced a furious message from Admiral Andrew Cunningham asking who was the officer who took it upon himself to usurp his responsibilities. I was called at once to Cairo to appear before the Deputy Quarter Master General. He was clearly hoping to enjoy himself, but when I explained about the ambulances he ranged himself on my side and the incident was closed with a friendly warning. I enjoyed over the next three years watching the ambulances carrying out their errands of mercy in Cairo - they were not desert worthy and therefore remained in the base.

Of the Egyptian ports, Alexandria was the best equipped but was largely given over to the Navy. In any case to take freighters, often with ammunition and scarce weapons through the Canal into the Mediterranean was a risk. A heavy burden fell therefore on Suez at the Red Sea end of the Canal. Lighters were also used in the Bitter Lakes to bring stores ashore in the Canal area. I found Suez fascinating. A strong smell of oil from the refinery hung over the port and the quays were piled high with war stores. A memorable day was the arrival of the first U.S. flag ship after the neutral U.S Government permitted their freighters to enter the war zone and thereby made available the vital addition of cargo ships to our diminishing resources.

At the east side of the Canal were the smart bungalows of the privileged and respected canal pilots - largely from the U.K. It was generally accepted that they alone were capable and qualified to take the ships through. This later led at the time of the Suez crisis in 1956 to the belief of the British

Government that the withdrawal of these pilots would cripple Nasser's attempts to run his newly nationalised Canal.   Nothing could have been further from the truth. Nasser's recruits did better.   As a retired naval officer explained in a letter to The Times many years later he never found difficulty in taking his ship through the Canal, he merely "aimed down the middle."

At the end of August, Marshal Balbo launched the expected Italian attack on Egypt. It was for him a disaster. He had almost twice as many troops as the Allies, but General O'Connor's counter offensive against the Italians starting in December 1940 reached a triumphant conclusion at Beda on February 7th 1941. More than 100,000 Italian prisoners were taken and the Italians were out of Libya. But in the same month the first Germans arrived in North Africa under Rommel.   They came well prepared with superior equipment. It is a matter of historical record that the Germans attacked Russia inadequately equipped for the inescapable weather conditions. In contrast, the Afrika Corps in Libya was fully prepared with appropriate specialised equipment for what was palpably a lesser area of conflict.

Regrettably the British victory over the Italians could not be exploited as the decision had been taken to despatch a force to Greece which had been attacked at the end of September. Our forces in Greece created a problem of supply and a fatal dispersal of our insufficient strength leading to the eventual chaotic evacuation from Greece and the fall of Crete. Shortly before the German airborne assault on Crete in May I was sent on a reconnaissance in Suda Bay and Canea (Khania). We sailed in convoy and were attacked en route by an Italian torpedo carrying plane which sensibly concentrated on a heavily laden supply ship in preference to the British India liner in which our troops were travelling. It scored an imperfect hit which caused the supply ship to be beached inaccessibly on the southern shore of the island. A tanker with 5000 tons of aviation spirit was also hit at the stern and miraculously did not explode. As we passed by a group of inscrutable Chinese crewmen leaned unmoved over its stern rail.

There were no air raid sirens on Crete and the warnings were given by the church bells in Canea. It was a picturesque scene as the bells rang out under a full moon which illuminated the red tiled roofs on the hillside of the little town. I returned to Cairo by flying boat, which was grossly overloaded with more than 90 passengers including one of President Roosevelt's sons. One engine failed soon after take off but we continued on three engines in the bright moonlight about 200 feet above a flat calm sea. Very few days later the Germans launched their airborne attack on Crete.

If our national fortunes were at a low ebb my personal affairs were in a happy state. I had been awarded the OBE (Mil). But more importantly I had become engaged in April to Angela McCulloch who worked in an intelligence organisation in the Embassy. Angela had been brought up in Helensburgh and in Kensington and had spent nearly a year in Germany. After working as a translator at the British Metal Corporation at the approach of war, she had been introduced to an Intelligence Department in London. Early in 1940 she had been appointed to our Embassy in Belgrade. At the last moment, she was, on account of her youth, switched to Egypt, where she arrived by sea at about the same time as I arrived by air. She crossed the Mediterranean from Marseilles in an Egyptian passenger ship, the last crossing before the sea was closed in advance of the Italian declaration. We had met at a small supper party given by John Cowley in our flat to which she had been invited as I could not muster anyone of my own choice. We had decided to marry in June at the Cairo Cathedral, and spent a week's honeymoon in Jerusalem and Tel Aviv. Amongst many memories I recall that every evening as dusk fell in that Jewish city, the windows of scores of houses were thrown open and countless violins could be heard as the refugees from Europe relaxed. We took advantage of being in Palestine to get a bottle of Jordan water against the day of a possible christening. It was kept in a gin bottle and later poured away by Ibrahim the house boy, who no doubt had surreptitiously tasted it and found it wanting.

After the disaster in Greece and the fall of Crete the battle in the Western Desert ebbed and flowed. The success of the Germans contrasted with failures, human and mechanical, on our side. These disappointments enraged the Prime Minister and the Chiefs of Staff at home. There was grave dissatisfaction with the performance of the Generals in Egypt. In mid June 1941 as a part of the search for the reasons the Prime Minister arranged with the U.S. President for Averell Harriman, one of Roosevelt's closest advisers to visit Egypt. He was asked to report confidentially to the Prime Minister on our leaders and also to ascertain what equipment was most needed to reverse the constant failures.

I was attached to a very small group who were to accompany Harriman to the base in the Canal. He was a relatively unknown figure to those in the Middle East. General Wavell and others failed, I believe, to grasp the opportunities offered by his mission. Being with Harriman was fascinating. He was accompanied by an irascible Australian born American civilian tank expert who, not without reason, thought he was not treated with the respect he merited. The party at one point was unexpectedly expanded by the Prime Minister's son Randolph Churchill who was serving with the Commandos. I do not think anyone of us were aware of the close relationship of his wife with Harriman in London. As a result of the arrival of Randolph, the tank expert and I were excluded from a formal lunch given by the Admiral in Charge, Canal Zone in his ship anchored in the Bitter Lakes. We had to be satisfied with an omelette at the French Club in Ismalia. It was an uncomfortable meal.

Many years later when I was at our Embassy in Washington I discussed this mission with Harriman. He had a vivid recollection of it and complained that he had found General Wavell "sphinx like." Harriman's report led to additional supplies for the Middle East but, more importantly, new appointments and better coordination of the military and civil effort.

The Prime Minister's dissatisfaction led to the appointment of Oliver Lyttelton as Minister of State in the War Cabinet, resident in the Middle East and the replacement of Wavell by General Auchinleck. But German successes continued. By June 1942 Rommel had moved rapidly towards Alexandria and seemed likely to take it. But his communications were over-stretched and many of his supplies destroyed crossing the Mediterranean from Italy. General Auchinleck took over command and German forces were checked at El Alamein. Australian troops rushed down from Syria contributed to the successful check. When congratulated on their contribution by the Commander in Chief the Australian general replied, characteristically, "That's all right General, the boys were interested."

These developments caused an immense volume of work but also created a personal crisis. The German threat to Egypt was sufficiently acute for arrangements to be planned for the evacuation from Cairo of General Headquarters in two parts: one would go North to Palestine and the other south via the Nile Valley to Khartoum. There was the possibility of civil disorders in the Delta. We were issued with side arms. The question of moving women and children from the possible areas of conflict became a matter of urgent discussion. Angela was expecting our first child and I agreed with her superiors that it would be wise for her to go to South Africa, a country which had shown willingness to accept some British evacuees. Her bosses said that her special qualifications made it legitimate for them to recall her if the danger passed after the birth of the child. It was a wretched situation but it would have been unforgivable if we had become separated and she had stayed and become involved in what looked to most of us as likely to be chaos. She was, as always, stalwart. Thousands of couples at home and abroad suffered similarly and worse. We were lucky for her to find a friendly welcome and safety in the Cape in the small town of Knysna. In retrospect I believe it was right for her to go, although in the event she could have stayed.

Rommel's advance had almost brought about the defeat of our forces in Egypt. His vulnerable supply lines had failed him but our mistakes had contributed to his success. He would not necessarily fail next time. We knew very well that our defeat would be a national disaster, far worse than the fall of Singapore and a terrible humiliation for us in the eyes of the Americans and Russians. The crisis brought the Prime Minister to Cairo. As a result in the next four months drastic changes took place. The imperturbable General Alexander and General Montgomery arrived. The existing generals, with varying degrees of justice were abruptly replaced. Men and equipment were amassed sufficient to ensure Rommel's defeat at the second battle of El Alamein on October 24th 1942. A special convoy of tanks in fast freighters direct from the U.S. was arranged between Churchill and Roosevelt. Its speedy unloading was most efficiently organised by our group under the direction of Col. John Gentry an officer recruited from the Port of London Authority.

The Allied landings in Algiers on November 8th made inevitable the eventual surrender of the Germans and Italians in Tunis although this did not come about until May 1943. When the new generals arrived in Egypt, General Headquarters had been thoroughly dispirited. General Montgomery addressed its staff in a characteristic way. I was very glad to hear him. There were cynics in the audience but most of us felt there was a good chance that the dark days were over. These dramatic events and the victory at El Alamein changed the whole atmosphere in Cairo. The Middle East theatre was to take a much diminished role in Allied strategy. The spotlight was moving off us and the excitement and tension was significantly reduced. People began to be moved away to prepare in great secrecy for the invasion of Sicily and Italy and to return to England to take part ultimately in the invasion of Europe.

During my three years at General Headquarters Cairo there was on my staff a young rather hirsute Maltese clerk named Vella who was inevitably the object of constant teasing by the British soldier clerks. From time to time he came to me to complain of this treatment and I tried my best to protect his feelings, but there was a constant turnover amongst the British staff and he continued to be mocked. I last saw him in 1943 when I left Cairo for Algiers. More than thirty years later I was sitting in the House of Lords chamber when I received a note saying a Mr. Vella wished to see me. I remembered the name and went out into the lobby where I saw a smartly dressed man in a dark business suit. I recognised him at once. He quickly told me he was visiting the U.K. and Europe from Australia but primarily to pick up his new Mercedes car from the factory in Germany. He had emigrated from Malta to Australia after the war and had built up a highly successful estate agency in Queensland catering for the large number of Maltese immigrants. He wanted to thank me for my kindness to him in Cairo and told me that he had named his eldest son after me. He said that he had no time to stay longer and walked quickly away.

CHAPTER 6

TRANSFER TO ALGIERS AND ITALY

It would have been the right time for me to try to make a move. But it was not until November 1943 that the chance came. My War Office chief, General Williams had come to Cairo for the discussions after the Teheran Conference. He told me that he wanted me to go on promotion as a full Colonel to Allied Force Headquarters in Algiers. This seemed an exciting prospect, but from a personal point of view it could not have come at a worst moment. After long negotiations Angela had just been allowed to return to Cairo to take up her old job. She had been permitted to bring our son Nigel, who had been born in South Africa. They had arrived by sea at Suez on October 2nd, 1943, Nigel's first birthday. Angela and I agreed it would be wrong for me to try to stay in Cairo where my job was of diminishing importance. She would remain in her old office at G.H.Q. and would share our flat with a colleague.

Eventually she and our baby son Nigel embarked on the hazardous voyage home by sea, landing in Scotland in July 1944. She went to stay with my parents who met her and my little son for the first time.

An incident on her arrival in Suez from the Cape made a pleasant impression on us both and contradicted the often held view on the honesty of the Egyptian fellahin. She had come ashore by lighter from the troopship, carrying the baby in her arms. She was wearing slacks and in their deep pockets she had put her personal jewelry and all her currency. Halfway back to Cairo in the car she suddenly fell silent. The contents of her pockets had gone. There was so much to be thankful for that it was not difficult to resign ourselves to the loss. I reported the matter by phone to the supercilious naval officer in charge at Suez. He laughed unsympathetically. Some few days later he rang me to say that an Egyptian lighterman had handed in some 'trinkets' and some notes. The total value was certainly equal to six months or more of the Egyptian's wages. I retrieved the 'trinkets' and passed the notes to the honest lighterman.

I left Cairo for Algiers in November. Allied Force Headquarters there had been set up under General Eisenhower after the Anglo/U.S. invasion of North Africa. It had played a key role in the preparations for the invasion of Sicily and Italy. The campaign in Italy was well under way but was not proceeding as fast as had been hoped. After the surrender of the Italians the Germans had quickly moved in and were offering strong resistance. Algiers had become an unquestionable backwater.

It was my first experience of an Anglo American war organisation and the British were in a minority. There was a whiff of Hollywood about the place and it seemed even more remote from the battle than Cairo had from the Western Desert. Compared with Cairo, Algiers was virtually a dead city as far as the Algerian natives were concerned. It was an eerie experience to go into the large branch of Galeries Lafayette and find the only goods on sale were locally made pottery. The Americans were easy to work with and their enthusiasm was contagious. Their response was more often 'can do' rather than 'no can do'. They had no experience of lean military years and the novelty of the war had not yet worn off. In Egypt we had been short of every military equipment. With the Americans in Algiers there seemed to be enough of everything and if there was not enough you could get more. Occasionally one encountered the unexpected. One evening when the meal in the mess was over we sat around talking to an American general who had been a professional soldier for many years. After he had left the room an American colonel with a New York banking background turned on us. Why had we been so respectful? As for himself, before the war he would never have had such a man in his home. Indeed one of the social results of the war in America, as I came to learn later, was the enhancement of the status of the professional armed forces.

At the end of 1943, General Eisenhower had left for the U.K. to take up his post as Supreme Commander of the Allied Forces for the invasion of Europe. The headquarters itself in Algiers was poised to move to Italy as soon as the Allied advance there permitted. The palace of Caserta near Naples currently General Alexander's Headquarters had been set aside for its reception. The change over took place in the summer after the fall of Rome and General Alexander had moved north. I paid several visits from Algiers to Italy before the final move. Before we left Algiers, I witnessed an exchange of British and German prisoners arranged through the Swedish Red Cross in their vessel 'Gripsholm' sailing to and from Barcelona. The British party arrived first. Duff Cooper the British Minister Resident in Algiers with Lady Diana went aboard to greet them. It was a moving sight to watch the British ex-prisoners come off the ship, but equally moving was the silent embarkation of the Germans. The majority were stretcher borne and many were limbless or eyeless. Their discipline was striking and at that stage of the war their hopes for the future cannot have been high.

Italy was at the nadir of its fortunes and my recollections are of the appalling poverty and degradation of Naples and its desolation aggravated during the winter of 1943/4 by rare snowfalls and intense cold. Brazilian troops arrived to take a token part in the war and looked alien and unprepared. The American Navy deeply insulted the Royal Navy by wanting themselves, for political reasons, to take over the escort of the ships carrying these troops within the Mediterranean. Their request was refused. In addition to Naples, one of the main supply ports of entry for the Allied troops and stores was at Bari on the Adriatic coast. It was the scene of a heavy air raid which one night sank an American freighter carrying a secret cargo of mustard gas bombs for the United States Air Force at Foggia. The harbour was polluted before the hospital authorities could be alerted to treat appropriately those crew members taken from the water. The casualties were heavy and the disaster was hushed up. Marcus Sieff who was port commandant gives a vivid account in his autobiography to which I have referred.

Bari and its neighbouring small ports were also supply bases for partisans operating in Yugoslavia. Although there were liaison officers these units were suspicious of Allied intentions and were not easy to work with. Col. Rycroft who had been one of the original members of our War Office Movement Control team in 1939 was killed during a reconnaissance in Yugoslavia. His hosts suspected that the reconnaissance might be a prelude to the unwelcome arrival of British troops. They were not over zealous in warning Rycroft and his naval colleague of the presence of land mines on his way back to the coast to pick up the craft that had brought them. His clever daughter, then a baby, eventually became one of the early female graduates to join the Diplomatic Service where I got to know her in the Foreign Office. She reached ambassadorial rank, but was tragically killed in a motor accident in Canada in 1990.

Our headquarters at Caserta Palace were, in spite of its faded elegance, a soulless place in which to work. I found it very inappropriate that a U.S. military band came to play in the courtyard during the regular afternoon tea break. This and the arrival of the Brazilian contingent made me feel it was time to move on. I paid a duty visit to England in mid summer travelling via Rabat and then on to the U.K. in a converted Liberator bomber. I had been away more than four years and found on landing early one morning my most acute impression was the sweetness of the Cornish air. I had time to meet hitherto unseen brother-in-law Ben Symes and sister-in-law Benita and to see that we could all fit in well together when the war was over.

I had not shared the dramatic experience which had in my absence dominated the lives of family and friends at home. I had missed the Battle of Britain, was absent during the companionship and dangers of the Blitz and had not shared the long drudgery of rationing of food and clothes. This is something which I have frequently regretted and of which I had sometimes felt somewhat ashamed. At the end of 1944 I was posted home and returned again by air to England. Before I did so I flew to Athens during the brief period between its liberation and the civil war. It was a sad city but the shops still contained some of the luxuries brought in for the German troops. The shopkeepers would only do business 'for gold or meat.' There was a brief and bitter row with the Americans about the loan of landing craft to move British forces quickly from Italy to Greece. They had a republican objection to our support of the monarchy. I was not sorry to leave this theatre of war and had never felt satisfied with my contribution to events there.

CHAPTER 7

FAR EAST POSTING

On arrival in England towards the end of 1944 I was eager to find out what future posting was intended for me. The battle in Western Europe was not prospering as hoped and who could foretell the pace of events in the Far East and what would be Britain's role. Nevertheless most people felt the end of the war was not too far away. Angela's priorities were not the same as mine. She wanted a home of her own and argued convincingly that it could not be wrong to buy a house in London. I hesitated as I was still assuming that I would rejoin the railway and London would not necessarily be our base. Her view prevailed. With the aid of the loan of a petrol coupon from a cousin we conducted a search for a house largely in the Hampstead area. At the end of a discouraging day we returned to Westminster where I had lodged with the Campbell-Johnsons in September 1939. By chance we stumbled on exactly what we wanted - an early nineteenth century terrace house in Maunsel Street which has since become a prize-winning street, favoured by M.P.'s. It had been made habitable after some bomb damage and further compensation was going to become available in due time. We bought it for little more than £2,000 with some modest parental assistance. We did not then realise our luck or how it would exactly fit into our future. On the day after we bought the house the first V2 rocket fell in the U.K. and for the next few months we held our breath. In later years living in a Division Bell area, we were roused at night from time to time by the slamming of front doors as the party faithful hurried to record their vote. One of our early neighbours was Bill Yates a Tory M.P. who later emigrated to Australia and eventually became the first M.P. to have sat both in Westminster and Canberra. But we were to be happy in this little house for many years. The street was often alive with the cries of Westminster schoolboys en route to their ancient playing field in Vincent Square. The picturesquely clad nurses of Westminster Hospital passed by chattering on their way to and from their day and night shifts. Neighbours included (Sir) David Hunt then at the Commonwealth Office and (Sir) Richard Bayliss confidently at the start of his distinguished medical career. Next door was an eccentric old Etonian who drove around at the wheel of an elderly 20 h.p. Rolls Royce with his black French African wife sitting tearfully in the rear seat. In reply to Angela's frequent inquires as to her well being she replied "Noir toujours noir!"

MAUNSEL ST., S.W.1.

Peggy Stack '46.

But to return to 1944, my new posting had yet to be made known to me. The War Office was eager for me to go to Allied Land Forces, South East Asia, then based at Barrackpore near to Calcutta. I did not much like the idea, but as there seemed no alternative, allowed myself to be persuaded. Every posting in Western Europe was committed to others. My new chief in India was to be Brigadier Langley who had first interviewed me in the War Office in 1939 and with whom I had served in the Middle East. That at least I could look forward to and surely the posting could not be for long.

In retrospect I regret I did not take part in the war in Europe itself. I did not see with my own eyes the havoc in the ruined cities and the vast human tragedy, not only of the vanquished, but the helpless millions of displaced persons. In later years in the Foreign Office when dealing with European questions I did not fully share the deep feelings of those who had seen these events and who sought to prevent their repetition by radical new developments in Europe.

The journey to the Far East was by flying boat in February 1945. My first sight of India was Karachi at evening. Having bathed at the Rest House I went outside onto the street. As I did so, to my astonishment, Howell Thomas, a form master from my old school at Bishop's Stortford, passed on his bicycle and we greeted each other. He was probably at that time the only man I knew on the sub-continent - a many million to one chance meeting. Next morning we pushed on to Calcutta. The heat and humidity on arrival was immeasurably greater than anything I had known in the Middle East. The squalor and poverty came as physical shock. The city had not recovered from the great famine of the previous year and there was every sign of its ravages. The headquarters at Barrackpore on its outskirts was in the grounds of Government House on the banks of the Ganges. A large new airfield adjoined it from which every few minutes an American cargo plane took off for its hazardous journey over the 'hump' into China. Every night at frequent intervals, the flames from the exhausts of their overstretched engines illuminated our huts.

But our discomforts in India were trivial compared to the army deeply engaged in the liberation of Burma. Barrackpore was the scene of some of the first disturbances in the Indian Mutiny of 1857 and I began to feel somewhat mutinous myself. Here on the lawn of Government house in May we sat on the grass to hear the Prime Minister's broadcast on the surrender of Germany. It was quietly received and seemed a long way off and strangely of little concern to us.

Headquarters at Allied Land Forces, South East Asia (ALFSEA) in Barrackpore was commanded by General Leese the former 8th Army

Commander from Egypt and Italy. Most of the people in the Headquarters had been serving in India for some time. They were in a somewhat disgruntled frame of mind. They had their backs to the wall for years, being starved of equipment and success. The tide was beginning to turn but the 'forgotten Army' complex had to some measure taken hold. In addition to the General, there were in Headquarters, others like myself who had come from victories in Egypt and Italy. Some of them were inclined to suggest that they knew all the answers. It was not the best mixture and took time to sort out. The turning point came belatedly in July with the controversial sacking of General Leese by Mountbatten the Supreme Commander. He was replaced by General Slim who was the local hero. The departure of Leese must have been a fearful blow to him, but the readers of his biography by Rowland Ryder know with what dignity he accepted it.

ALFSEA was responsible to Lord Mountbatten at Supreme Headquarters South East Asia (SEAC) at Candy in Ceylon and itself moved from Barrackpore to Candy in mid summer. SEAC was another theatrical headquarters but the personality of its commander gave it a special style and quality. There were several friends at Mountbatten's headquarters including Alan Campbell-Johnson with whom I had lodged in Westminster in 1939. He returned to England to fight the General Election in July 1945. In my position I saw little of Mountbatten, except on one occasion, a group of us was stopped in Burma and told that the Supreme Commander would shortly pass that way and would say a few words. There were mutterings. Most felt the war had gone on long enough and the time of pep talks was past. He arrived and in a few minutes was speaking to enthusiastic new converts. The objectives of Lord Mountbatten at SEAC were the liberation of Burma, Malaya and Singapore. ALFSEA, of which I was part, was the subordinate headquarters to plan for these operations.

Preparations were being made for the seaborne liberation of Rangoon and ultimately for landings in Malaya. This entailed visits to Delhi, Bombay, Chittagong, Akyab and Ramree. It was flying into Burma that I heard on the plane's radio of the death of President Roosevelt and remember well the hush which fell on all of us. In the event the brilliant success of the 14th Army led to the freeing of Rangoon by land. The city which I visited at its liberation presented a most dismal spectacle in the drenching rain. Ten years later when I again visited it from Singapore, very little effort had been made to restore any of it. Two small incidents at the time of its liberation remain in my mind. First, the sight of a lone nun leading a crocodile of spotlessly laundered small children and picking their way around the pools of filthy water. Secondly, my companion, an officer who had worked on the

Burma Railways, suggested we went to see how the house he had once occupied in the railway quarter of the city had fared. We found it with no difficulty and whilst we were exploring it a small Burman ran up and greeted my colleague with great emotion. Then suddenly he vanished, but after a few minutes returned carrying a heavy bundle of silver and cutlery. These he had kept hidden throughout the Japanese occupation and was now handing them over to their owner. The belief that the British would return was then very deep seated. Later in Penang a not dissimilar incident occurred. With a colleague who had formerly been in business there we explored the area in which he had once lived. He was apprehensive. At the approach of the Japanese in 1941 the British community had slipped secretly out of the island one night on naval vessels, without warning their employees. My friend feared this deliberate deception would have created lasting resentment. On the contrary his emotional reunion with his staff reduced us all to tears.

The sudden surrender of the Japanese in August after the atomic bombing brought not only joy but immediate practical problems. Detailed planning had been carried out on how to handle those civil and military people released from the Japanese camps in South East Asia. But the shortage of suitable passenger ships was acute. There were competing demands between the repatriation of impatient and near mutinous British troops in camps in India, the released prisoners and the Dutch forces urgently hoping to re-establish their control in Indonesia. Decision on priorities lay in London and, rightly or wrongly it was the Dutch who suffered. During my later Diplomatic career I was not infrequently reproached by some of their diplomats for these events. At the time I was eager to get to Singapore to help with some of the problems. The shock of hearing of its fall in 1942 had been more startling to me than the collapse of France and the evacuation of Dunkirk. In 1945 the city was a dilapidated spectacle. The houses that had been occupied by enemy troops had a strange smell and the inhabitants of the city were busy reclaiming furniture and household effects which had been 'borrowed' from them by the invaders. Japanese prisoners were hard at work tidying up with little or no supervision. Their demeanour was in vivid contrast to the shattered Italian prisoners I had seen in 1940 after Wavell's desert victory. The Japanese were working without a trace of sullenness or self pity, saluting British officers smartly at extreme distances. The Chinese street traders were at once setting up their stalls anxious to do business with the incoming British troops. I bought several yards of white silk to take home which proved on washing, to have rotted hidden in storage during the Japanese occupation.

I left Ceylon in November 1945 by air when released from service and arrived home several days later after a seemingly endless flight. I can recall only one incident on the journey. In Cairo we took on more passengers including a young English mother and a very small baby. From the moment of take off the child started to cry ceaselessly until a large sailor reached across and folded it into his tattooed arms, where it instantly fell into a long sleep. To be demobilised was the next priority after I had first seen my second son born in June 1945 and planned with Angela how to occupy our own house in Westminster, which we had bought nearly a year ago.

CHAPTER 8

1946 - DEMOBILISATION AND A NEW CAREER

The actual process of demobilisation was a simple and well organised anti climax. I took my papers to a small office in Hobart House near Victoria station. Having established that I had no grounds to make a future claim on His Majesty's Government for any disability I was signed off by a young officer who it turned out, had once worked for my father in the City. I cannot recall how or where I collected my free suit, shirt and shoes. The shirt was of an unusually tough material with a simple pattern on one side only. It proved virtually indestructible and was finally given away with hardly a sign of wear. The suit was seldom worn by me. My mother had faithfully kept my civilian suits during my five years' absence. But she never satisfactorily explained where my college sweaters and other cherished items had gone. I suspect she answered war time appeals for merchant navy sailors, but she would never admit it.

Five years service overseas entitled me to several months on fully paid leave. But there were urgent plans to be made. Most important was the problem of future employment. I reported quickly to the LNER boss whom I had left so suddenly in York in September 1939. I was relieved that he remembered me but remarked reproachfully that I had been away a long time. He agreed that my long absence was not entirely of my own choice. With the election of a Labour Government the prospect of nationalisation had brought all personnel questions to a stop. I was anxious about my job; so was he about his. He had no suggestion to make but certain things were clear to me. My railway pay was likely to be about a third of my army pay. We certainly could not manage on that. Under nationalisation the modest advantages accorded to an LNER traffic apprentice were unlikely to survive. In addition, the staff would for all time be divided between those who had served in the armed forces and those who had borne the heat and burden of the day at home. A special bonus payment had been paid for the intense devotion of the Operating Superintendent, Mr. Wilson, in the Stratford London area which had suffered dreadfully from enemy bombing. The sum was £100.

I left the offices in York with nothing decided and began to look for alternative employment. I would regret leaving the railway industry. I had shared the romance that so many feel for railways and I knew I would miss it. An alternative came more quickly and surprisingly than I had expected. I called on General Williams, my first boss at the War Office. He made a halfhearted attempt to persuade me to stay in the Army. Finally he suggested that for the time being I should come into the War Office and write up some aspects of my service in Egypt. I agreed and for one morning faced a blank sheet of paper with diminishing enthusiasm. The second morning looked like being a repetition. My head was full of other things.

I suddenly decided to ask a Cairo Embassy friend, now in London, Andrew Chapman Andrews, to lunch. He had had the experience of escorting Haile Selassie back to his throne in Addis Ababa and I wanted to hear his news. I did not know that he had now become head of the Personnel Department at the Foreign Office. At lunch he asked if I had ever thought of joining the Foreign Service. I had not. Nevertheless I was conscious that my recent experiences overseas had aroused an interest in international affairs and the problems that the aftermath of the war would bring.

There was an additional reason why the idea of working for the Foreign Office appealed to me. One of the redeeming features of serving in the Army during the war was that the central objective of one's efforts was abundantly clear. To serve one's country was a simple and satisfying purpose. Working in the Foreign Service would be a continuation of this purpose. It seemed preferable to promoting the interests of a railway company even if, as seemed probable, that company became a nationalised organisation.

Chapman Andrews explained that a new department, called the Middle East Secretariat, had been set up in the Foreign Office on the initiative of Ernest Bevin the new Foreign Secretary. They needed someone to work in it who knew the area. Would I like to be considered? It would not, he explained, mean permanent establishment but could possibly lead to it. Suddenly I saw the chance of everything falling into place. Our house in Westminster, bought on Angela's hunch, was within walking distance of the Foreign Office. The pay would be more than twice the amount the railway would be likely to offer. I agreed to be considered, was accepted on an unestablished basis and started work at the end of 1945. My first chief was Sir Kinahan Cornwallis, a giant Arabist from the Sudan Political Service who had won fame as Ambassador in Iraq during the war at the time of the German inspired Raschid Ali revolt. After a few months the question of establishment came up officially. I was just above the age which necessitated a written examination and a 'house party' weekend.

I accordingly applied formally to the Civil Service Commission for establishment in the Foreign or Colonial Service. After interviews with the Civil Service Selection Board the Colonial Office replied affirmatively and offered me a posting to the Colonial Secretariat at the King David Hotel Jerusalem. An understanding Colonial Office official, (Sir) Patrick Renison (later Governor of Kenya) suggested that I might prefer, before finally agreeing, to await news from the Foreign Office. In due course there was a favourable reply from them which I decided to accept. Had I gone to Jerusalem I would almost certainly have perished with others in the famous Jewish terrorist attack on the Secretariat in the King David Hotel. I was pleased that the Foreign Office recruited at the same time a particularly gallant soldier (Sir) Peter Wilkinson. (Sir) Oliver Wright and (Sir) Brooks Richards highly decorated naval officers also joined.

Although I had studied nineteenth century colonial history as my special subject at the University, I had been largely indifferent to foreign affairs in the immediately pre-war years. The rise of the Nazis did not seem to agitate my friends at Oxford as much as our counterparts at Cambridge. Amongst us were few fierce arguments about fascists and communists. Looking back, this disinterest must reflect badly on us, and perhaps on Oxford as a whole. As far as I was concerned, the war had changed all that and I approached the Foreign Office appointment with some excitement.

My first day at the Foreign Office was less strange than the first day at the War Office in 1939. The military had been an unknown quantity but to win the war was clearly the immediate objective. At the Foreign Office the objective was not so abundantly clear. None of the senior officials was known to me. I was directed to the Middle East Secretariat which was not in the main building but in the government offices in George Street. This was unpromising. I realised at once that few people were going to seek out a new and unknown department far away from the centre of things. This indeed proved correct.

The idea behind the Secretariat, for which I had been recruited, was a favourite theme of Ernest Bevin's. He believed simplistically that the way to avoid future political problems in the Middle East was to raise standards of living as quickly as possible. British technical assistance was one way to do so. The Secretariat was to interest Middle East governments in such assistance and to find British specialists willing to advise and, if necessary, work for Middle Eastern governments.

It was a sensible idea and had been identified in many aspects by the civil staff of the Middle East Office set up in Cairo in 1941 under Oliver Lyttelton, to which I have earlier referred. In practice it proved far easier said than done. Middle Eastern politicians were more interested in political than economic matters. In particular the problem of Israel was beginning to dominate their minds as well as the struggle for personal advancement within their own domestic arenas. Nor was the idea fully accepted in the Foreign Office, Colonial Office and the embassies abroad. It was new and, for that reason alone, was to be looked at with some care. The 'old hands' were keen to get back to familiar ways and the appointment of Sir Kinahan Cornwallis as Head of the Secretariat had raised the spectre of outsiders with undue influence. Nevertheless a certain amount was achieved. For example, the Iraq government were persuaded to recruit an irrigation expert who produced promising and imaginative plans for development, some of which were later fulfilled. Others revised Nile waters' schemes for Egypt and various kinds of specialist services were made available for Trans-Jordan, Syria and the Lebanon. But the effect was negligible compared with the need.

In addition to myself, the Secretariat included two intelligent and enthusiastic ladies, Josey Crouch and Charlotte Waterlow, the daughter of a famous Ambassador to Greece. Her knowledge of Foreign Office ways was invaluable. She was later decorated for her work in this Department. Coming straight from the Services I found, at first, the universal use of Christian names to senior officers somewhat surprising. At first the pre-war members of the Service with whom I dealt were somewhat distant in the usual British way. The most forthcoming was (Sir) Peter Garran. The explanation was simple. He was Australian and one of a few who had been recruited pre-war.

The existence of the Secretariat led to my appointment in December 1946 as Secretary of a War Office Working Party on Cyrenaica. The basic objective of the Working Party was to put the British Military Administration of the territory into respectable and internationally praise-worthy order before it was visited by the representatives of the United Nations, who would decide on its future. Our recommendations, after forty years, read quaintly as no one could foresee the oil bonanza which would transform the poverty stricken and war-scarred territory eventually into the Libya of Colonel Gaddafi. By the standards of the time, our suggestions were progressive enough but limited by the understandable Treasury constraints. The Working Party was led by Sir Bernard Reilly an ex-Indian Political Service officer who had spent most of his life in Aden. He was an Arabist of note and was the architect of the first treaty (1934) between the UK and the Yemen. He and I had a bond between us, as he was a Railway enthusiast. Over many years he had spent his home leaves pursuing his favourite hobby. I asked him how he maintained his morale as he sat, in 1940, a lonely and isolated Governor in Aden, hearing the depressing news on the radio from London. He replied that he kept on his desk a model of the best LMS Express Locomotive. When the bad news came flooding in from London he took comfort from looking at this model and saying to himself "a country which can build an engine like that cannot go down."

The Working Party did not over estimate the chances of Sayed Idris, the so called King, returning to Cyrenaica from his wartime refuge in Egypt. Sir Bernard and I visited him in Cairo. He was an ascetic looking man with beautiful long hands and a soft voice. We were entertained to tea which included a large wild strawberry flan. He cut for us two small segments and then a similar one for himself. But on to his own plate he swept all the remaining strawberries leaving behind the empty crust.

Sir Bernard's second enthusiasm, after railways, was the British Empire (now Commonwealth) Society for the Blind for which he devoted much time and effort. He also kept a sympathetic eye on the Yemeni and Adeni community which had become established in South Wales. He was an ideal choice as a leader of such a Working Party as he was immediately acceptable to the local Cyrenaican population and kept his own delegation constantly entertained by his anecdotes of the Raj, the Arabian peninsula and more recent times. A favourite story was of a colleague who had been torpedoed and, after six hours in the water, was on the point of giving up. Then he thought of his relatives getting premature access to his prized wine cellar, which gave him the necessary strength to survive.

The Working Party returned from Cyrenaica at the end of January 1947 into the latter part of the famous freeze and fuel shortage which must have been one of the lowest points the country ever reached including the worst deprivations of the war. I found my family in moderately good spirits but Angela slightly resentful of having to push a pramload of coke from Battersea Power Station to Westminster. She wrote an amusing short poem addressed to Emanuel Shinwell the Minister of Fuel and Power who, when shown it some years later, took considerable umbrage. An extract was

JACK FROST AT THE WINDOW KNOCKS,
I GO TO BED IN RUGGER SOCKS,
ALAS, ALACK, EMANUEL,
DO YOU WEAR RUGGER SOCKS AS WELL?

Soon after our return I accompanied Sir Michael Wright, an Under Secretary at the Foreign Office on a visit to Washington DC. He was to have secret meetings in the Pentagon about the Middle East. I was supposed in some way to distract the attention of the State Department by talking about the Middle East Secretariat with those members involved in Arabian affairs. The State Department had several highly qualified Arabists strongly sympathetic with Arab nationalism and some with family links to long established American missionary and educational institutions in the area. They warmed to Mr. Bevin's ideas. I also accompanied the late Lord

Davidson on a goodwill mission to Iraq and saw him exercise the persuasive gifts which made him such an influential member of the Conservative Party.

At home in my modest position, I naturally saw little of the Foreign Secretary but I had been lucky in October 1946 to take the notes at some of his discussions with Sidky Pasha the veteran Egyptian statesman on the subject of the revision of the Anglo Egyptian Treaty and on the future of our military bases in the Canal Area. In the event Sidky was unable to get domestic support for the agreement reached with Bevin but the talks gave me a good opportunity to observe the great force of Bevin's sensible and understanding personality. He had the engaging ability to illustrate his arguments with anecdotes of his early life including his time delivering mineral water by cart in Bristol. In later years I observed that Dean Acheson and President Lyndon Johnson had the same ability to use personal anecdotes which did much to create in their listeners an impression of friendship and intimacy. My visit to Washington, my first time in America, filled a gap in my experience. I was kindly invited to stay at the home of (Sir) Denis and Della Allen. He was the Head of Chancery and he and his wife were friendly tutors to me in the ways of an overseas Embassy. My stay also had the very important practical result of enabling me to buy for my children incomparable snow suits as we had just heard that we were to be posted to the Legation in Sofia, Bulgaria as our first overseas diplomatic appointment.

CHAPTER 9

FIRST OVERSEAS POSTING - BULGARIA

My posting to Bulgaria as Head of Chancery at our small Legation was the sort of thing we had expected. It showed that I had been accepted as an average new recruit and was clearly not a mark of special favour or disfavour. Bulgaria was currently the scene of great political changes and would be new to us both. It had played a minor part in the war as a belated and reluctant ally of Germany. There had been a very small communist inspired partisan movement in which a British Officer, Major F. Thompson, a brother of the historian E.P. Thompson, played a significant role. He was an idealistic Oxford educated communist who volunteered for service in the Balkans after training with SOE in Egypt. He was wounded shortly after crossing from Macedonia into Bulgaria in 1944 and was captured and executed. He was commemorated by the Bulgarian Communists who had clearly been impressed by his unusual and sympathetic character.

By the end of the war, Bulgaria had declared itself a Republic and fallen inevitably totally under Soviet influence. British and American diplomatic/military missions had, however, been established in Sofia. By 1947, together with other Balkan states, a peace treaty had been signed with the Allies which granted independence under a measure of Allied supervision. It was agreed that the country would continue as an area of predominantly Russian influence, but the Allies vainly were hoping that some semblance of democratic government would be evolved. This was not the intention of the Russians.

The climate was said to be healthy for children and the living conditions were reported to be adequate. Some food and drink was imported from the U.K. to the Legation. The office pressed us to go as soon as possible as my predecessor had already moved to his new posting in Portugal leaving his wife in Sofia in the flat allocated to us. This had the advantage of making it difficult for Bulgarians to occupy it. But our departure from London at short notice posed logistical difficulties for us. We were short of money. Our house had to be let, expensive heavy winter clothes had to be purchased, and a small car ordered. But most difficult of all was to recruit someone to help with our two small sons.

An advertisement, not disclosing the destination, brought a flood of applications from suitable ladies understandably seeking the sun and escape from rationed Britain. All fell away when we disclosed our destination. At a cocktail party near to the date of our departure we mentioned our problem to an army friend. He offered to speak to a girl in a neighbouring flat to his own who had been complaining to him of her job in the City. Within twenty four hours a strikingly pretty girl named Barbara Burd called at our house and said at once that she was willing, in spite of her mother's hesitations, to come with us. She confessed that she had no experience with young children but would do her best. Her eagerness impressed us and we agreed. She proved a great success. Within two years she had married the French Military Attache, Marcel Cima, a charming Corsican. They have remained our good friends ever since. By such tricks of fate are destinies settled.

There was no way of getting a family to Sofia except by train. The famous Orient-Express was said to have resumed service. But it was not initially revealed that, after Venice, it stopped at most stations and was reduced to one sleeping car with no restaurant service. After Ljubliana it proceeded seldom at more than ten miles per hour owing to the work on the track and especially on bridges which the war had wrecked. The journey seemed interminable until after three days the train came to a halt in the total darkness and deep snow some distance from Sofia station. After waiting some time it was explained we would have to wait longer as Sofia station was fully occupied with the ceremonies marking the departure of the Communist Albanian Head of State.

Just as our spirits reached rock bottom we heard English voices outside and saw torches and the outlines of a large old fashioned Daimler limousine. We were quickly helped out of the train by legation colleagues into the snow and crunched through it with our portable luggage to the waiting cars. It was an inauspicious start but we were encouraged by the warmth of our welcome and our enterprising rescue.

We spent our first few nights in the Legation residence and met the Minister, John Sterndale Bennett and his gentle wife Dorothy. They were admirable but were totally preoccupied with the work of the Legation in which she acted voluntarily as his supplementary secretary. Sterndale Bennett, a brisk Yorkshireman, had joined the Diplomatic Service after the end of the first World War, in which he had been decorated and so seriously wounded at Salonika as to be deprived of the full use of one arm. After being hit he had lain all night in the freezing snow but, as he remarked, he might as well have been in a refrigerator as his wounds were sterilised. He was a 'workaholic' par excellence and his seniors in Whitehall were from time to time ungratefully impatient with him. But he was determined that they should understand developments in Bulgaria which were hard to visualise in London if they were not accurately reported. If Whitehall judged them unimportant he, at least, had fully informed them.

Communications between Whitehall and Sofia were difficult. There was no reliable telephone connection. We had diplomatic wireless for emergencies and a weekly diplomatic bag which was brought by the King's Messenger on Friday evenings and who departed for London again with our bag on Sunday. The King's Messenger was accompanied by a guard. The Minister characteristically wanted questions raised by Friday's bag answered in time to return with the King's Messenger on Sunday. This meant that all our weekends were disrupted and Mrs. Sterndale Bennett's voluntary contribution proved more than welcome.

Our departure from London at short notice had precluded an adequate briefing and any rush language courses. Indeed at that time the Foreign Office was not organised properly to equip their people before they left for new postings. There will always be occasions for hurried departures, but I would certainly have profited from being better informed before our arrival. There were several legendary stories of pre-war diplomatic life in Sofia. I like best the incident when a revolutionary Bulgarian had been shot seeking refuge in our Legation and had fallen dead on the front steps of the Residence. On being told, the Minister raised his eyes briefly from his papers and said,

"See that the body is removed before the children go for their walk."

When the Legation staff under the Minister Sir George Rendel were evacuated from Sofia to Istanbul during the war a bomb was hidden in their luggage. At the very last moment on arrival it was detected and a disaster averted. There has been argument about who placed the bomb. The Bulgarians have always denied it. The Germans were blamed but Sir George is said to have attributed it to the carelessness of our own S.O.E. The Minister's daughter Ann, a strong minded girl, became well known to us in Cairo and eventually married Jack Triggs a close and valued friend from Christ Church days.

The main problems that were facing us in Bulgaria were clear. First and foremost the Bulgarian Communist Party was engaged in eliminating all domestic opposition. Non communist political party leaders were executed, imprisoned or forced to flee the country. A 'Fatherland Front' containing bogus democratic party members concealed a total communist dictatorship. This was contrary to all agreements embodied in the Peace Treaty. This policy inevitably meant the severing of all Bulgarian links with the West. Persons who had been educated in the West were suspect and deprived of employment. Academic links were broken. There was a notable Shakespearean scholar at Sofia University. His contacts were cut off. Dealings with Western countries were confined to carefully monitored official channels. Thus it was unwise and ultimately impossible to have Bulgarian acquaintances. Travel in the country without surveillance was impermissible. But the peace treaty with Bulgaria permitted the British, Americans and French to have attached to their Missions, treaty enforcement military personnel whose duties were theoretically to check Bulgarian performance. Needless to say they were obstructed at every turn.

The result was that the members of Western Legations plus the Swiss, Turks and sometimes the Austrians, drew together in self defence, entertaining each other and exchanging opinions and such information of Bulgarian and Soviet activities that they could glean from a variety of sources. The company of fellow diplomats, many of similar age and common interests was by no means dull. The French legation included Romain Gary who later became internationally known as a novelist and the later husband of Jean Seberg the Hollywood actress. In Sofia his wife was Lesley Blanche, the authoress of *The Wilder Shores of Love*. Sofia was no place for such a bohemian couple. It was a sad city still recovering from the war and bewildered by political developments and offered little recreational or cultural activities. The British Council struggled manfully but all its modest efforts were treated with hostility and suspicion. Angela delivered a lecture on Hogarth with great aplomb with a text and slides provided from the Council in London. It was well attended. The long established American school gave up the struggle and closed down.

The British and the American diplomats in the immediate aftermath of the war, were closest to each other. The French maintained a certain independence. The Turks with their large Turkish minority in the country had special advantages and problems. The Italians were anxious to restore their reputation and obscure their role in the recent war. The only British subjects in Bulgaria were very few locally born ladies who were widows of British Danube pilots. They were very poor, had few friends in the U.K. and did not know whether to stay in Bulgaria or face an England they hardly knew. We warned one who had decided to go that she should be careful not to attempt any smuggling out of precious objects. At the last moment she arrived breathless at the Legation with a not inconsiderable quantity of gold bars. The Bank of England grudgingly agreed to accept them by instalments at current rates through the Diplomatic bag.

It was extremely painful to watch the elimination of potentially friendly individual Bulgarians for whom we had no responsibility and were powerless to protect. An example was the Reuters correspondent in Sofia, a Bulgarian national, Filcheff, who had been educated partly in the U.K. and was probably the only cricketer in the country. His Bulgarian wife gave piano lessons. He indicated to the Legation that he thought it inevitable that he would in due course be arrested and asked for our help. We made suggestions to his head office in London. They declined to cooperate pleading that any cooperation would prejudice the position of their agency in future. In due course he was arrested, charged with currency offences and eventually disappeared. For a time his wife was allowed to continue to give piano lessons in the one room retained in their Sofia flat. The remainder of the flat was taken over by Communist officials. One day she came to the Legation in a state of great distress. She had been ordered to leave Sofia that evening by train to a distant part of the country unknown to her and where she had no friends. She had to comply and, as we heard later, was arrested on arrival as a 'prostitute' having no means of support. She committed suicide. This was not an isolated case and Bulgarians linked with the U.S. suffered worst of all.

There were, of course, purely Anglo-Bulgarian matters for the Legation to discuss with the Foreign Ministry. There were questions of compensation for properties and factories of British ownership seized by the Government. At that time all representations were fruitless. The Bulgarian government was also allowing Jews to leave for Palestine at a time when the British Government still held the mandate and were doing their utmost to prevent immigrants reaching Palestine in view of the overcrowded situation there. Although the streets of Sofia were lined with crates marked 'Tel Aviv' etc. the Government denied all knowledge of any such movement and manifestly welcomed our embarrassment.

There were also debatable cases of persons claiming British nationality who were seeking exit permits. These were almost without exception refused by the Bulgarians in spite of compelling humanitarian reasons. On my visit to the Foreign Ministry to discuss these cases I was usually received by the Head of Protocol who had long been a pre-war member of their Diplomatic Service and spoke good English. He hung on to his post by virtue of his technical knowledge but he always gave the melancholy impression that he expected that particular day to be his last.

The Bulgarian Government was headed by Georgi Dimitrov supported by other Bulgarian Communists who had been members of the Comintern and who had spent the war in the Soviet Union awaiting an opportunity to return to take over their native land. Dimitrov was probably the Bulgarian, with the possible exception of Kings Ferdinand and Boris, best known in the U.K. His brave performance at the notorious Reichstag trial in Nazi Germany in 1933 had been headlines at the time in the British Press. The admiration for him then had been well deserved. As members of the Sofia diplomatic corps we got occasional glimpses of him when the Bulgarian Government gave receptions to foreign dignitaries in the faded splendour of the former Royal Palace.

On these occasions at an appropriate time, Dimitrov took briefly to the floor, and danced traditional dances with ladies in gay peasant costumes. There was no doubt about the genuine enthusiasm of the party faithful. One of my clearest memories of the palace was the impossibility of finding the route to the only gentleman's lavatory without a journey of hundreds of yards through dismal ill-lit corridors.

One of those Bulgarians who returned to Sofia from the USSR after the war was a certain Georgi Andrechin. He occupied a post which could be called 'Special Assistant' to the Foreign Minister Kolarov. He spoke perfect American. I took him British newspapers whenever I could. He was a man of great personal charm and good looks. His life story, as told to me in part by him is worth recording. King Ferdinand had made a habit of touring in his country and visiting the town and village schools to question pupils in any class. Any child who showed unusual intelligence was picked out by him and trained for his civil service. Andrechin had been such a pupil. The King kept track of his scholars and from time to time called them for interview. In his late teens Andrechin attended such an interview at which the King said bluntly

"Mr. Andrechin, I hear you are a Socialist."

To which he received the answer, "No, your Majesty, not a socialist but an anarchist."

"In which case," the King said, "You had better leave this country and go to America."

Andrechin did so and joined the famous American Communist International Workers of the World. He was employed on building railroads and engaged in political agitation. In due course he was picked up by the police but not before he had attracted the attention of a wealthy American widow who put up bail for him. He took advantage of this to flee to Europe where he eventually became a member of the Comintern.

When Averell Harriman visited the Soviet Union in the nineteen twenties seeking compensation for the seizure of Harriman properties, Andrechin acted as interpreter. Harriman returned as U.S. Ambassador to the Soviet Union in 1943 and enquired after Andrechin. The Russians at first denied any knowledge of him. He was in fact undergoing punishment in a labour camp in the North from which he was hastily recovered, dusted down and in due time produced for the Ambassador. After the war had ended he opted to return to Bulgaria and started to serve in the Foreign Ministry. When

I used to visit him regularly in his office the Chinese Communists were making their spectacular advance against Chiang kai Shek. He had a large flagged map on his wall and lectured me excitedly on the significance of this Communist triumph.

We entertained him once to family lunch in our flat where he quickly fascinated our two small boys. Sometime later he was suddenly no longer in his office. Bulgarian officials denied any knowledge of his whereabouts. I could find out nothing about him. Many years later I learned from a former Bulgarian Ambassador in London that he had been one of Stalin's selected victims. The KGB distrusted his close U.S. connection but Stalin had a special grudge against him for his authorship of an unauthorised communique used by TASS in 1941 warning their readers of the impending German invasion. Both Dimitrov the Bulgarian dictator and Vasil Kolarov his Foreign Minister tried to intervene in 1948 on Andrechin's behalf, but in vain.

A great deal of our time was spent in trying to protect our British staff from persecution by the Bulgarian secret police and, in some cases, from their own follies. Everyone, to a greater or lesser extent, was spied upon, sometimes in the clumsiest ways. Little attempt was made to conceal surveillance by binoculars or shadowings and our few Bulgarian staff in the office or in our homes were under constant pressure. When I had first arrived, Sterndale Bennett had told me, somewhat apologetically, that I would find some 'odd things going on.' For the most part they were left overs from the period before the Peace Treaty had been signed and the Diplomatic missions and their staffs were more like occupying forces and sometimes behaved as such. Robert Conquest, the poet and clearest eyed historian of the Soviet Union was briefly one of this undisciplined group and was permitted certain favours by the Bulgarians and succeeded in removing a local girl out of the country. This he did without informing anyone in the Legation. His wife had a miserable time in Sofia and we were relieved to see the back of them.

One of my unmarried colleagues, Ffreebairn Simpson, had a Bulgarian girl besieged in his flat. They had become friends and on her way home one night she had been stopped and threatened by the secret police. Next day she fled to his flat where she had remained ever since, being afraid, with reason, to leave it. He had now received his orders from London to go to another post and a decision on her fate had soon to be taken. He had ceased to do any work in the Chancery and vanished each day to deal with what he termed "his problem." Day after day passed until he announced that she had received permission to marry him but nothing had been said about an exit permit for her. The ceremony duly took place and in the evening she came to a little party at the Minister's residence. On the day fixed immediately thereafter for their departure the permit was, at the last minute granted, but no one felt safe until the train had crossed the border into Yugoslavia. He was obliged to leave the Diplomatic Service but continued to serve with distinction in many ways in former Colonial territories and both he and his wife were decorated by H.M.G. The marriage was long lasting. She died in 1991.

In the curious atmosphere of the city, tensions were often high amongst the staff. At one time the KGB in the Soviet Union obviously ran a course of 'faking' compromising photos and the 'graduates' rejoined eventually their national secret police to put their skills to the test. A rash of such photos broke out in our missions in Eastern Europe. The case in Sofia had some special features which represented a modest victory of good over evil.

Our new Minister, (Sir) Paul Mason who had succeeded Sterndale Bennett in 1948, was stopped one Saturday afternoon in the street by a tearful lady who handed him a sealed envelope. He tried to divert its delivery to the Chancery but she firmly refused. Having opened the letter in his residence he at once sent for me. We studied it together. It was a photograph of a man and woman partly undressed. The lady was certainly the wife of one of our staff but the man's face was conveniently turned away from the camera. The embarrassed husband was called in to examine it with us and quickly removed any possible doubt by pointing out that his wife's hair had not been done in that distinctive way for a long time. The photograph of her must have been taken when she had undergone a medical examination in a Bulgarian hospital some months before. It was not long before Paul Mason was summoned to the Ministry of Foreign Affairs. He took me with him. The Chief of Protocol to whom I have referred above made an unctuous speech and regretted that the officer and his wife would have to be withdrawn. When he had finished, Paul Mason rose to his full height of well over six feet, and towering over the man, delivered in a magisterial way a beautifully worded rebuke, the gist of which was that only a low born cad would stoop to a trick like this. He expected to hear no more of it. Nor did we. The threatened staff remained.

Thousands of British tourists have learned what a beautiful country Bulgaria is since changed political conditions have made it a low cost holiday destination for westerners. At the time of our posting, tourist travel was out of the question, not least because of road conditions, lack of hotels, but also because of political obstructions. Comparatively near to Sofia was a primitive mountain resort, Tchamkorya, at which it was possible for diplomats to spend weekends in summer and winter. Access in winter by car was hazardous because of rock falls and deep snow drifts. Advance parties were necessary to light stoves and prepare food. Skiing was possible but there were no lifts and only primitive facilities. Travelling further afield was strongly discouraged and required official permission.

The following is not untypical of the harassment to which diplomats were subjected. A small party of us decided to visit Varna on the Black Sea by way of Plovdiv and Turnovo. The party went in a convoy with an Oldsmobile coupe belonging to the U.S. First Secretary Ray Courtney and our two Humber 4 x 4 military cars with heavy desert type tires. There were seven passengers including my sister Barbara and two Bulgarian drivers. One of the military vehicles carried a load of full jerricans as the Bulgarians would provide no fuelling arrangements en route. The roads, with the exception of a few miles out of Sofia were unsurfaced. All went well including the mountain passes until we arrived at Varna although at Turnovo male members of the party had a hard job to make the hotel lavatories fit for use. On coming out of the hotel at Varna on the first morning we found the tyres of one of the military vehicles had been cut. It was no mean task to repair them. On the first stop on the way home we decided to put the vehicles under the care for the night of the local police, having explained the incident of the tyre slashing. This was a stupid mistake. In the morning the drivers found the tanks of the military vehicles had been filled with sugar - a strictly rationed commodity. The police excused themselves by saying that men had come in the night saying they had 'adjustments' to make. It was necessary to clean out the tanks with our reserve petrol in the jerricans. Finally we had to abandon the Bulgarian drivers and the military vehicles en route for lack of fuel and proceed to Sofia in the Oldsmobile arriving late at night with rapidly diminishing supplies of fuel. Next day the drivers and their vehicles had to be recovered with a new load of jerricans from Sofia.

The vehicles of the treaty enforcement military officers were frequently dangerously sabotaged by interference with braking systems and filling the sumps with nuts and bolts and other foreign matter. No amount of protest to the authorities made the slightest difference or produced any admission of official guilt. Interference was attributed to 'spontaneous public hostility' to us. With no contact with the man in the Bulgarian street or anywhere else we found it hard to detect any hostility or any lack of it but it was always necessary to remember that gratitude if any, was reserved for the Russians who had twice liberated their country - first from the Turks and second from the Germans. There were few traces of German occupation in Sofia except the totally and deliberately neglected German military cemetery which the

Bulgarians refused to maintain. An occasional homesick German straggler came out from the protection of a Bulgarian lover.

One felt very isolated in Sofia and it was hard to realise the dangers of the situation elsewhere in Europe between East and West which culminated in the Berlin air lift. Moreover visitors from the U.K. were few and far between and not always informative. Papers from home were late and the BBC Overseas Service was not always adequate. Far Left MP's in the persons of D.N. Pritt and J.D. Mack came as guests of the Bulgarian Government and expressed their enthusiasm. Mrs. Mack was said to own a hat shop in London but the Bulgarians found her style hard to match with her claimed left wing credentials. A correspondent of the Times of the same persuasion paid a brief call as did an aristocratic lady from the Council of Civil Liberties. The latter asked me if there was not a spirit in Bulgaria that was absent "in dear old England." When I told her bluntly what was in fact happening to civil liberties in Bulgaria, she replied "I don't believe you." Since then I have always felt rather doubtful about the Council.

More welcome was Harry (later Lord) Walston who came with strong recommendations from Ernest Bevin to study, albeit briefly, Bulgarian agriculture. He arrived, with driver, in a large pre-war Mercedes-Benz open sports car. In post war Sofia it was a sensation. I doubt if his studies were profound and he showed us no report. I was later to work with him in the Foreign Office when he was a junior minister in Harold Wilson's Government. In the House of Lords he was always sensible and courteous and although Labour seemed close to the Liberal view.

Welcome also was the late Lord Stansgate (Wedgwood-Benn) who came with his younger son David. They were expected one evening on the Orient Express which they were to board at Belgrade. Accompanied by Bulgarian officials we searched without success for them amongst the passengers on its arrival. A later train was expected from the West near midnight but it was explained that it stopped at all stations from Belgrade and when it crossed the frontier into Bulgaria it was used by the peasants to bring their merchandise into the market in Sofia. I thought it prudent to meet it and persuaded the sceptical Bulgars to do so. On arrival a swarm of peasants came off carrying live ducks, chickens and all kinds of vegetables. After some delay we saw two small, rather travel stained figures who duly identified themselves. In a loud voice in front of his hosts Lord Stansgate exclaimed "I cannot think why we have been invited." But the visit seemed to satisfy them.

For the first time in my life I became seriously ill in Sofia, but, thanks to Angela, escaped disaster. The attack came after dining at the Egyptian Embassy and I was soon convinced that I had appendicitis. The British legation shared with the Americans a Bulgarian doctor who had two, and possibly only two, qualifications. He spoke good English and had access to the American stocks of the new wonder drug 'penicillin.' In retrospect, I suspect he might never have been more in the past than a hospital orderly. We tried to get in touch with him during the night but failed to do so. Staff of the Legation managed to persuade two Bulgarian doctors to come urgently to our flat. They were unprepossessing in the extreme and carried what looked to me to be a plumber's bag of tools. Fortunately before they could make a move the regular doctor arrived. He immediately prescribed a glass of castor oil. I reminded him that if it was indeed appendicitis, as I was convinced it was, such a dose would probably kill me. He guaranteed "one hundred per cent" that it was only "spastic constipation." I hesitatingly drank the glass and in a short time clearly became very ill indeed. Angela then seized the doctor and asked him if he knew what he was doing. He admitted doubts and she and a colleague managed to summon Dr. Tomov, who was the most senior surgeon in the city. He came at once, called an ambulance and went ahead to the hospital having warned me that a local anaesthetic might be necessary. He performed the operation at once and excused the absence of an effective anaesthetic on the lack of supplies and the need for very rapid action. After one bad night I was back at work in not much more than a week. Dr. Tomov came to my bedside in hospital always accompanied by a younger man to whom he seemed to defer. On one occasion Tomov came alone. He told me with tears running down his cheeks that the other man was a Russian who had been put above him to run his hospital and who forbad Tomov to correspond with his distinguished doctor friends in London or to receive western medical publications. He was devastated. I was happy to be told many years later that Tomov recovered his independence and renewed his old contacts. No bill for treatment of any kind was ever sent by the Bulgarian authorities to the British Legation.

Soon after this an entirely different blow fell which changed everything. The Bulgarian Government, in company with its fellow Soviet satellites, were systematically destroying such influence as their Christian churches possessed. Earlier the Bulgarians had successfully dealt with the Orthodox Church replacing a significant Exarch by a more obedient figure. At the end of 1948 we got news that 15 Protestant Pastors in Bulgaria had been arrested and that a show trial was impending.

The church was small and those arrested constituted the whole of its ordained members. There were links with the British and U.S. Baptists and other nonconformists which the Bulgarian Government was determined to destroy. Our Legation sought unsuccessfully more information about the rumoured trial. Questions were asked in the Westminster Parliament and gossip in Sofia suggested that members of the U.S. and British legations would be implicated in charges of espionage. We pressed for representatives to be present at the trial but were refused.

A strange elderly British clergyman arrived suddenly in Sofia to 'observe' the trial. When we asked him who had sent him he was evasive, but it was difficult to judge whether his evasion was deliberate or arose from an overall mental confusion. He claimed his qualification to judge the fairness of the trial derived from the fact that his wife was a J.P. in Norfolk. As the trial progressed I was greatly disconcerted to learn that I was alleged to have instructed the most senior pastor to carry out certain acts of espionage. There was not a word of truth in any of the accusations. It was a strange experience read in the press 'verbatim' remarks which, in the course of evidence, were attributed to me.

All the prisoners confessed and pleaded guilty. Fortunately none of the accused suffered the death penalty but the senior pastor, Ziapkov, was sentenced to 25 years imprisonment of which, I believe, he served no less than 18 before release. Some of the 'evidence' against him was supplied by a young man who had infiltrated himself into the family home in the guise of the Pastor's daughter's fiance. Of the 15 pastors, I had met only Ziapkov twice. First at an official lunch when we were visited by the Bishop of Gibraltar in whose diocese British Anglicans in the Balkans were included. The Bishop incidentally carried with him episcopal equipment specially adapted for air travel including a telescopic crook and a special mitre. He discovered that I had never been baptised nor confirmed. He promised to send me suitable literature which would enable me to prepare for such events. I was unwilling. Ziapkov was a humble man wearing very thick glasses through which I allegedly asked him to count coastal gun emplacements on shore by swimming out in the Black Sea at Varna and looking shorewards. Subsequent to the official lunch he came to our flat for a meal in order to give my sister, visiting us from the U.K., a message of goodwill to a relative in England who had requested my sister to elicit it. His short-sightedness compelled him to crouch low over his food to identify it. The trial inevitably led to a demand for my withdrawal but initially no time limit was set. A bitter exchange of protests began but then died down. It seemed for a short time that the Bulgarians were not going to insist. But a letter to the Times from Lord Vansittart was published sharply critical of the

Bulgarian Government. I was then compelled to leave. I was disappointed and angry as I had tried hard to report fairly and to be unprejudiced in my approach to the regime.

One of the reasons for my expulsion was no doubt the fact that Paul Mason our new Minister had recently arrived and as I had been in Bulgaria for nearly 18 months it was desirable not to allow too much experience to be carried over from his predecessor's time into a new regime.

Personnel Department is always irritated by the unexpected return of officers from abroad. Carefully laid plans are thereby disrupted. Much to my chagrin I was told to prepare to go to Caracas. I did not speak Spanish and all reports of Venezuela were depressing. Happily, on second thoughts, in the light of the mild notoriety I had acquired by my expulsion it was felt I would make a more interesting recruit to the Embassy in Washington where apparently my brief visit in 1947 had made the right impression. As a result my career prospects were substantially improved. The Bulgarians had unwittingly done me a good turn.

There was an interesting sequel to my Bulgarian experience more than twenty five years later. The last nine years of my diplomatic career were spent in senior positions in the Foreign Office in Whitehall, ending as Permanent Under Secretary. Not infrequently I had dealings with a succession of Bulgarian Ambassadors. Two, at least were men of ability and understanding. I made a special point of never referring to my treatment in Sofia and continued to deal with them in an unprejudiced way. Shortly before I was due to retire in 1973 I was astonished to be invited with Angela to pay a week's visit to Bulgaria as the government's guest. With the Secretary of State Alec Home's permission, we accepted and were received with elaborate kindness and shown with pride the notable improvements in the infrastructure of the country.

There was of course no sign of the unfortunate pastors and it was wiser not to make enquiries. As a gesture to the Christian Church we were however driven some distance to take lunch with the Abbot of Rila Monastery who obviously greatly enjoyed the augmentation of his rations for the occasion. Finally I was received by the now disgraced Prime Minister Zhivkov. It was afterwards explained that it was unusual for an official of my rank to be so received. We left that day by train for Belgrade - Angela loaded down with bouquets of gladioli. We considered a chapter had been closed and honour had been partially satisfied.

CHAPTER 10

WASHINGTON EMBASSY - FIRST POSTING 1949-52

To move from the Legation in Sofia to the Embassy in Washington was like going from preparatory school to university in one stride and required adjustment by us all. We made the journey to New York in the traditional way. The farewells at Waterloo, the boat train to Southampton Dock and up the gangway into the comfort of the second class on the Queen Mary. A happy voyage culminated in a spectacular dawn arrival in New York with the skyline of twinkling lights in the city skyscrapers. Train took us to Washington where we moved at once into the furnished house occupied by my predecessor Tom Bromley, within short walking distance down Massachusetts Avenue to the famous Lutyens Embassy. The omens appeared good and memories of Sofia were soon obliterated by the easy hospitality of an attractive city and a full and interesting work load.

Washington, during the war, had been almost a duplicate Whitehall and the main point of coordination of our war effort, civil and military. When we arrived our huge staffs were winding down slowly and were as far as possible concentrated in the Chancery building which was joined physically to the Lutyens mansion. There were also offices downtown and overflow temporary buildings adjoining the Chancery, which lasted in fact for a further fifteen years. Washington was, without doubt, the 'flagship' Embassy of the British Foreign Service and we felt glad to be there.

At the head, as Ambassador, was (Lord) Oliver Franks the one time Glasgow and Oxford don who had made an enviable reputation in Whitehall during the war. He came to Washington from his dominant role in the Marshall Plan and was therefore well known and greatly admired by all the American establishment. Further distinctions lay ahead. Intellectually he was more than a match for anyone with whom he might have to do business. During all my career in Government Service and elsewhere, I have never met a clearer headed man and one who concealed his astonishing analytical ability with such modesty. The remainder of the Embassy staff proved to be very compatible and we seemed to be in for a happy time.

It was pleasant to work with the Americans. Most of us had been used to being close to them during the recent war and the comradeship of that time still persisted. I doubt if at any time previously two countries had easier access to each other's thinking. This happy state of affairs could not continue indefinitely as the relative influence of each country became more apparent and in many sensitive areas of the world, ideologies and interests

68

began to diverge.

My job was to take over the 'Middle East desk' in the Chancery. The Middle East was one of the areas in which we were finding it increasingly difficult to see eye to eye. The three trouble spots were Israel, Iran and Egypt. The course of events is well known to students of Foreign Affairs and it is unnecessary to go over them in detail but there are general observations on each which it would be appropriate to make here.

Handicapped by its economic problems the British Government had the task of trying to make a controlled descent from a position of world power. The Middle East was an area in which British power had far exceeded that of the U.S. In this hard task it hoped and expected to receive the help and sympathy of the U.S. Government. The Americans on the other hand found difficulty in accepting the responsibility which their all powerful position logically forced upon them although they had commercial ambitions. Moreover they believed that the British were clinging in the Middle East to outmoded 'imperialist' positions which conflicted with their own more liberal conceptions.

Britain's abandonment of the Palestine mandate was inescapable but few British were aware of the intensity of feeling in the U.S. on the founding and recognition of the State of Israel. Bevin had become the object of intense hatred and abuse. The strength of the Zionist lobby in Washington was an eye opener to those unfamiliar with U.S. domestic affairs. Even the humble 'middle East desk' at the Embassy was 'marked' and personal visits to me were made at each stage of any crisis. At the same time in the same city there were clearer signs of anti-semitism than I had ever encountered in the U.K. Not a few criticised President Truman for his support of Israel. I was baffled one day at a cocktail party at the approach by an unknown elderly American lady who said "It is a pity that President Truman is not a Jew." I was at a loss until she added, "If he had been a Jew his haberdashery business would not have failed and he would not now be President of the United States."

Surprisingly a young Zionist organisation in due course invited the Embassy to send a speaker to one of their meetings in New York city. I was sent and had the expected hostile reception during my remarks. It became a good deal worse when I stepped down from the platform. But I was rescued by a very elderly bearded Rabbi who stretched a protective arm in front of my chest saying in a loud and heavily accented voice,
"In Russia before the Revolution we thought of Queen Victoria as our Queen and of Englishmen as more than brothers." This enabled me to withdraw with dignity.

The Israelis, on their acceptance as an independent state, opened a

diplomatic office on Massachusetts Avenue. It was not difficult to have good relations with visitors like Teddy Kollek, who is now known as the most famous mayor of Jerusalem and Chaim Hertzog who became President of his country. I was rather tactlessly introduced to the latter by one of his colleagues who said
"You must meet him, he used to be an Englishman."
Gradually hostility to us over Israel diminished but for a long time was deeply seated and from time to time came to the surface.

The second problem which gave trouble was Iran. Pent up nationalist feeling had burst out and concentrated on the activities of the Anglo Iranian Oil Company (AIOC) which was accused of exploiting the oil wealth of the country. No agreement between the company and Iranian Government could be reached and eventually the company was seized and nationalised. Desperate for sterling oil Britain felt that she was entitled to full U.S. support not only in her own interests but in the interests of the U.S. itself. Such support was not forthcoming in the way in which HMG hoped. Reasons for the U.S. attitude were clear. The Democratic Party was traditionally anti-imperialist and in certain circles there was an underlying sympathy for Iran's bid for a greater share of the profit from her own resources. British opposition to such a bid was, in Washington's view, the quickest way to open Iran to communist influence and to the bogey of a Russian takeover. The U.S. oil companies, long envious of AIOC were only held back by fear that Iran's policy would set a precedent and would threaten their growing interests in Arabia. Mossadeq was the embodiment of Iranian nationalism but characteristically the U.S. refused for long to believe he was not open to compromise. The negotiations dragged on for from 1949-52 until Mossadeq was removed in part by Anglo-U.S. inspired action.

My recollections are now of the quality of the Iran negotiations between Secretary of State Dean Acheson and Oliver Franks and the wisdom of the latter's advice to Whitehall where the inability of Departments to agree amongst themselves complicated the task of the ailing Bevin and his successor Herbert Morrison. It was without doubt a problem of the greatest complexity and failure to reach a quick settlement was inevitable.

During the negotiations, Mossadeq visited the U.S. and the U.N. Assembly where his dramatic appearance and his theatrical posturings supported a clever portrayal of the 'underdog.' At first, he successfully gained American press and public sympathy. I attended with considerable misgiving his speech to the National Press Club in Washington where the leading journalists from all parts of the country customarily assembled. For once his instincts deserted him. He opened by accusing all of them of being in the pay of the Anglo-Iranian Oil Company. From this he never recovered during his speech and subsequent questioning.

After Bevin's retirement, Herbert Morrison who had succeeded him as Secretary of State, came in September 1951 to Washington in an effort to get decisive U.S. support over Iran in advance of the approaching British election. It was difficult not to feel sorry for him, but also not to feel a little ashamed. He was clearly exhausted but totally out of his depth. Even with the support of Franks and Roger Makins (later Lord Sherfield) he was no match for Acheson and there was no compatibility. At a luncheon in the Embassy, at which Franks was not present, he outrageously criticised before British and U.S. guests, his fellow members of the Labour Government, particularly Sir Stafford Cripps. Suddenly, feeling he was losing his audience, he turned to Lady Franks and asked whether she did not agree. A quiet, "No," caused him to change the subject at once.

A very minor legacy of Morrison's visit as far as I was concerned was that his lady typist, an old time colleague from the L.C.C. left a drawer full of chocolate bars in my desk which she had temporarily occupied.

I had left Washington by the time the oil question was brought to a temporarily successful conclusion by the substitution of the AIOC by a consortium of companies in which the British held a strong position but the Iran Government revenue was ultimately considerably enhanced.

The same factors which made Anglo-American discussions difficult on Iran came into play on the question of the British Military Base in the Suez Canal Zone in Egypt. Repeated efforts to reach a compromise failed and the way was gradually cleared for the advent of Colonel Nasser - a much more formidable embodiment of Middle Eastern nationalism than Mossadeq. The return of Churchill and Eden to power in London in 1951 made it no easier for agreement to be reached with the Americans on a mutually acceptable approach to the Middle East. Our differences culminated in the Suez crisis in 1956 and the fall of Eden, but by that time Acheson had left office and been replaced by Dulles who was much less understanding of the British case.

Life at Washington was always interesting. Visits by Prime Ministers Attlee and Churchill and Princess Elizabeth contributed to the excitement.

Prime Minister Attlee came unostentatiously at a critical time in the Korean War. It has become a legend of the Labour Party that he prevented Truman from using the atomic bomb against the Chinese. This is less than the truth as Dean Rusk tactfully explained in his very frank television cross-examination on the BBC by Kenneth Harris the biographer of Attlee.

Churchill's visit could not help being more sensational both in the city and in the Embassy where his presence infected the whole staff. The

Princess greatly interested the Americans and the impression she created pleased us all and gave great hope for the future. Very moving was the presentation to her of an extremely old black messenger who had delivered Embassy letters throughout Washington for many decades. He confided later, it was not for him the most memorable occasion in the Embassy in his life. This, for him, had been the marriage of the Ambassador's, (Lord Pauncefote) daughter, more than half a century earlier.

Work in the Chancery was absorbing and hospitality in the city - received and given - was stimulating, informal and amusing. My routine in the Chancery was to call frequently on the officers in the State Department who dealt with Middle Eastern matters. Sometimes these visits were made on instructions from the Foreign Office but, more often, to compare notes regularly on developing situations and to argue out interpretations of policies. The American officers had a great deal of expertise in the area although they were inclined too often to think that the British must know best on the basis of their long experience there. These officers became good friends. They were supervised by an Under Secretary, George McGhee, a powerful and enthusiastic former Rhodes Scholar from Queens College Oxford. After leaving the university he had quickly made a fortune in the oil industry and married the beautiful daughter of the legendary American oil expert de Golyer. He was at the beginning of a distinguished career in diplomacy being Ambassador in later years in Bonn and Ankara. At the time of the Iranian oil crisis, the authorities in London persistently mistrusted his motives, believing him to be too close to the U.S. oil companies and, worst still, an Irishman. In fact his family came originally from Scotland. He has been devoted to Oxford all his life and admits his heroes when he studied there were Clive and Warren Hastings. But by the time he took control of Middle East Affairs in the State Department he was one of the strongest believers that the U.K. had not adjusted their imperial views sufficiently to the spirit of the times. In retrospect, he was probably right. At that time the CIA was expanding and becoming a new factor in Anglo/US relations. On our embassy side liaison was developed by an intellectual young first secretary Adam Watson, who had been in Moscow in critical times during the war. He eventually left the Foreign Office for academic life, often in the U.S. We had known him slightly in Cairo.

When not fully occupied in Washington I went, like all my colleagues, on speaking engagements across the country usually at Universities. These were for the most part on Middle Eastern topics with occasional exceptions. I shared a platform at Denver University with Dr. Mohammad El-Sayyat, from the Egyptian Embassy, who later became Foreign Secretary. He caused great disappointment by refusing to quarrel with "his good British friend." Particularly memorable was the celebration of William Shakespeare's birthday at a University in Florida. There were two speakers, a well known film actress with the first name of 'Liz' and myself. Two Jewish students born in New York City had specially composed a dance tune entitled "Happy Birthday Willie." We each received a recording of it. I spoke first and went back to sit next to Liz on the platform. At this point her PR man leaned over her and whispered "Your No. 2 speech Liz." She rose and faultlessly delivered, without a note, a not entirely inappropriate address. What her No. 1 speech contained I never learned.

Our scene was changed when Guy Burgess arrived to join the congenial world of our Chancery. The story of his time in Washington has been frequently recorded, often inaccurately, by the many 'spy writers.'

It was then normal practice, as a matter of courtesy, for the details of any officer being proposed for his staff to be sent to the Ambassador for formal approval. In Washington the question was handled by the Minister Derick Hoyer Millar (Lord Inchyra) and the Head of Chancery Bernard Burrows. Both these men were senior regular members of the Foreign Service, unlike Oliver Franks. On hearing of the proposal, Hoyer Millar exclaimed

"We can't have that man. He has filthy fingernails."

The subject was developed further and Burgess's application was turned down. Whether Hoyer Millar knew of Maurice Bowra's alleged remark that Burgess "had shit in his fingernails," I do not know. Our refusal produced a sharp rebuke from London to the effect that Burgess was now an established member of the Foreign Service and it was not for the Embassy to refuse to accept him. He had in fact been established comparatively recently in the junior Branch B having failed the tests for Branch 'A', the administrative grade. Whether this rebuke or his recruitment had, as has been suggested, political backing I do not know but he was well known to certain M.P.'s. Shortly before he arrived I had a visit in my office from Kim Philby, an intelligence officer, who worked in a nearby room but with whom I had no official contacts. I knew Philby slightly, but did not like him, although mutual friends, especially ladies, spoke well of him.

Philby asked if I knew Burgess. I replied that I had seen him from time to time in the corridors of the Foreign Office when he worked for a Labour Minister, Hector McNeil. He explained that he had been a friend of Burgess at Cambridge where he had been considered one of the most brilliant undergraduates of his time. However, said Philby, this early promise had for some reason not been fulfilled - much to his friends' and his own disappointment. Would I try to take a sympathetic view of him and help him when I could? He understood that Burgess was to work with me. This was the first I had heard of his working with me.

Burgess had been coming to us from the Far Eastern Department in London and it was first intended that he should work with the Counsellor Hubert Graves (Sir) who dealt with that area. However he knew Burgess and absolutely refused to have anything to do with him. The Head of Chancery, Bernard Burrows, therefore intended that he should help me instead. I protested, not because I personally had any unfavourable reports of Burgess, but because any success that I might have with my contacts in the State Department depended much on our personal friendships. They would not like to be fobbed off with a new, more junior man who had no knowledge of the Middle Eastern area. The Head of Chancery quite reasonably insisted and in due course Burgess turned up in my office.

He was a most unprepossessing sight with deep nicotine stains on his fingers and a cigarette drooping from his lips. Ash dropped everywhere. I took an instant dislike and made up my mind that he would play no part in my official duties. It took little longer time to find out that he was a drunken name dropper and totally useless to me in my work. But he certainly had an enormous range of acquaintances. He made no secret of being a homosexual but at that time there was no link in official minds with security. Over months it was difficult for anyone to find anything constructive for him to do. I noticed that from time to time he asked me to show him classified telegrams on matters which were not his concern. I declined to do so, not because I thought he might be a spy, but because I felt sure he would not be able to resist the temptation to show off his knowledge to the friends of whom he boasted. He explained his morning lateness in coming into the embassy by 'sinus' trouble, caused by a blow to his head, when a colleague (Sir) Fred Warner had 'deliberately' pushed him down the stairs of a London night
One redeeming gift was an ability to caricature. He drew several
for my small sons. Included among them was a Christmas
for Father Christmas. I should have paid
ater 'borrowed' from me and

c Arthur by President Truman
of what to do with Burgess. Our
ers blaming the dismissal on the
mbassador ruled that replies were to
were to be ignored. Burgess was to sort
erflowing ash trays. After many days he

Dear Robin
This is Daddy's New
Railway Line, the Clinkie-Clinki
Guy

ONE OF SEVERAL DRAWINGS SENT TO MY SMALL SON, ROBIN
BY GUY BURGESS IN WASHINGTON 1951/2
(THIS ONE IN BLUE CRAYON ON MUCH FOLDED
KITCHEN PAPER)

drafted a private letter to Donald Maclean, Head of the American Department in the Foreign Office analyzing the correspondence. He showed it to me, but I did not absorb it. Whether it was ever sent, I do not know. He mentioned with some surprise that it was favourable to the U.S. Administration. Donald Maclean was his companion on their eventual flight to Moscow.

Burgess occupied a part of Philby's large house. Angela and I dined there once. It was for the hosts an alcoholic evening watched in almost complete silence by Philby's delicate Irish wife. In the light of later events, several have speculated on whether her early death was completely natural.

Finally Burgess was sent home after the Governor of Virginia had officially complained of repeated excessive speeding in his huge Lincoln Continental coupe. Burgess was fascinated by fast cars and his stepfather had designed the unsuccessful rear-engined Birney streamlined car. It is now widely accepted that he deliberately provoked his return to the U.K. as a part of a pre-arranged plan to warn Donald Maclean that his treachery had been detected and to escape with him to Moscow. I have always been reluctant to share this view but I am assured it is so by those best placed to judge. Recently (1991) redundant ex-KGB men in Moscow have confirmed it to visiting journalists in return for hard currency. The Ambassador's premptory dismissal of him appeared to me to come as a sharp shock. I saw him immediately after he had left the Ambassador's office. He burst into my room. He was furious. Referring to the Ambassador, he cried out, "That man had the nerve to criticise me," and so on. If he was acting he had missed his true vocation. Later he tried to make light of it to me saying his only regret was that he would find it hard to explain to his friends in London. Before he had left for Washington he had told them of his expectations that he would soon be mixing with Acheson and the top American policy makers. To report failure would, he said, be embarrassing. It always gave me comfort to think how he must have hated living in the Soviet Union and how, on further acquaintance the KGB must have wondered why they had put confidence in him.

My American opposite numbers were, of course astonished at this miserable episode. They knew very little about Burgess, but those who had known Maclean realised the seriousness of their flight as he had collaborated with them on very sensitive matters. Revelations about Philby were to come later after we had returned to England. He came near to being appointed Head of British Secret Intelligence but was blackballed by the instinctive judgment of (Sir) Patrick Reilly who had experienced him in Athens and was later in a position in the Foreign Office to veto the proposed appointment.

From a professional point of view, our stay in Washington was of the utmost value. I had been a part of our largest Embassy and learnt from an outstanding Ambassador. I had seen at close range negotiations with our most important ally. In this process I had made the acquaintance of contemporaries of many nationalities, who would clearly be future players in international affairs. What I had seen in the Legation in Sofia was child's play compared with Washington. It was reasonable to expect on my return that a middle level departmental job in the Foreign Office would be within my experience and capability.

We were due to leave Washington towards the end of 1952. The question of fitting the boys for entry into a British preparatory school had been ever present in our minds. My elder son had begun schooling in Washington in the neighbourhood public (free) school where he found friends but learned little. He joined the local boy scouts. At each of their gatherings he was required to salute the American flag and swear loyalty. Since he could not do that a stupid scout master ruled that he could not remain. I pointed out that the scouting movement had been originally a British conception, but he was not impressed. The problems of my sons' learning more was happily solved by the offer Angela received to work in the headmistress's office in one of the best private schools in the city, which was beyond our means. In exchange for her services, our boys were accepted without payment. No Latin was available, but Angela took the responsibility for that in our home. As my elder son won a classical scholarship to Oxford some seven years later, she can rightly claim a large measure of the credit.

Holidays were spent on the Maine coast where we had been given an introduction to an American family, which together with their friends and relatives, created a happy community in a small harbour village. The many children of similar ages were in their element and we made life-long friends outside Washington diplomatic circles. For many years after there was always a British family there in the summer.

*ANGELA ENJOYING HER FAVOURITE SPORT IN MAINE
SKETCH BY B. VIETOR. 1951.*

CHAPTER 11

RETURN TO THE FOREIGN OFFICE

On our return to London I was assigned to further Middle Eastern work which was continuing to be an area of activity and of special interest to Anthony Eden the Foreign Secretary. Great changes were ahead in the Persian Gulf where the question of boundaries between Saudi Arabia and the Trucial States for which we were politically responsible, were matters of dispute not only with the Saudis but also their American patrons. Oil claims were an important factor although the scale on which they would develop was not then fully imagined. One of the areas of highest tension was the Buraimi oasis. At that time, before the discovery of oil, nobody would have believed that one day it would be reached, not over the desert, but as now by a four lane highway leading to a Hilton Hotel. The Saudis were exercising great pressure to establish their claim to the territory of our Trucial rulers and armed clashes seemed probable. But our view eventually prevailed but not before HMG had removed an unreliable Trucial ruler and installed a substitute of our choice.

The selection of the successor was the choice largely of a young political officer, Michael Weir, who recommended by telegram a local sheik. Eden minuted on the telegram, 'Sounds a good man.' He became the Ruler of Abu Dhabi and eventually one of the richer men in the world and the largest shareholders of the BCCI Bank which collapsed in 1991. Such was the measure of our influence at that time. Tribute must be paid to the Foreign Office for the training of a corps of Arabists who were able at a critical time to exercise a successful paternal influence in this important area.

Such work in my new posting in London was absorbing, but the Coronation of the Queen provided an unexpected relief for two or three weeks in June 1953. Each country invited was represented at the ceremony by a Delegation. The U.S. Delegation was led by the famous General Marshall. Two British officers were attached to it. Royal Marine General Sir Leslie Hollis was the leader and, by virtue of my recent experience in the States, I was appointed to assist him. Marshall, the perfect American gentleman, was head and shoulders above the other U.S. Delegates. They were the rugged General Bradley, the war leader, Governor Warren of California and the engaging Fleur Cowles the then wife of the proprietor of 'Look' magazine and later the wife of Montague Meyer, a British industrialist. Wives accompanied them and the Governor's pretty young daughter, known throughout America as 'Honey Bear,' was also included. Mrs. Bradley kept an embarrassingly sharp eye on the General's drinks. A U.S. marine major provided the liaison with me. The whole event was a unique experience and the festivities seemed limitless. Angela was able to share in some of them but unfortunately could not be seated in the Abbey for the crowning. The whole U.S. Delegation, less General Marshall and his wife, had a splendid view from a gallery in the Abbey. We had to arrive early and could watch the senior representatives of all other countries, move to and from their places below. It was an enthralling procession of world leaders.

In my opinion, the two guests who made the most striking impression were Pandit Nehru and Princess Marina, the widowed Duchess of Kent. The former's clothes of sober coloured material were a vivid contrast to everyone else and his solemn pallid face bore an enigmatic and unchanging expression. The Princess looked beautiful, with magnificent jewels and an unmatched regal air. After a time, watching the movement in and out of the Abbey below, suddenly and simultaneously caused a feeling of faintness in our group, who snatched from me the smelling salts which I had brought for my own benefit.

There were many bizarre moments during the two critical days. On the first evening, General Hollis took General Marshall away and I was left to brief the others over dinner on the plans for the ceremonies over the next days. Governor Warren had brought a young and inexperienced civilian aide from his office in Sacramento. He asked question after question until the U.S. Marine remarked to me in an audible whisper,
"Gee I guess this guy doesn't know his ass from page two." It was an expression new to me but it seemed to be entirely appropriate.

On the evening of the Coronation itself there was a crowded reception at Buckingham Palace at which the Heads of visiting delegations were presented to the Queen. When it came to General Marshall's turn, the Queen asked to see his wife, a request which (stupidly) none of us had anticipated. Mrs. Marshall was a partial invalid and had to remain seated. Where she was no one seemed to know and I was despatched urgently to find her. I did not then know the geography of the Palace reception rooms and rushed frantically from room to room seeking news - without success. Finally I looked behind a large door to find myself face to face with Archbishop Fisher of Canterbury who was seeking refuge from the throng in meditation. By the time Mrs. Marshall was found, the presentations to the Queen had moved on.

Another memory of those exciting days was the journey to the Abbey for the ceremony. I rode with General Marshall and Fleur Cowles in a large Daimler limousine. Whilst we moved slowly down the Mall she quite reasonably tried her utmost, by every wile to secure his memoirs for 'Look' Magazine. The repeated refusals were firm and curt. His records were to be reserved for a special library in Virginia. The preparations for the ceremony were my first contact with the Palace staff. They were extremely courteous and efficient on what was a very complicated occasion. However they had an irritating habit of putting an abrupt end to any suggestion which they personally did not like, by quietly saying, "The Queen would not like that."

Back in the office I had my first opportunity to see Anthony Eden in action as Secretary of State. To me, with pre-war and wartime memories, he was a legendary figure. I had heard favourable stories also from the scout on my staircase at Christ Church, who had looked after him in his undergraduate days! I found that he was not slow to praise a junior officer when he thought praise was due and gave it with great charm. Equally, he could be unreasonably sharp and impatient as I learned when one Saturday afternoon he found me in the office after he had failed to find anyone else. The telephone conversation began,

"This is your Secretary of State speaking" and continued in that hectoring vein. Very many years later I was taken to his bedroom in the Provost's House at Eton, where he was staying. He was then a very sick man. He was courteous and wonderfully well informed on current international affairs especially in the Middle East. During 1953 he took me with him twice to Defence Committee meetings in the Cabinet Room presided over by Prime Minister Churchill who was slowly recovering from his illness. On the first occasion, before we went into the Cabinet room the participants had gathered outside the door. Eden was standing at one side of the group talking to the Home Secretary. The Prime Minister was at the other side when suddenly he called out in a voice of overwhelming authority,

"Anthony, what are you saying?"

"We are," Eden replied, "discussing whether flags should be flown at half mast for the death of Gottwald the President of Czechoslovakia." Churchill was silent for a moment and then snapped,

"Gottwald - filth." The matter was not pursued.

The subsequent committee was conducted by the Prime Minister with complete mastery. It was adjourned however until a later occasion when it was a very different scene. Churchill was preoccupied by the recent death of Stalin. He rambled on and talked of his wish for a summit meeting with the Americans and the Russians. He recalled how he had greeted Molotov en route to the U.S. in 1941. He had met him at the gate at the rear of No. 10. "He took my hand and squeezed it. I knew he was my friend," he added.

Eden tried in vain to bring the Prime Minister back to the agenda of the meeting which was the Persian Gulf. Further confusion was caused by Field Marshal Lord Alexander, the reluctant Minister of Defence, who thought the Sultan of Muscat and Oman was two separate persons whom he erroneously believed to be in treaty relationship with the U.K. It was fascinating, but at the same time, disturbing. Finally, Eden signalled me to leave the room as he had failed to focus the discussion.

In another encounter with Eden I was let down by my superiors. To deal with a certain matter it had been decided to send a special emissary to King Ibn Saud of Saudi Arabia. There was an argument about the choice. I ventured the suggestion that the King would be flattered if a member of our Royal Family was sent. I suggested Lord Mountbatten and this was greeted with approval. The Permanent Under Secretary, (Sir) William Strang, a Deputy Under Secretary, (Sir) James Bowker, the Head of the Department Archie Ross and myself, proceeded to Carlton Gardens where Eden was propped up in bed awaiting removal to hospital for a serious operation. The four of us sat on chairs in descending order of seniority at the foot of the bed. "It is suggested," said the Permanent Under Secretary, "That an envoy to Saudi Arabia should be a member of the Royal Family."

Eden gave a cautious nod.

"Who had you in mind?" he asked. The Permanent Under Secretary turned to the Deputy Under Secretary, who turned to the Head of Department, who turned to me,

"Who had we in mind?" they chorused.

I gave the name and there was a furious outburst from the bed. They were all well aware of the antipathy between Eden and Mountbatten, but left it to me to weather the storm. I felt somewhat resentful. No envoy was sent.

Eden took an almost paternal interest in the Middle East. I was with him twice when he received the Sultan of Oman in the Foreign Office. The Sultan ruled his country with a rod of iron and excluded even his family from everything. Eden was concerned lest his dictatorial ways would cause his family and his people to reject him - as indeed it eventually did. Eden took advantage of the Sultan's visits to his favourite Dorchester hotel to lecture him with increasing vehemence on the need to reform and particularly the education of his people. The answer was always the same - a softly spoken "I see," but never any action.

It was the custom of the office at that time to circulate annually to all members of the Diplomatic Service, a 'post preference form.' The recipient was required to say in order of his preference at which post he/she would like to serve and why. I had consistently chosen a year's course at the Imperial

Defence College. During the war I had served with several army and navy officers who had been students there. I had liked them and they had spoken with pleasure of the time spent there. The Foreign Office sent two members each year and sometimes contributed to the directing staff. It was not a posting for which, until some years later, there was much competition. Head of Personnel Department, John Henniker, rang me one day and asked if I really wanted to go. On my confirmation he unenthusiastically agreed. It was a decision never regretted. It proved to be of the utmost value especially in the final nine years of my service in Whitehall when I was in close contact with the military Chiefs of Staff who had been, almost without exception, fellow students.

Students at the College were drawn from all the Commonwealth countries, including an Afrikaner Colonel and from the U.S. Service personnel predominated, but civilians were included. There were of course, at that time, no black Africans. My Foreign Office colleague was Stanley Tomlinson a charming and gifted Far Eastern expert. The course had a simple and practical structure. Mornings were devoted to visiting lecturers of the greatest prominence and high standing. Two lectures remain in my memory. The Archbishop of York, the saintly Dr. Garbett, was spell-binding. Equally dramatic in a different way was a lecture on the lessons of the Korean War by General Mike West, a fellow student, who had commanded the Commonwealth Division in the conflict. Clement Attlee and Field Marshal Montgomery lived up to their reputations for crispness. The Field Marshal was especially critical of the Foreign Office and all but himself.

Such study as there was fell to the lot of the students organised into syndicates in the usual service style. It was not until years later that Denis Healey as Minister of Defence and Alastair Buchan as Civilian Director introduced a more disciplined syllabus. Important aspects of our course were the visits to a selection of civil activities in the U.K. Although I had, from my railway days a good knowledge of pre-war industrial life, it was important for those like myself of who had spent some years abroad to be brought up to date on developments in our own country.

One of the industrial visits was to Short's aircraft factory in Belfast. In their plant, substantial parts of the pioneer jet airliner, the Comet, were being manufactured. Two of these planes, designed by de Haviland had recently disappeared in mid air, including one piloted by a boyhood friend of mine Maurice Haddon from Bournemouth. These planes had been the subject of great British pride. Whilst we were touring the factory, work was suddenly halted by an announcement coming over the loud-speaker telling the work force that all work on the planes was to be suspended. I recalled at once a conversation with a USAF fellow student to whom I had boasted of the plane's success. He had remarked that his wartime experience had always been that de Haviland planes were too flimsily made. This indeed was the basic defect of the Comet. It was a sad day in Belfast and the U.K.

However, the highlight of the year was a long inter-continental tour in an RAF Viking aircraft. The group of which I was a member went to Turkey, Egypt (the Canal Zone base), Sudan, Aden, The Persian Gulf, Somaliland, Kenya, Uganda, Rhodesia, Nigeria and Ghana - all places which were to be in the news in the early years to come.

Ghana was of particular interest. It was the first large African colony to be on the eve of independence. British colonial policy, moving at an unexpectedly rapid rate, was about to be put to the test. Ghana gave every sign of being capable of success. There was in Kwame Nkrumah, the Chief Minister, an apparently effective and friendly leader bubbling over with self-confidence. We posed with him in a cheerful group photo and he was only too willing to talk. There was a well trained civil service, a sound economy and considerable financial reserves prudently accumulated by the colonial government. Yet a few years later, the independent country was to be in political and economic ruin. The powerful corruption of absolute power was never more vividly illustrated.

Within a month or two from the end of the Imperial Defence College course I was told my next appointment would be Head of Chancery at the U.K. Delegation to the Council of NATO, then situated in the Palais de Chaillot in Paris. This had many attractions, not the least in the joy of living and working in Paris without the need to concentrate on relations with the French Government. NATO was beginning to find its feet. The Germans had lately joined with a skilfully chosen Delegation whose disclosed wartime service had been largely in the Far East. Everything seemed set for interesting and constructive work. The Head of the British Delegation was the elegant and highly professional Sir Christopher Steel. Those familiar with Terence Rattigan's successful comedy 'French without Tears' set in a pre-war French crammers were not surprised to learn the attractive central character, a Foreign Office student, was based on the real life Steel. Other Delegation leaders of the NATO Council were men of distinction in the histories of their respective countries.

The Secretary General of Nato was General Lord Ismay, a leading figure in wartime Whitehall and in the settlement of Indian independence. As a chairman of a multinational committee of distinguished allies he was without peer. He conducted meetings in a way which left all participants of large or small countries with the impression that they had all been sympathetically and equally consulted on the matter in hand. He was assisted by a hard-bitten Royal Naval Officer, Captain Coleridge, fully trained in the ways of the British governmental machine in Whitehall. For the British Delegation, all looked as if it was going to be plain sailing and, for many months, it was. My counterparts in the other delegations were compatible and included a Turkish diplomat of my own age, Zeki Kuneralp who was in future years to be twice Ambassador in London and whose father, a servant of the Turkish Sultan, had been murdered in the Ataturk uprising. Zeki himself escaped assassination by an Armenian terrorist when he was Ambassador in Spain but his charming wife and her brother perished. He developed multiple sclerosis but, with an amazing determination, he carried out his diplomatic duties to the full.

The Greenhills as a family, had time to travel widely in France and spent our first August with our boys at Cap d'Ail in a small villa. The hills behind the little town were ideal for picnics and butterfly collecting and gave a grandstand view of the annual fireworks at Monte Carlo. From the villa itself we could, if we wished, each evening see Greta Garbo distantly entering the sea, stark naked, from the rocks of the villa she shared with her American friend. During the day she could occasionally be seen heavily disguised doing some local shopping. In Paris after one or two false starts we had found a beautiful apartment on the left Bank looking down on the Seine and Pont Alexandre I and the Place des Invalides. It involved occupying a floor in a large hotel particulier belonging to an aristocratic French family. It was the first time they had willingly allowed aliens to invade their privacy. They were most courteous although there were some cultural clashes, sometimes over the treatment of staff. It was some time before we could negotiate for our one maid to sleep within our flat rather than in alarmingly primitive quarters beneath the roof. To bring our shopping up to the fourth floor in the lift rather than carrying it up backstairs was another hurdle which had to be overcome. But these happy conditions lasted a little more than a year. Suddenly, without notice, my chief was asked by the Foreign Office to release me to go to the Commissioner General's Staff in Singapore and serve as chairman of the regional Joint Intelligence Committee, a sub branch of the Whitehall committee. It was made clear that after only a short time in Paris I was not being ordered to go, but that the Commissioner General, Sir Robert Scott, had been without a committee chairman for several months and had particularly asked for someone who had been at the Imperial Defence College. The Commissioner General and the three Service Commanders-in-Chief in Singapore were located closely together and their work was well integrated. The Foreign Office request for me appeared reasonable on paper to all parties and the logic of it could not be denied. I was not unfamiliar with parts of South East Asia from my previous military career. However, I was strongly advised by Steel and my friends in Paris to refuse to go and the temptation to stay put in such agreeable conditions was great. Angela took a very unselfish view. Eventually we decided to go but, as a concession, the Foreign Office said for two continuous years only, instead of two tours of eighteen months, each separated by ample leave.

Into these discussions a bombshell fell without warning - namely the Suez crisis and the Anglo-French action against Nasser. None of us in Paris had pre-knowledge of this and even our Ambassador Gladwyn Jebb and Steel were not fully aware of the Prime Minister's plans. I had stumbled on at least one clue which I had been firmly discouraged from pursuing. Steel's daily routine was to arrive in the office about 9.30 a.m. and on most days go off to golf at St. Cloud with fellow diplomatic colleagues, having satisfied himself that there was nothing requiring his attention until after lunch. From time to time this routine was varied and he spent the morning in the office. These were the days when, by some instinct he seemed to sense that Eden was going to telephone him. Shortly before the news about the Anglo-French action broke I had come into my office earlier than usual and heard talk coming from within Steel's room - a highly unusual thing. I looked in at once to find him in discussion with Sir Patrick Dean the Under Secretary for Defence and Intelligence from London. I was dismissed quickly and went back to my desk. Having seen Dean off the premises, Steel came back to me and said,

"Under no circumstances tell anyone that you have seen Sir Patrick here today."

I speculated to myself as to what might be afoot without coming anywhere near the right answer and, in any case, was much pre-occupied with preparing to leave Paris for Singapore. But as soon as the Anglo-French action hit the headlines, the NATO Council became immediately occupied with it and met daily. Steel found himself isolated but, more discouraging, was the strong criticism of British policy by Ismay. This struck me as uncharacteristic and his role would have been more appropriate responding to the views of the Council rather than leading them. It was for Steel to put the British view. Steel put up a strong and well argued defence and by the time the operation was called off the Council was markedly sympathetic. Bob Dixon, our representative at the U.N. had an even worse problem. He thought of resignation. I do not think Steel ever did. The French public, press and politicians did not share the reactions of their British counterparts and in the Council their representative kept a very low profile. The whole episode was an unhappy finale to our stay in Paris.

On getting back to London I found the Foreign Office officials in disarray and much talk, but little action on resignations. Very few officials had been in the know. Amongst them was Patrick Dean who I had seen with Steel that morning in Paris. His participation affected his career when the Labour Party came to power in 1964. Paul Gore-Booth then a Deputy Under Secretary and later Permanent Secretary describes vividly in his autobiography the doubts that assailed him as a highly principled official and how near he came to leaving. Those Conservative junior Foreign Office Ministers who resigned were most affected by the fact that Eden had not taken them into his confidence. All this made it more welcome to get out of London to an entirely new scene in South East Asia with the Commissioner General.

CHAPTER 12

SINGAPORE AND THE FAR EAST AGAIN

The Commissioner General's office in Singapore had been formed soon after the end of the war. Whitehall had been impressed by the undoubted success of the office set up in 1941 under a Cabinet Minister in Cairo to coordinate British interests in the region and to harmonise departmental policies. In 1956 the Middle East office was continuing, however, with a greatly diminished role under Sir Hugh Overton a Home Civil Servant of high reputation but unfamiliar with the area. But the South East Asian area was an obvious candidate for a regional organisation which would bring together the often conflicting interests of the Foreign, Colonial, Commonwealth and Defence Departments. Great economic issues were also at stake. Obviously much would depend on the character and status of the man in charge. Initially in Singapore, Lord Killearn, the dominating wartime Ambassador in Cairo, had been appointed, but in retrospect there were many reasons why he was not the best choice. He was followed by Malcolm Macdonald who had the prestige of having been a Cabinet Minister and had a pacific character in contrast to his predecessor. He enjoyed an unrivalled reputation for winning the affection and admiration of widely differing people, ranging from Averell Harriman to African and Asian revolutionary leaders. When he was our roving Ambassador in Africa at a later date, I had the privilege of being with him when he called on several African leaders. It was not hard to identify the reasons for his success. He always took care to avoid the most sensitive subjects and, to my mind, often wrongly dodged issues which required argument. His technique is summed up in a discussion once with me when he said
"I disagree with what you say, but you express it all so beautifully." It was difficult not to be disarmed and think kindly of him. In his company on this trip I was able to see parts of Africa where my father had served during the Great War including the German barracks at Tabora - one of the few German colonial relics on the continent.

One of the main reasons for Macdonald being chosen to go to Singapore was to break down the outdated colonial attitudes of many British expatriates who had returned after the war but had found themselves in new political circumstances. By his informal clothes and the choice of his local friends he gave much offence to the 'old hands,' but at the same time, did much good. The Japanese victories had delivered a mortal blow to British prestige. The 'wind of change' was blowing in all imperial territories in

South East Asia, British, French and Dutch, with just as great force and possibly greater than in Africa. By the time I arrived at the end of 1956 the powerful communist rebellion in Malaya was at last collapsing thanks to the exceptional and ruthless character of Field Marshal Gerald Templer and the adaptability of British National Servicemen. But the days of Somerset Maugham were gone for ever. Templer had no truck with the British newspaper correspondents. He had the likeable but probing Louis Heren of the Times withdrawn who, when we were later in Washington, was banned for a while from the White House by President Kennedy.

Macdonald was succeeded by Sir Robert Scott - a truly remarkable man. He had spent most of his life in the Far East in the China Consular Service. It is relevant to recall his career at least from the outbreak of World War II. When he was dying of cancer in 1982, I rang The Times newspaper and asked if they had an obituary prepared worthy of him. They had virtually no records. I did my best to supply some of the missing facts which I thought the public should know. Some of them are set out below.

At the beginning of the Second World War, Scott was conducting British propaganda in Japan but in 1941 was transferred to Singapore to set up a branch of the Ministry of Information. As the crisis deepened in Singapore he became a member of the Governor's War Council consisting of the three Service chiefs. From contemporary accounts he outshone the others in vigour and imagination in the face of the impending catastrophe.

When the city fell to the Japanese he attempted to get away to Australia on the last passenger boat to leave the stricken port. His wife had already gone on ahead. Then began a period in his life which gave him his place in history. His ship was intercepted by a Japanese cruiser. He volunteered to row across with others to the warship in an attempt to persuade the enemy captain to allow the refugee ship to proceed. The sea was rough and the warship opened fire on the ship before Scott's small boat could reach her. The passenger ship sank and there were few survivors. Scott succeeded in reaching Sumatra where he was briefly in hiding until he was returned as a prisoner to Singapore.

After a period of solitary confinement he was put in Changi jail with other civilian prisoners. But Scott was always regarded with suspicion by the Japanese who equated the Ministry of Information with intelligence and spying. He quickly became a leader in the camp. Discipline was not unduly aggressive initially and the inmates did much of their own administration. Contact was maintained with those outside. Towards the summer of 1943 the Japanese became apprehensive about the activities within the camp and were planning a careful raid to crack down on them. But in late September matters came quickly to a head. A commando, daringly led by Captain Lyon reached Singapore from Australia undetected and blew up tankers in the harbour. The Japanese were astounded and mistakenly thought that the raiders must have had accomplices in the camp. Scott was assumed to be the ring leader and he was found to have a radio.

For weeks he was terribly beaten and tortured but no confession was ever obtained. He was put on trial by the Japanese and eventually sentenced to six years in Outram Road prison. Throughout this ordeal Scott conducted himself very calmly and established a moral and intellectual ascendancy over his persecutors, who found his arguments and predictions most disturbing. A duel of words and wits developed between him and his chief tormentor, Colonel Sumida who was later hanged as a war criminal.

During part of this time in Changi he was held in solitary confinement at the top of the prison tower where from time to time he could be seen by his fellow prisoners in the yard below. He became known throughout the city as 'the man in the tower' and was a symbol to the British and Chinese of defiance and resistance. When the Japanese surrendered, the prisoners broke out of Changi jail and made their way towards Singapore harbour. On the way they met a group coming to release them including The Times correspondent Morrison. He greeted Scott with the words,
"You can't be here I have already published your obituary."
"That's all right" Scott replied, "I will write yours one day." Morrison was later killed in the Korean War and, on hearing the news on the radio, Scott phoned The Times and was able to fulfil his promise.

Scott's wife Rosamund in Australia was all this time unaware of his fate and drew a widow's pension. The first communication he received from the Government on his eventual return to England was a demand for back tax payments on the salary he should have been receiving, had it been realised he was not dead.

At the end of the war Scott was a principal witness in the war crimes' trials which were then staged in Singapore. His testimony was given without rancour and with such fairness that all were astonished - not least the accused. He attended their execution and he recounted to me one evening how, from the scaffold, the condemned sought him out amongst those attending and bowed ostentatiously towards him. In fact, Scott never subsequently showed animosity towards the Japanese. Some years later with the help of the British Ambassador in Tokyo, Sir John Pilcher, he arranged a meeting with some of his former gaolers who had escaped execution. After a slow start, it proved a satisfactory reconciliation.

Scott's appointment to Singapore as Commissioner General was greeted with warm approval by the people of the area and by British Colonial officials and Service chiefs who recognised his deep knowledge and admired his courage. He made me welcome on my arrival and encouraged me to travel as widely as possible. As a result, during my appointment, in addition to Australia and New Zealand, I became familiar with Burma, Malaya, Thailand, Laos, Vietnam, Hongkong, Tokyo, Jakarta, Borneo, Sarawak, Brunei and Hawaii. All the ex-colonial or undeveloped territories were just awakening to a new world and new opportunities, but had not yet been carried forward on the political and economic revolutions which were to transform them in the next decades - with the exception of Burma. I am glad to have seen them in the mid-fifties, with the imprint of their colonial histories still remaining, and in the next thirty years to revisit them from London in various roles and been encouraged by the unbelievable changes. My military service, my travels at the Imperial Defence College and now these journeys in South East Asia meant that when I returned to London in 1964, I had seen a great deal of the world, with the notable exception of Latin America.

On the way to Australia for an Intelligence Conference, our plane, an RAF Viking, had to stop at Cloncurry for refuelling at its small airfield on the edge of the outback. It was a base for the Flying Doctor and a nearby monument paid tribute to the service provided. I talked to an Australian airport worker who was washing it down. In the course of our conversation he asked if I knew how many calls had been received on the Doctor's radio in the past year. I had no idea. He then replied with a figure of many hundreds - he then paused and added, "Seventy per cent were to place bets."

In January 1958 Macmillan visited Singapore in the course of his one and only Commonwealth tour. His visit was the occasion for calling a regional conference of all senior British officials in the area. This meant the Ambassadors, the remaining Colonial Governors, High Commissioners and the Service Chiefs. Amongst them was Peter Carrington the young British High Commissioner in Australia - a political appointment. He made an immediate favourable impression and it was not difficult to see that he would have a distinguished career ahead. The meetings were held at Eden Hall, the Commissioner General's spacious Singapore residence. The like of such a gathering was not seen again. Macmillan arrived, having just encountered in London his famous 'little local difficulties' when Thorneycroft, Powell and Birch had resigned from his Government. I do not think any of those of us who had assembled for the conference, fully appreciated the significance of the events in London or the anxiety which they occasioned in Macmillan. But very soon, it was apparent that the only things that really interested him were the telegrams from home. When he rose to give the 'key note' address to the conference, it is doubtful whether he had given its substance a moment's thought.

He started off slowly in a melancholy voice, saying that being Prime Minister in the U.K. was like being the owner of a great house, who found that circumstances compelled him to close room after room and wing after wing. He clearly had Chatsworth in his mind's eye. He continued in this vein, casting gloom on everyone. Suddenly, there was a change of pace. When Calais had fallen in 1558, all England, he observed, believed it was the end of greatness, when in fact it was the beginning of the Elizabethan era and all its wonderful achievements. Were we not perhaps now on the verge of another great Elizabethan era? The meeting broke up in a mood of pride and optimism and all trooped into lunch. A Private Secretary and I remained behind to tidy up the papers. In doing so we discovered a note from Sir Norman Brook, the Cabinet Secretary as follows: 'P.M. I think your opening was rather too gloomy. Why not end on the Fall of Calais and a new Elizabethan era?'

But Macmillan was feeling the strain of the journey and of events at home. By next morning he had developed a fever. His staff were advised to get in touch with the medical inspection room at the Army General Headquarters nearby. The conversation went as follows, "The P.M. is here and is not feeling too well."

North Country sergeant at the inspection room, "Well he better come down." Macmillan's secretary, "I don't think you quite understand, the P.M, the Prime Minister, is here and not feeling well."

After a pause, strong North Country accent in response, "In that case, we better come oop!"

In military circles, P.M. could only have meant 'Provost Marshal.'

Travelling in the area I sometimes accompanied the army Commander in Chief, the giant General Festing whose size and geniality won him friends easily. He was an enthusiastic Roman Catholic convert and took his faith seriously which sometimes seemed to have strange side effects. On one occasion he and his party, of which I was a member, were invited in one of our colonies, to a buffet supper given by a senior British official, the District Commissioner. His large bungalow opened on to a long lawn which terminated in a bank with the sea beyond. We had been at the party only a few minutes when the General burst out,

"I must go, I can't stay, there is something evil here."

All attempts to pacify him failed and he left with his ADC. We later found a possible explanation in that the room, quite unknown to the General, had been used by the Japanese for the interrogation of British and others during the War. After interrogation the victims were led into the garden and executed at the end of the lawn. No one else had felt an evil presence but his sudden distress and alarm was genuine.

A more agreeable occasion was a visit in Sarawak to another District Commissioner who lived in the interior. He proved to be a dashing looking bachelor, sporting a black monocle. He was originally a recruit of the Brooke family who had operated the territory as a private fief with carefully selected staff. At the end of the war, the Colonial Office under the Labour Government had taken it out of the Brooke's private hands. The natives showed their disapproval by assassinating the first official London appointed governor. After tea the Commissioner surprisingly suggested a game of polo. The general, his ADC and the U.S. Military Attaché who was with us accepted and, after some delay, were kitted out and provided with ponies. The party then proceeded to the edge of the village where a suitable field existed. It resembled an English village cricket ground. Waiting there were a number of Chinese in white cotton shirts and black cotton shorts standing with their ponies, rope bridles, sticks and no saddles. The General and the Commissioner picked up sides and a game took place which would have done credit to Cowdray Park.

On the same occasion we visited Brunei which was beginning to enjoy the rewards of its oil production. An Englishman had been seconded from the Treasury in London to oversee the state's expenditure. He looked thoroughly miserable. In conversation he explained that education, health care and all welfare was free in Brunei. A costly huge mosque in memory of Churchill was being completed. Throughout his career in London the Treasury official had been trained to save money. Here in Brunei he was at his wits end seeking ways of spending it. He was sadly frustrated in trying to change the habits of a lifetime.

The reduction of British Forces overseas was a lively political issue at home. The British economy could no longer afford expensive establishments abroad and heavy cuts were inevitable. Singapore was an obvious target. The Prime Minister chose Duncan Sandys as his hatchet man and there was great agitation in the Defence establishment in Singapore when it was known he was to visit the base. His confrontation with the local chiefs of staff was memorable. The three faced him across a table and he started a brutal cross examination. "What is the Royal Navy doing in Singapore?" Such a fundamental and unimaginable question completely silenced the Naval Commander in Chief. A similar question about the Land Forces was addressed to the Army Commander in Chief who made a passable reply. It was then the RAF's turn. Their Commander in Chief was the Earl of Bandon a roguish man of great courage, foul mouth, with fewer academic gifts than his colleagues. But he knew very well how to handle the likes of the Minister. "Why do you need all your planes?" Bandon replied that if the Minister wanted them, he should take them. A dialogue continued on these lines and Sandys, finding no resistance, became irritated as the responsibility for assessing needs was being passed to him.

"Surely the Commander in Chief wants some squadrons?" to which the reply was, "If the Minister insists." In the end the RAF ended up with more than they needed. As he left the room, the Minister ignored the other two and pointedly invited Bandon to see him when he next came to London. He was conscious that he had met his match.

Living in Singapore, the tragic memories of the war were sufficiently recent to induce a certain melancholy from time to time. In the centre of the island lies the beautifully maintained war cemetery and I reminded myself of the last desperate weeks for the Allied Forces by reading the appropriate volume of the Official War History which has a vividness which is unusual in such laborious and detailed works.

When standing on the lovely beaches on the east coast of Malaya and looking out across the glassy sea, one could imagine only too vividly the mental and physical agony of the crews of HMS Prince of Wales and Repulse as they lay at the mercy of the Japanese bombers. But to balance this it was always encouraging to think of the penniless and fatherless Stamford Raffles who, from a start on a high stool in the office of the East India Company, by immense effort, talent and imagination laid the foundation of British influence in South East Asia at the beginning of the 19th Century and whose prophetic vision for the future of Singapore was fulfilled less than two centuries later by a Chinese student educated at Cambridge University, Lee Kwan Yew.

Towards the end of our posting the Japanese were showing signs of cautiously returning to Singapore. They had blundered badly by a disastrous choice of representatives who they had sent to open up again in the Philippines. No such error was made in Singapore. One of the earliest arrivals was a former Cambridge graduate. As a famous victim of their cruelty Scott initially made a gesture by including a Japanese in a foursome at the Island Club golf course. It proved to be an exceedingly close match, the outcome of which came to depend on a shot by the Japanese. He bungled it and his ball ended deep in a bunker. He uttered a cry "I think I commit hari kari" with such intensity that we instinctively ran towards him. Sometime later one of his fellow countrymen could be seen on the course accompanied by a cameraman who filmed his every shot for later analysis.

We all knew that Britain could never establish a political influence and military strength comparable to the pre-war situation. It was neither possible nor desirable. The communist rebellion in Malaya had nearly succeeded and the party's influence was still evident in Singapore. The U.K. had the objective of moving Singapore and Malaya towards a non communist independence and an avoidance of racial friction between Chinese and Malay. The Japanese economic threat was not appreciated and few would have forecast that British products would in little more than a decade, vanish from the shops, shelves and showrooms of the city in favour of Japanese. The racial problems of the local population were illustrated by the composition of the Singapore police force - the constables were Malayan and the detectives Chinese. One night when we heard stealthy sounds around our house, we dialled for the police. On their rapid arrival we reported 'suspicious sounds.' "Malay or Chinese?" was the question first asked.

The quality of the British members of the Malayan Civil Service was particularly high. Those who survived the war and returned to Singapore and Malaya seemed to feel a special and urgent responsibility for the local people who, in their view, had been let down by the British failure to resist the Japanese assault. These included Sir Robin Black and Sir William Goode who both were Governors of the Colony whilst we were there. The former became in due course an admirable chairman of the Clerical Medical Assurance Company which I was invited to join as a director after my retirement. The attitude of the local people was often misunderstood in London. For example when Malaya became independent the Commonwealth Office decided as an act of policy not to appoint anyone to the new High Commission who had served in the area during the colonial period. Scott was approached by a mystified Tunku (the overall ruler of Malaya) who asked him what had they done which caused the British Government not to send any of their 'friends' to staff the new Mission.

Life in Singapore was leisurely and left long time for recreation. August brought a flood of children from British boarding schools to join their expatriate parents. The journey out with an overnight stop in Calcutta caused the parents more anxiety than the children. On arrival they found their entertainment to have been highly organised. The organisers were usually based on the various clubs, the swimming club, the more exclusive Tanglin Club, the Island Club and various Services groups. At the same time it was interesting to see the increasing educational pull that Australia was exercising on ex-patriates and, but more particularly, on the well-to-do Chinese. English education was no longer a must. Our two boys were going through a butterfly and moth collecting phase. We took them and their equipment up into Malaya and stayed at a small Government guest house which gave easy access to the jungle. There we found a wealth of exotic butterflies, many with long trailing wings like wedding dresses. All had the irritating knack of flying very slowly just out of reach of our nets. Nevertheless the results were good. But on the eve of their return to school, we were still without an Atlas moth - one of the largest insects available anywhere. At a very late moment a colleague telephoned us at dawn one morning to say an Atlas moth had found its way into their loo. It was quickly secured and put head down into our high powered cyanide killing bottle which could not take the whole insect and therefore could not be sealed up. The moth did not struggle but after hours was still not dead. Other methods were tried without success. I sought the help of the staff at the appropriate department of the university. They were only too ready to assist. The moth was transferred to a jar of chloroform where it remained motionless for an hour or so whilst we chatted with the staff. They told us the insect's life span was not more than 48 hours and in due course they pronounced it dead. They were wrong and to our consternation it quivered on for a further twelve hours or more. It was duly mounted in the U.K. and has lasted more than 30 years. We have all felt a little guilty about our failure to make a cleaner job of its execution.

The end of 1958 was the completion of my two years assignment to Singapore. I left with some knowledge and some experience of all the countries of South East Asia and of Japan. I saw some of the winding up of our Eastern colonial empire and recognised what had been achieved in the past and had a glimpse of what might happen in the future.

CHAPTER 13

RETURN TO THE FOREIGN OFFICE 1

We reoccupied our house in Westminster and I began work in the Foreign Office on intelligence matters, dividing my time between the Foreign Office itself and the Headquarters of the Intelligence Services. The purpose of the appointment was to ensure that the activities of these Services were consistent with Foreign policy and were approved by Foreign Office Ministers or Home Office Ministers, where necessary. The need for such an appointment had been given special emphasis by the death of Commander Crabb in 1956, who had, without ministerial authorization, undertaken an unsuccessful intelligence operation against a Soviet warship in Portsmouth during Khruchshev's visit to the U.K. The result had been a considerable embarrassment to the Secretary of State, Eden, who had to admit ignorance to Parliament. New procedures were quickly put into force. The appointment was fascinating, but out of the main stream of Foreign Office work. I expected it to last for a least two years. This was not to be.

After eight months, I chanced to meet the Head of our Personnel Department John Henniker outside the Travellers Club. We had a general gossip about the Service, during which he asked what I thought the most desirable post in the Service at my rank. I suggested, with no thought of myself, the Head of Chancery in Washington. About two weeks later he rang me up to offer me the post. I accepted at once. I learned later that he had been offered the job himself, but did not wish to leave the U.K. He had been glad to find a willing substitute acceptable to Sir Harold Caccia, our Ambassador since 1956. I had met Caccia before, only briefly. I knew he had an adventurous time in the war and had served Harold Macmillan in the Mediterranean Theatre. He was admired by him and indeed by all. He was also strongly and correctly tipped as the next Permanent Under Secretary and was not expected to remain in Washington long after the Presidential election in November 1960.

Caccia was a remarkable all rounder and one of the few Diplomatic Service officers who excelled in many sports, especially rugby football. He constantly used sporting phrases. His frequent response to anyone seeking advice on an intractable problem was "to kick it into touch." He proved a joy to work for both as my Ambassador and later in London when Permanent Under Secretary. At his Memorial Service in Eton College Chapel in 1991, the Foreign Secretary, Douglas Hurd, read the lesson taken from Wisdom of Solomon Chapter 3 V 1-9, the Souls of the Righteous. He remarked to me afterwards that Harold Caccia was aptly described by the sentence in Verse 7, which reads, "in the time of their visitation, they shall shine and run to and fro like sparks among the stubble."

We left in October for the U.S. travelling by one of the Queens. En route we listened to the General Election result, which returned Harold Macmillan with a surprisingly increased majority. Selwyn Lloyd was to continue as Foreign Secretary. At no time in my Foreign Office career did I have close contact with him.

The Washington Embassy staff remained as large, if not larger, than we had left it in 1952. New office buildings were being constructed. As Head of Chancery, my preoccupation was to try to be certain that the right hands of the various branches knew what the left hands were doing. The Ambassador had taken up his post in 1956 at the time of the Anglo-French invasion of Suez. Indeed, such was the secrecy of the operation that the first he knew of it was en route by sea to take up his post. On arrival, he found not the welcome of our closest ally, but the hostility of President Eisenhower and Foreign Minister, Foster Dulles. At that point, the US/UK relationship was at its nadir. By the time we arrived it was being gradually restored by Harold Macmillan, after his serious misjudgment of American reactions at the time of Suez. He was drawing on his long war time friendship with President Eisenhower. The Ambassador was playing his part with notable success, so that the atmosphere in the Embassy was cheerfully businesslike. He was assisted by the Minister, Lord Hood, especially experienced in European affairs and by the Economic Minister, the worldly wise Lord Cromer, who had come direct from the City of London. Outstanding also was the gifted Paul Gore-Booth then Head of the British Information Services, who later succeeded Caccia as Permanent Secretary at the Foreign Office. As Christian Scientists, both he and his wife, Pat, continued to handle the massive Washington press corps without the help of any alcohol. Tom Brimelow, who was recognised by the Americans as an expert Kremlinologist was a powerful member of the chancery.

The Eisenhower Administration was in its last year and the mood in Washington was one of frustration and disappointment. The country was at the height of its power, but lacked self-confidence. Although Eisenhower was admired and respected, people were looking for more than a 'golf and poker' President. John Foster Dulles had passed from the stage and had been succeeded by Christian Herter, a gentlemanly figure, but not internationally dominant. The President's frequent press conferences had become something of a laughing stock and leadership of the Western Powers was notably absent.

Following the reassurance of his election victory, Macmillan had set his heart on a summit meeting with the Russians. By visiting Washington he tried to persuade the President, held back by the Pentagon and conservative Republicans, to agree. A preliminary summit without the Russians was held in Paris in October 1959. Eventually, after Khruschev had visited the U.S. a full scale summit took place again in Paris in May 1960. This was wrecked by the incident of the U.S. spy plane, which gave Khruschev an excuse to walk out. The foolish explanations attempted by the U.S. administration were a public measure of its weakness and an encouragement to Khruschev's aggressive and self assertive mood. All this involved great diplomatic activity during the first year of our appointment.

Towards the end of the year, Khrushchev announced his intention of coming to the UN assembly in New York and it was clear that he intended to make the most of the occasion . Macmillan correctly judged he should be in the U.S. at the same time for three main purposes, namely to speak at the Assembly himself, to take his leave of Eisenhower as President and most importantly to pursue with him the future shape of Anglo-U.S. cooperation and the handling of East-West confrontation. Fortune smiled on him, as Khruschev chose vulgarly to interrupt the Prime Minister's thoughtful and conciliatory speech by beating his shoe on his desk and heckling him in Russian. Macmillan, watched by a huge TV audience, put him down in a grand and characteristic manner, which delighted his audience and impressed his personality on the U.S. public and made Khruschev wary of him in the remaining days of his leadership.

It was not the first time that the televising of U.N. proceedings in New York had come to the aid of British diplomacy. In the early nineteen fifties Sir Gladwyn Jebb's (Lord Gladwyn) mastery over the Russian Andrei Vyshinski greatly enhanced our reputation. A Chicagoan lady once described to me how she rang her lawyer husband in his office to 'drop everything' and come home to watch Sir Gladwyn. Much later (Sir) Nicholas Henderson in Washington had a not dissimilar TV success during the Falklands War.

I remember Macmillan and his team returning to Washington from New York, slightly dazed by their success, like a triumphant football team coming off the field after a tough match. Macmillan's visit made it evident that the future East-West policy and especially defence arrangements, were to be a major and sensitive issue for the new President, whose election was less than a month away. Throughout the summer and autumn, the attention of the American public had been concentrated on the preparations of the parties for the election. This was, of course, of intense interest to us in the Embassy. Mindful of past history when alleged partisanship had cost an

Ambassador his job, our public and private posture was of strict neutrality. In fact, neither candidate, Nixon or Kennedy, was then much admired in the U.K. The Kennedy family reputation had been marred by the candidate's father, Joe Kennedy, the U.S. Ambassador in London at the outset of the war, when his Irish origins and known doubts about the U.K. caused him to be regarded with suspicion.

All this rubbed off on his family which, however, was popular in some aristocratic British circles. Nixon's record in public life had done nothing to endear him to us. This was the first Presidential election in which TV played a decisive role. Neither candidate was a clear victor in the face to face debates. Nixon's lack of make-up was a disaster, giving him a dark unshaven appearance. It is hard to understand how it came to be allowed before the public presentation.

It was a measure of Macmillan's foresight that after Nixon's defeat and later failure in California, he was received some few years later in No. 10 when he had been written off by his fellow countrymen. Nixon was always mindful of this.

Immediately the narrow victory of Kennedy was known, our attention was focused on the identity of the appointments of special interest to us - namely the Secretary of State for Foreign Affairs and the Secretary of Defence. No obvious choices had been publicly discussed during the campaign. As for the President himself, Macmillan had not met him and it was inevitable that he would attract to the Administration a younger generation of advisers who were unknown personally, except to a very limited number of British politicians, academics and officials. It is always one of the most difficult tasks of any Embassy in the advance of a bitter election to have friends in both camps without giving offence to the current government. It is particularly difficult in the USA where a new President recruits a very large number of new people for all departments from the breadth of a whole continent and there is thus only a very limited continuity at the head of the major departments of State. The new President intended to create a revolution in official Washington. In the event, the two appointments of special interest to us came as a surprise to everyone. Dean Rusk, his choice for Secretary of State was reassuring. A Rhodes Scholar, he was known to many British personalities from the war, from the Truman Administration and from the Rockefeller Foundation. He was never regarded by Kennedy's self styled 'New Frontiersmen' as 'one of us.' In the long run he proved to be a firm and reliable friend and outshone his early detractors. Alec Home described him as, 'a splendid man to do business with' and he was right. The selection of Robert McNamara from the Ford

Motor Company as the new secretary of Defence, astonished everyone. He was unknown beforehand, even to the President. It was of great importance to us in the middle of sensitive discussion over nuclear weapons and strategy to have someone familiar with past wartime history and our post war cooperation. With McNamara it was only too plain that our long established links with the Pentagon were going to be subject to a highly intellectual re-examination and rejustification, at this critical time, by a person of unusual talent and original methods and ideas. His connection with Ford did not strengthen in advance his reputation as the company had recently produced the Edsel, one of its most notable failures, destined to a short life and universal contempt. It quickly became a used car bargain, greatly favoured by the coloured population only.

Below these top level posts, there were several welcome appointments at the State Department and elsewhere, including George McGhee and others we had known in the Truman Administration. An influx of Rhodes Scholars was welcome to us and later could be relied upon to liven up the annual Oxford University Dinner in the capital.

The new President's inauguration was a huge success - beautifully stage-managed in peerless winter weather. His eloquent speech, delivered in ringing tones was rapturously received, not only in his own country, but throughout the free world. Although numerically his majority had been narrow, even suspect, the country rose to him and his beautiful wife.

Much has been written of the mood and character of the new Frontiersmen who began to flood into Washington, changing its official and social atmosphere. It was initially impossible not to share some of their enthusiasms whilst being amused at their understandable name dropping and their anxiety to be near the 'throne.' Amongst these competitive folk it was even considered a coup for the British Embassy that the small child of Heather and Geoffrey Brigstocke, one of our attachés, was invited to join the little school for Caroline Kennedy, the President's daughter at the White House. It was perhaps fortunate that for the long term, within six months the President and his new Administration came up against the major fiasco of the Bay of Pigs invasion of Cuba by U.S. trained exiles. In most democratic countries such a failure would have destroyed the Government. In retrospect, it is incredible that such a bungle should have been allowed to happen. One is tempted to conclude that few of the highly intelligent newcomers to Washington found the courage, in their probationary period, to speak out to call a halt and stayed silent rather than risk their new found eminence. The formidable presence of Allen Dulles and Richard Bissell of the CIA inherited from the Eisenhower regime, no doubt gave them pause, but the animosity between rival parts of the new establishment was summed up in a remark by Bissell to one of our Embassy staff -

"State Department, I hate their bloody guts."

I served in Whitehall in 1964 and 1970 when the British Government changed parties on each occasion. I can, as a result, compare the effect of the arrival of new men in London with the results in Washington of the invasion of Kennedy's appointees in 1961. The British system which brings the ministerial newcomers into immediate contact with an experienced Civil Service sometimes diminishes their enthusiasm and obstructs not only their unwise proposals. The U.S. system, with a clean sweep at the top of most departments permits some reckless driving before the brakes of experience can be applied. This was a factor in the events of the Bay of Pigs.

From the moment of Kennedy's election, the Prime Minister set himself skilfully and painstakingly to build up a relationship with a President he did not know, which would be as strong as his twenty year friendship with Eisenhower. He began a correspondence at a high intellectual level designed to impress the President with his anxiety and care for future international developments. This was, we have since learned, not entirely successful, but at the same time we pinned hope on his first face to face meeting which was scheduled for April 1961 in Washington. In the event we did not have to wait until then and it came suddenly and unexpectedly in March. The Americans were becoming anxious about the communist threat to Laos and were unsuccessfully seeking support from the Europeans. Kennedy learned that Macmillan was about to fly to the Caribbean after a wearing session at Westminster. He invited him at very short notice to divert his plane for a meeting at a U.S. naval station, Key West in Florida.

The invitation was accepted with alacrity. Harold Caccia and I were flown down at once in a U.S. military plane and awaited the Prime Minister on the runway which was alongside the small white building in which we were to meet. The Prime Minister came off the plane looking the perfect English gentleman, wearing his Guards tie which over later years I recognised as a sign of an important meeting. Soon afterwards, the President landed bringing McGeorge Bundy with him into the meeting room. The President spoke first, with impressive fluency, illustrating his points effortlessly with selected statistics. He made a strong, eloquent case for British military assistance in Laos. The Prime Minister listened intently. He began his reply in a low voice, taking the President through the history of his life and times and dwelling emotionally on his experiences at the battle of the Somme. It was a moving speech, versions of which I later heard on several occasions over the years, in widely different settings - at a Gaudy in Christ Church Hall and finally when he addressed the House of Lords at ninety years of age. When the two men had finished, it was not difficult to see that both admired the performances, for that is what it was, of the other. The Prime Minister, whilst showing sympathy, gave more than a hint of a negative response to the President's request and took refuge in emphasising his duty to consult his Cabinet. It was the first signs of the deepening of the Vietnam crisis but neither could foresee the extent to which this would ultimately develop.

I like to think that this meeting convinced President Kennedy that, as Eisenhower had recommended, Macmillan was a man whose advice warranted attention and convinced Macmillan that Kennedy was a significant personality and with whom he needed no longer fear that age was an obstacle to understanding and cooperation. The way ahead was clear.

Before the Prime Minister left Key West to start his holiday, he decided to dictate a summary of his discussion to his secretaries. He did so after lunch and paced the room as he dictated. Slowly, in the doorways, the Philippine stewards, which all U.S. naval establishments employed, gathered with shining eyes and watched this extraordinary scene.

The Prime Minister came, as originally scheduled, to Washington in April 1961. One of the by-products of this meeting was the appointment of David Ormsby-Gore (later Lord Harlech) as Ambassador in succession to Harold Caccia, who was to return to the U.K. to take up as expected, the post of Permanent Under Secretary. We were all sad to see the Caccias go as they had presided over a happy, and we thought, efficient Embassy. No member of the Diplomatic Service could dispute the appropriateness of Ormsby-Gore's political appointment. He was known to be an intimate friend of the Kennedys and had been a popular junior minister in the Foreign Office. He soon established an unparalleled relationship with the President and came to be virtually a member of the family. This unique position he held with the greatest discretion. In a furiously jealous city he never abused the confidence placed in him. The fact that he was an amusing, talented and original personality with a charming and religious wife, turned aside much of the envy and gossip. He was happily more than match for the new frontiersmen who did not conceal their self esteem. In some ways it was dispiriting to work for him as it was almost impossible to surprise him with any information that he had not already received from the President or his brother Robert. The Orsmby-Gores showed their unconventionality and caused a mild sensation by entertaining the Beatles at the Embassy. Their youngest daughter, with typical family enterprise, later sold me one of their autographs to send to the child of a colleague in Peking.

Naturally enough there was intense social rivalry to be seen to be near the Kennedys. To entertain Vice President Lyndon Johnson instead, was an admission of a certain failure. But those who did invite the Vice President, whether diplomats or socialites were, after the assassination in November 1963, to reap their reward. Amongst those who did not secure President Kennedy's favour was the protocol conscious French Ambassador, Hervé Alphand and his elegant wife. Angela and I were invited for dinner by the McGeorge Bundys when the Vice President was the guest of honour. It was the first time we had seen him in a social setting. His personality was magnetic and his affability great, but I wondered whether he felt all in the room were mentally comparing him with the young man who was then the toast of the town.

The Cuban missile crisis in October 1962 put the Ambassador's and Macmillan's standing with the President to a severe test. Americans do not deny Ormsby-Gore's influence on U.S. tactics nor the value of Macmillan's daily contacts by phone, although the extent of the latter were concealed at the time by the President from his colleagues. In later times, Macmillan admitted he may himself have exaggerated his influence. I recall that when the Russian ships turned back, Ormsby-Gore came into my room and exclaimed,

"Thank God, they've turned back, just before the Prime Minister gave way!"
It had been an immensely exciting week and I remember at one point, being seized by a sudden fear that nuclear war was upon us and thinking distractedly of our boys at school in England.

A pleasing consequence of the crisis was the demonstration of the superiority of our Diplomatic communications world wide. As a result, President Kennedy ordered a complete overhaul of the State Department's systems.

The resolution of the Cuban missile crisis was a milestone in the battle of wits between Kennedy and Khruschev dating from their meeting in Vienna in June 1961. One of Kennedy's achievements, as time passed, was to bring relations with the Soviet Union from a blind fear and hostility to a more intelligent understanding and a better intellectual appreciation of the significance of nuclear weapons. In both these advances, the U.K. played a beneficial role. The Soviet threat to Berlin was continuously monitored by a small Allied group meeting in the State Department under Assistant Secretary Kohler, at which the British Minister Lord Hood, was our representative. A large volume of our work in the Embassy flowed from this. The U.S. diplomatic machine had received an access of strength with the imports of the new Administration, but it took the President some long time before he was satisfied with the organisation of the State Department and associated departments. But our long-established easy access was at no time diminished, and it was confirmed and strengthened when the President's relationship with the Prime Minister and the Ambassador became well known to the Americans. Dean Rusk, George Ball and Averell Harriman were an effective and friendly combination at the U.S. top level in the State Department. McGeorgeBundy at the White House was always accessible and a man of evident quality. Lesser people with whom I mostly dealt, like Walt Rostow and Harlan Cleveland, with their academic backgrounds, were inclined to treat foreign officials more as pupils than equals. The former was the high priest of the 'domino' theory for communist advance in the Far East, whereas the latter had a typically liberal Democratic faith in the United Nations.

Amongst the New Frontiersmen there was a powerful group who did not welcome the privileged position of the U.K. amongst the Europeans and sought to diminish it. It was a defensible object from the U.S. point of view. Their attention focused on the British determination to maintain an independent nuclear deterrent. Our position was particularly vulnerable as the cost of developing alone a British missile was beyond us. There was no unanimity amongst our Service Chiefs as to the best alternative with the Royal Navy and the RAF in contention. Especially attractive to the RAF was the U.S. Skybolt missile, under development for the USAF which was apparently capable of being married to our 'V' bombers. The Navy favoured the submarine-launched Polaris.

In spite of information from the Embassy and other sources, it was strongly believed in London that the U.S.A.F. would get Skybolt as in the past they had always got what they wanted, no matter the cost. The cancellation of the project by Macnamara came as a great shock to the British and Macmillan was left to make the best deal he could over Polaris Submarines. After much bad-tempered sparring, the matter was brought to a head in a meeting arranged between the P.M. and the President in Nassau at the end of December 1962. The Ministry of Defence delegation on their way, passed through Washington. It included my old chief in Singapore, Sir Robert Scott, now the reluctant Permanent Secretary of the Ministry. Discussion with them showed a disturbing division in their ranks. The U.S. Delegation to a man, were said to be opposed to meeting British wishes and believed that they had the President on their side. The outcome of the famous meeting is known to all and the merits of the agreement reached will be forever debated. For good or for evil, it was an emotional appeal from Macmillan, direct to the President and deft work by Ormsby-Gore that secured U.S. consent to what was at best an untidy understanding. Looking at it through the eyes of our Embassy it seemed a famous victory and a just reward for the Prime Minister's patient and skilful handling of Kennedy. Nearly thirty years later it is not difficult to argue that French hostility to the agreement made impossible a timely entry into the European Community, the ultimate consequences of which we have yet to see.

The year was to be eventful for us from a personal point of view. With the departure of Lord Hood to London, I had been appointed Minister, the number two post in the Embassy. With the post came a pleasant official house, once the home of the donor of the Davis Cup. Next door was General Mike West, my former colleague at the I.D.C, his wife Christine and their long legged daughter Carinthia. It was in a part of Washington where the only black faces to be seen were domestics or delivery men going about their business; but the race question was at the centre of American politics. In August, a quarter of a million blacks converged on Washington, led by Dr. Martin Luther King. While white Washington held its breath, they marched in perfect peaceful order on the Lincoln Memorial where they heard King deliver his famous speech, "I have a dream." It was an historic day. The Autumn brought bad tidings. The British attempt to join the EEC was soon to be stopped in its tracks in face of General de Gaulle's opposition. Although a Test Ban Treaty had been signed with the USSR and the disarmament discussions had been resumed in Geneva, bizarre events like the Great Train Robbery and the Profumo affair kept Britain's name in the transatlantic headlines in an unwelcome way. Profumo, as Secretary of State for War, had recently visited Washington, where in the absence of the Ambassador, I had escorted him to the Pentagon where he was entertained in the usual unsuitable way by the Pentagon string orchestra. But he made an excellent impression in the official talks and the Americans liked him. His disgrace shocked and saddened us. I am glad to have met him not infrequently in later years and witnessed how he has recovered from that setback.

Macmillan's surprise resignation came in October. The way in which we first learned of it in Washington was not without wry humour. I had gone into the Ambassador's study and found him on the phone at his desk. He was sitting bolt upright, repeatedly saying "No," with some emphasis. I was not surprised when, as he put down the phone, he turned to me and said, "That was the President. He says Macmillan has resigned. Randolph Churchill (who was at that time visiting Washington) has told him. Have we heard...?" We had not, but soon did.

I learned some years later how Churchill was first with the news. When in Washington he usually stayed, not always as a welcome guest, with a friend in Georgetown. She told me on that particular day he had been very restless, pacing the room and saying, "I'm sure something bad is happening at home." Finally, he could contain himself no longer and picked up the phone to call No. 10. The lady went into the next room to listen on an extension because, as she said, he had the habit of making long overseas calls and trying to leave her the bill. He had got quickly through to No. 10 and spoke to Julian Amery, who had just left the Cabinet room. Amery told him the news and Randolph lost no time in calling the White House. Thus it was that the President was probably the first person in the world, outside the Cabinet, to hear. The resignation, unnecessary as it proved to be, seemed likely to hamper Anglo-U.S. relations. But the choice of Alec Douglas Home, the Foreign Secretary, as his successor, was a comfort to those of us in the Diplomatic Service and Americans who knew him.

It was not long before the new Prime Minister and his wife came to Washington on an introductory visit. They made, as expected, an excellent impression on those who had not met them before. They were accompanied by Mr. and Mrs. R. A. Butler, the new Foreign Secretary. He shocked some of us by his indiscreet and patronisingly loud comments on the new Prime Minister, who had deprived him of his chance of succeeding Harold Macmillan. It is not always a happy arrangement for a Foreign Minister to accompany his Prime Minister on an overseas visit as it is inevitable that the senior man attracts the most attention of the hosts and there are possibilities of jealousies. I am told that this indeed was what happened, years later when Prime Minister Callaghan visited Washington with his young Foreign Secretary, David Owen.

Shortly afterwards, it was time for us to go on home leave and it was in my father's study that I saw on his T.V. the terrible events in Dallas of 22nd November. Like so many everywhere, I bitterly thought of the morrow. But was the Kennedy reign so wonderful? For some time it seemed so. The spectacle of a handsome and articulate young man and his beautiful wife at the head of the most powerful country in the world was so full of promise. In the light of subsequent events, it is reasonable to question whether the regime had the innate quality and stamina to cope with the events which proved to be its legacy to the Vice President, Lyndon Johnson. I regret that I missed the drama of the funeral and did not see at first hand the emotional devastation of all Americans. One of the most saddening things was, on our return to Washington, to find many of those who seemed to have sworn fidelity to Kennedy were so soon ready to deny it. During the Kennedys' time in the White House, the press behaved with a reticence which is inconceivable now. For the final verdict on the Kennedy regime the jury, as a recent historian remarked, "is still out."

The assassination of the President and later of his brother and Dr.

Martin Luther King was a reminder of the violence and hatred endemic in U.S. politics. I recalled my shock and surprise in 1945 when I first heard vitriolic and unbridled criticism of Franklin Roosevelt. In some minds he had been clearly a candidate for physical attack. Even Truman was shot at in 1952 as he drove to Arlington cemetery to unveil a statue to British Field Marshall Dill. Along with a Delegation including Anthony Eden I waited long in the cemetery until rumour was stilled by the President's late arrival in his car festooned by security men.

By mid 1964 we had been in Washington nearly five years. Together with our previous three years, there was a real danger of 'going native'. The atmosphere of Washington was seductive and we had many friends. It was easy not to grasp fully what was going on at home, particularly changing attitudes towards the U.S. and Europe. I was reluctant to leave, but Angela could see more clearly that it was time for me to go.

CHAPTER 14

RETURN TO THE FOREIGN OFFICE II - 1964

We returned from Washington in 1964. Angela and the boys had returned in time for the school summer term. I came back in the autumn. We were glad to re-occupy our house in Westminster and I had the pleasure of resuming my walk across St. James Park each morning to Whitehall.

During our time in Washington I had not given much thought to the future stages of my career. It seemed that I was considered to have done quite well and was known to senior people in the Service. I was therefore fairly confident that there was a chance of getting an interesting appointment in the Office. I had no particular objective and I was not dissatisfied, but not overjoyed by being made Assistant Under Secretary with my main responsibility being United Nations affairs.

As there was some time before I could take up my new appointment, and the General Election was near, I took the opportunity of visiting Moscow for the first time at the beginning of October 1964. I was met at the airport by a Secretary from our Embassy. After he had helped me to negotiate customs and immigration he mentioned rather mysteriously that he had been held up by an 'incident' at the Embassy. He did not elaborate on the journey from the airport into town as the car was driven by a Russian chauffeur. On arrival the 'incident' became only too apparent. A fire had occurred in a small wing of the Embassy building which commanded an uninterrupted view of the Kremlin. Clearing up operations were still going on. The fire had broken out in a high security area devoted to sensitive communications equipment. Although the Ambassador, Humphrey Trevelyan, had been rushed to the scene from the Bolshoi theatre there was no alternative to admitting Russian firemen. They had completed the destruction of the equipment by holding off the British and particularly Tom Brimelow, the Minister, by the simple expedient of relentlessly hosing them down. The fire has sometimes without certainty been attributed to the Russians sending a high charge of electricity into the apparatus from outside the Embassy premises. It was an appropriately hostile introduction to the life in Moscow which members of the Embassy regularly endured.

After a few days I left Moscow early on the cloudless morning of British Election Day and on arrival in London found to my astonishment that Khrushchev had been sacked on that very morning. There had been no hint of this on the drive to the airport and it was clear that the population had been as ignorant as I was.

"Trains always held a fascination for me."
D.G. right with brother Brian.

D.G. on left with parents

brother Brian

and sister Barbara

at Ashfields

1938/9

With John Hennell
on our tandem
near Aachen
1933.

Miss Crump's School at Woodford, 1920.
D.G. on extreme right front row.

Duke of York's Camp at Southwold, 1936.
D.G. second from left.

The Bride
is given away by
her boss,
Desmond Adair.
Cairo
4th June 1941.

Emerging
from
Cairo Cathedral
after our wedding.

Angela with Nigel and Robin 1953/4
(Photograph by New Zealand friend Lyn Corner)

The Author

with grandaughter

Aster.

1982.

Minister Paul Mason

and Legation staff leaving

Presidency in Sofia

after presenting credentials

1949

On the way to Moscow,

equipped by Moss Bros.

1966.

ROBIN - 1948
FRENCH LEGATION
SOFIA

Robin in the French Legation Garden

Sofia.   1948

BRITISH EMBASSY,

Above. After the party. Ronald Searle's insight into Diplomatic life. (Presented to Angela by The Diplomatic Wives' Association).

On left. Angela on the dance floor with U.S. General Marshall. Coronation week. 1952

Alexei Kosygin face to face with Harold Wilson, Moscow 1966
Author on Prime Minister's right.

Andrei Gromyko at Moscow Airport with Foreign Scecretary George Brown
Viscount Hood (Foreign Office) extreme right. D.G. in background.

Belgrade 1965.
The Author, H.M. Ambassador Sir Duncan Wilson and
Foreign Secretary Michael Stewart.

*1969. The Ambassador of the United States, Walter Annenberg
presenting his credentials to The Queen at Buckingham Palace.
The author on the left*

Washington 1951

Visit of

Their Royal Highnesses

Princess Elizabeth

&

The Duke of Edinburgh

Princess Elizabeth greeting Charlie Brown

(Embassy Messenger)

Prime Minister

Sir Alec Douglas-Home

and the Author

consulting at Heathrow,

before Sir Alec's

departure

for New York

September 1970

With Angela and

the Prime Minister

in the

Washington Embassy

1963

Greeting General Amin
at the Hyde Park Hotel
in London
1971.

The Author
received by
Ian Smith
in Salisbury
(now Harare)
in 1971.

December 1971. Meeting of Prime Minister Heath
and President Nixon in the White House.
The British Delegation (clockwise) Lord Cromer
Anthony Barber, Sir Burke Trend
Robert Armstrong, John Graham,
The Prime Minister, Sir Alec Douglas Home and the Author.

February 1973. Dinner given by President Nixon
for Prime Minister Heath at Camp David.
L to R. Henry Kissinger, Lord Cromer, U.S. Secretary of State
Rogers, Sir Burke Trend, Robert Armstrong,
Ambassador Annenburg, Prime Minister Heath, President Nixon,
Sir Alec Douglas-Home and the Author.

Angela on the Great Wall of China.

November 1972.

*Visit to the Temple of Heaven, Peking, with the wife of the
Chinese Foreign Minister.*
*Lady Home and Angela with, left, Julian Morgan (Counsellor's
wife) and right, Elizabeth Wright (2nd Secretary) and Chinese
Interpreter* *(Photograph John Dixon)*

Monochrome picture of the Permanent Under Secretary's room at the Foreign and Commonwealth Office, by Jean Reddaway. November 1973

With Angela at the Lord Mayor's Easter Banquet, Mansion House, Spring 1973. (Photograph Desmond O'Neill).

Lord Carrington,   The Author   and Lord Roll

17th February 1975.   Angela (President of the English Speaking Union's
George Washington Ball) greeting Foreign Secretary (later Prime Minister)
James Callaghan, U.S. Minister Ron Spiers, and Dr. Henry Kissinger.

Aster with her parents, Nigel and Jeanne at the Gothic Folly,
Stowe. *September 1991.*

ROBIN AT NEW COLLEGE, 1965

With P.B. colleagues at the Alaska pipeline, Prudhoe, September 1977

It is always difficult after some years abroad to catch up with the changed opinion in Whitehall. Many of my colleagues in the Office seemed to welcome in the new Government. They had been disappointed by R. A. Butler as Foreign Secretary who had seemed somewhat disinterested in the post having failed to become Prime Minister. Nicko Henderson, in his perceptive book *The Private Office* explains how his attitudes and manner of work discouraged the more aggressive members of the Office. I had no strong feelings about either the outgoing or incoming governments. All liked and admired Alec Home and the narrowness of his defeat surprised most people but was evidence of the respect in which he was nationally held in spite of a strong effort to deride him in the media.

With the advent of a new government it was not only the identification of the new ministers which was of interest to the office. Harold Caccia was due shortly to retire. There was naturally speculation about his successor. Some few months before the election Harold Wilson and Patrick Gordon-Walker had together visited Moscow where the Ambassador was Sir Humphrey Trevelyan. Not surprisingly they were much impressed by his strong character and wide experience. He had entered the Diplomatic Service from a high post in the Indian Civil Service and had later been Ambassador in Baghdad and Cairo. It became common knowledge that he was favoured as Caccia's successor by the Labour leadership not least because of his open disapproval of Eden's Suez adventure. His age was against him as he also was near to retirement. His retention would seriously aggravate the promotion block in the higher ranks of the Service. He was much favoured by those who had served with him, but was less well known in Whitehall and had not played a leading part in our diplomacy in the U.S. and Europe. According to his diary Gordon-Walker who was greatly interested in Commonwealth relations favoured a short appointment of Trevelyan to be followed by a younger man. It is widely believed that Trevelyan declined the appointment, but for what reason I can only guess. In the event Paul Gore-Booth was given the post. This was welcome to me because of our service together in Washington and my admiration for his talents and our friendship with his family.

I had met Harold Wilson and George Brown, the dominant members of the new government, when they had come separately to Washington a few months earlier. As I was Chargé d'Affaires at the time we had entertained the Wilsons and their younger son to dinner, together with the Brimelows. Tom Brimelow, the most senior member of our Chancery, was the acknowledged expert on Soviet Affairs and a north countryman like Harold Wilson. It had been a pleasant quiet evening. In contrast George Brown, obviously impatient for an electoral victory talked a lot about his plan for creating an Economic Affairs Ministry. He also upset some Washingtonians by missing appointments and some flamboyant and erratic behaviour of a kind with which the British public was later to become only too familiar.

I was personally excited by the fact that the new Foreign Secretary initially appointed was Patrick Gordon-Walker who had been my history tutor at Christ Church. Sadly, as I have explained earlier, he failed to secure, at second try, a seat in the House of Commons and had to give way somewhat unexpectedly to the lesser known Michael Stewart. When this had occurred I was called to the office of George Thomson, the Minister of State, who had quickly shown himself to be a particularly friendly and genial member of the new Ministerial team. He doubted whether I knew anything of the new Foreign Secretary. I replied that I had in fact, sometime before, read a complimentary piece about him in the Economist. There my knowledge stopped. The Minister said that I should know that there had been no significant development in the Labour Party in opposition on which Stewart had not played an important part. We would all like him. This, indeed, proved correct, but he remained the least appreciated Foreign Secretary of recent times. As a speaker and debater he had few equals as later events were to show. Nicko Henderson who was, for a time his Private Secretary, gives a just assessment of him in his book to which I have already referred. The obituary notices in the Press on his death, showed a belated appreciation of his worth.

The delay whilst Gordon-Walker made his second attempt to enter the Commons, brought about a valuable reform in Foreign Office procedure which became an established part of the system. In order that he could be quickly briefed by his Private Secretary whilst he was electioneering in the constituency of Leyton, East London, the Permanent Under Secretary, Harold Caccia, called a daily morning meeting of his senior colleagues to review the international scene. It is amazing it had not been done before, but once started it has not been given up.

Journeys abroad by Ministers are sometimes criticised in the Press. Their use is self evident and especially so for new personalities. To be of maximum value, careful preparation is essential. I tried hard when the responsibility was mine, to see that the briefing materials and briefing meetings before departure provided the background that a new Minister would need. During Stewart's first spell in the Foreign Office I accompanied him to Yugoslavia, Czechoslovakia and Poland. He was little known to his hosts but in each case they were clearly impressed, if not disconcerted by his quiet authority and the skill with which he advanced his arguments and criticised their policies. The visit to Poland included Warsaw and Cracow and was greatly helped by our Ambassador George Clutton who had started his career in the British Museum before moving into the Foreign Office. He had a profound knowledge of Polish history and art and soon silenced our guides and the government officials by his superior knowledge of their own country. The final departure from Warsaw airport had elements of drama, the full extent of which was not fully recognised at the time. As we looked out of the cabin porthole window there appeared to be some commotion amongst the farewell party centring on the Ambassador. But after some significant delay the plane took off. A clue to the incident became apparent when the cabin steward in full uniform appeared with a muddled tray of drinks and clear signs of drunkenness. He was hastily withdrawn by his colleagues. It later transpired that he had been a Polish resident in the U.K. since the war had ended and our visit was the first time he had returned to his native country. He had fallen amongst his countrymen who had welcomed him into an almost incapable state. He had been observed by one of the official farewell party unsteadily mounting the steps of the plane and had been mistaken in his smart uniform and peaked cap for the pilot. The message that the pilot was drunk had been immediately communicated to the Ambassador who was urged to agree to halting the departure. After some hesitation, his faith in British Airways prevailed and he dismissed the accusation and watched, with relief, a perfect take off.

The new Labour Government had decided that, as an indication of its priorities, a Minister, rather than an official, should be appointed to be the British representative at the United Nations organisation in New York. Sir Hugh Foot was chosen. A member of a distinguished West Country Liberal family, he had been a former Governor General of Nigeria and Governor of Jamaica and Cyprus. He was well known in New York when Harold Macmillan had appointed him as a member of the U.K. Delegation, as especially qualified to help deal with the delegates of newly independent colonial territories. It was a good idea, but it broke down when he later ostentatiously resigned as a protest at British policy in Rhodesia. As the relevant Assistant Secretary, I was clearly going to have to work closely with him. Not unreasonably, I imagined that he had hoped one day, to be the third Foot brother to sit together in the House of Commons, but the narrowness of the Government majority made it impossible to find him a seat. This in any case, would have taken time. To be a Minister at once he would have to be a Life Peer. He told me that he would always consider himself 'a Roundhead, rather than a Cavalier.' He proposed therefore, on the announcement of his peerage, to issue a press release which indicated his disapproval of peers and his reluctant acceptance of the honour in the wider interest of the Government's new policy towards the United Nations. He showed me a most unsuitable draft. For his own good I protested, but he looked determined to go ahead. The only way I persuaded him to abandon the idea was to suggest that H.M. the Queen might be greatly offended. As a former Colonial Governor and Governor General his loyalties held him back. I gave accidentally, further offence by saying in jest that I hoped he would keep the 'Foot' name in his title and not choose something 'fancy.' He replied curtly that he had already chosen 'Caradon.'

In the event he proved the most delightful Minister to work for although, from time to time, he demonstrated that, in trying to pursue his personal policies, the means justified the ends. On his appointment, he was certainly given, by the Prime Minister, a false impression that he would have a freer hand than his predecessors in making policy in New York and not always have to submit to instructions from the Foreign Secretary in Whitehall. In fact, he never failed to obey orders from London but often when visiting London carried a letter of resignation in his pocket which he showed me 'in confidence' but never delivered. He was a compelling speaker and was a major figure in the United Nations in New York to the benefit of the British reputation particularly in the Third World. He was largely responsible for the famous Resolution 242, which, in spite of some ambiguity, may yet be the foundation for a Palestine/Israel settlement. But he could never entirely forget his Colonial service days and when ex-colonial delegates from newly independent countries did not follow his advice, he was greatly aggrieved. It was characteristic of some members of his family that at his funeral I am told that his coffin was wrapped in the flag of the Palestine Liberation Organisation.

Caradon decided he would form in the Foreign Office a consultative group of outside people interested in the UN to discuss British policy with him when he visited London from New York. It was an unusual but sensible idea. He involved members of other political parties including Jeremy Thorpe, the Liberal leader. He also invited Lord Chalfont, a newly created life peer, who had been appointed Minister for Disarmament in the new Labour Government. During the election campaign, Chalfont had acted as an adviser to the Liberal party in his capacity as the Defence correspondent of a leading newspaper. His sudden emergence as a peer and a Labour Minister caused some critical comment and as he entered the room for the first meeting of Caradon's committee, Jeremy Thorpe the Liberal leader raised his eyebrows and remarked, in the hearing of all, "Et tu Brute."

During the next two years I spent a great deal of time on the question of Rhodesia and the attempt by the government to use the United Nations organisation to bring pressure on Ian Smith the rebel Prime Minister. Indeed I was preoccupied with the problem until my retirement in 1973, and again briefly in 1976. Ian Smith had visited London during the Commonwealth Conference in 1965 and missed the opportunity to put his case for independence fairly and squarely to Ministers. It would not have been accepted but an ill tempered break might have been averted.

In November 1965, satisfied that he would get no response from a Labour Government Smith made his Unilateral Declaration of Independence. The Government should have been more prepared for this move and done some better contingency planning, for the consequences both domestically and internationally were bound to be serious. Departmental responsibility for Rhodesia at that time did not lie with the Foreign Office but rested with the still separate Commonwealth Office. But the consequences of Smith's action internationally were clearly in the Foreign Office court. The Labour Party had close links with the Black African leaders who were most directly affected. President Kaunda of Zambia and President Nyerere of Tanzania had many personal friends amongst the Labour leaders and had been helped by them over several years. Furthermore the Party was sensitive about its relations with all the new Commonwealth members and proved to be easily moved by threats of 'breaking up' the Commonwealth. Strong action by the British Government against Smith was expected and demanded by them. The use of force against the rebels was seriously considered and abandoned not only because there was no guarantee of quick success but because of domestic reaction in a difficult electoral situation. The reaction of our armed forces if used against white Rhodesians could not be foreseen. One of the strongest advocates of the use of force was Jeremy Thorpe the Liberal leader.

The United Nations offered a safer but by no means certain alternative. The Secretary of State decided to go personally to New York and I was glad to accompany him. It was very satisfying for an official to work with a Minister who commanded respect and whose debating talent was obvious to all. Michael Stewart was such a person. But throughout the Rhodesian crisis at that time and later I think the Government misjudged the interest and sympathy of the important members of the UN organisation in our problem. Some like the Soviet Union used it to embarrass us and others were content to call for sanctions with no real intention of imposing discipline on their own nationals. Standing aside was South Africa, who was ready to supply the rebels with most of their needs and was capable of inflicting material damage on us at a time when our economic position was weak.

The United Nations Organisation itself was declining from its peak immediately after the war and its limitations were increasingly apparent, not least in the quality of the national representatives. Negotiating with so many other delegations was indeed fascinating but at the same time had an air of unreality. False bonhomie with loud, mirthless laughter was the order of the day and it was virtually impossible to have a conversation without an arm being thrown round one's shoulders. There was also a folie de grandeur in some representatives speaking as if they and the Organisation were indeed running the world. Nevertheless, in retrospect, had I not later had the opportunity of being the Permanent Under Secretary I would have been very happy if I had been considered as a suitable Representative at the U.N. Organisation in New York. It is encouraging now to see the Organisation after the Gulf War climbing slowly back towards the role for which it was originally designed.

How was it that the Labour Government failed to settle the Rhodesian question during its more than five years of office? The reasons were complex. At all times the government over estimated the effect of sanctions on the white Rhodesians. Rather than contemplate the hazards of using force, the Cabinet accepted the widely optimistic estimates of sanctions damage to Smith made initially by senior economic staff of the Commonwealth office. At the same time we all over-estimated the international support Britain would in practice receive at the United Nations. The countries like France, Japan and the U.S. were inclined to the view that Rhodesia was a purely British problem and it was up to Her Majesty's Government to solve it and pick their own chestnuts out of the fire. In the meantime they were often ready to exploit the markets which we were abandoning. The nations most enthusiastic about sanctions were those who had little or no trade with Rhodesia. Totally uncooperative were, of course, the South Africans and the U.K. was in no economic position to risk the possible consequences of a head on clash with them. Ian Smith could count on receiving much of his vital needs across the Beit bridge from the Republic and the Swiss above all could relied upon to help in the evasion of international restrictions. At the same time the Rhodesians were not without their own assets. Those who had known the Rhodesian forces in the Middle East during the war were not surprised at their determination and ingenuity in resisting pressure. Many years later, when I visited Rhodesia on business, I heard them talking amongst themselves about their successful evasion of sanctions with the same pride our countrymen told tales of the London Blitz.

The Prime Minister decided to attempt direct negotiations with Smith towards the end of 1966. In retrospect the attempt was mishandled. The rendez-vous was in HMS Tiger off Gibraltar and the Rhodesians could be excused for feeling this was a piece of attempted intimidation. In addition, the Prime Minister's personal staff and kitchen cabinet belittled Smith's personal capacities and advised him that it would be like negotiating with 'a local councillor.' An agreement was in fact reached with Smith but was repudiated by his hardliners on his return to Salisbury. In fact Wilson and Smith had nothing in common and their contempt was mutual and remained so. Smith was a capable negotiator but never convinced the Prime Minister and many others of his trustworthiness.

The second attempt at direct negotiations was in October 1968 again at Gibraltar Harbour in a naval assault ship 'H.M.S. Fearless.' Smith's party was in a destroyer moored alongside. I felt sorry for the young naval padre who planned a Sunday service on the quarter-deck with the best will in the world, at which the Prime Minister and Smith were to read the first and second lessons. At the last moment the Prime Minister found out what was planned and instantly cancelled it. The thought of a photograph in the British press of the two in a joint religious service on the quarter-deck threw him and his personal staff into a near panic. It was not difficult to get the impression that the sympathy of the vessels' crews lay with Smith.

I was present at the meetings. Smith certainly held his own with the Prime Minister and the Attorney General Elwyn-Jones. The latter never forgave him for his derogatory remarks about the Judicial Committee of the Privy Council and did his best for sincere reasons to block a settlement. But agreement came near at the Fearless talks and it was Smith who finally rejected the terms offered.

After the breakdown, George Thomson, Maurice Foley M.P. a junior Minister and I visited Nyerere and Kenyatta to explain the terms which, after their rejection, 'remained on the table.' In Tanzania we had to drive to Nyerere's spartan country retreat where we met Miss Joan Wicken, his British adviser, whose views echoed Kingsley Martin and the New Statesman of the late nineteen thirties. Nyerere was strong in his criticism of the proposed agreement. He taunted Thomson and Foley asking how was it possible for a Labour Government to consider such terms.

Before being received in Nairobi by Kenyatta we called on Daniel Arap Moi, the Vice President who was to be his eventual successor. He gave then a very uncertain impression. But many years later when I had retired from the Diplomatic Service, I was received by him as President, with Alfred Shepperd (Sir), Chairman of the Wellcome Foundation who were extending their pharmaceutical factory in Nairobi. To my surprise, I was considerably impressed by a new strong and confident personality and by his courtesy. I had been keen to see Kenyatta, but by that time he was greatly aged. Our interview recalled for me Winston Churchill at the Defence Committee Meeting in 1953 to which I have referred. From time to time he dominated the discussion then suddenly his attention wandered right away from the point only to return again. The ministers who surrounded Kenyatta were embarrassingly sycophantic and laughed almost hysterically at his every sally. I could not get out of my mind my visit to the famous Thika Mau Mau concentration camp in 1954 on our IDC tour when, for the first time in my life, I felt an almost physical wave of hatred which rose from the imprisoned Kikuyu tribesmen hunched on the ground in small silent motionless groups.

Was Smith right to turn his back on an agreement with the Labour Government? It would at best have been a fragile understanding. Smith for too long counted on some of his friends in the U.K. but more on those in the United States and South Africa. Even many years later when all hope of British approval had passed he clung to the expectation that the Americans and the South Africans would stand by him. He was to be disappointed by both. He established his own man in Washington, who did not find it difficult to find kindred spirits in Congress. From them he received consistently bad advice. After the election of a Conservative Government in 1970, HMG tried again for a settlement. In these efforts I was again involved and will refer to them later.

During one of the visits to Rhodesia, I stayed at Government House in which the legitimate Governor, Sir Humphrey Gibbs and his wife were living under virtual house arrest, deprived of almost all facilities by the Smith regime. It was an inspiring experience. His loyalty to the Queen and his love of Rhodesia, where he had farmed extensively since long before the war, persuaded him to stay on and try without bitterness to influence a settlement with Smith. Ultimately he had to leave, but returned to Rhodesia after it had become an independent republic and, in spite of the personal danger, stayed on until his death in November 1990. A grave, tall man with a natural quiet authority, he put many of the white Rhodesians to shame and earned the respect of the blacks. President Mugabe, on the news of his death, sent a sincere and moving message to his family.

In August 1966 George Brown became Foreign Secretary and displaced Michael Stewart by swapping posts with him. The Department of Economic Affairs into which George Brown had put so much thought and effort had failed against the almost universal opposition of traditional ministries. He brought to the Foreign Office his passionate political partisanship and his jealousy of the Prime Minister who had defeated him for the Party leadership. He brought also energy, ability and a strong purpose towards Europe and to Arab reconciliation. These qualities he diminished by erratic and undignified behaviour. But it was easy to forgive him in many cases. He was to have a decisive effect on my own career.

During the previous two years I had been promoted from Assistant Under Secretary to Deputy Under Secretary and was in charge of defence and intelligence matters when he arrived at the office. Late in the evening on his first day gave me a hint of the shape of things to come. As I was preparing to leave my office a white faced lady secretary came in and said the Secretary of State wanted to see me at once. I went up to his room which was almost in darkness except for his desk lamp which illuminated his papers and a single bottle in front of him. He seemed to be the worse for drink and my mind flew back to undergraduate days at Oxford and I found myself wondering how we were to get him down the stairs. My fears were unjustified.

He entered into a fierce and logically argued attack on our policy towards the Soviet Union. I disagreed with him and we eventually gave up. Neither of us had convinced the other. I went home troubled but impressed by the way that he had maintained his argument whilst apparently so far from being sober. I met him in the corridor early next morning.
As he passed me he said, "Last night you were right and I was wrong!"

Stories of his being under the influence of alcohol were in my experience often exaggerated. Very little liquor, usually sherry, quickly created an appearance of intoxication. Indiscretion and abusiveness followed. Yet he was able to sustain a logical argument throughout.

Meetings with him were almost always boisterous and his language often brutal. After one such discussion as I was leaving the room he remarked, "I saw you sitting there looking like a bloody methodist." He had got the denomination wrong but he had found that I had been brought up as a nonconformist. After any argumentative discussion he could dictate an impressive speech with great fluency and clarity. Brown's especial interests were Europe and the Middle East and in these matters he tended often to disagree with the Prime Minister and did not fully share Wilson's preoccupation with Vietnam. He could be relied upon to argue his Foreign Office policy in Cabinet strongly and this was encouraging to his officials.

The contrast between him and Michael Stewart can be shown in the way he dealt with defeat in the Cabinet. Michael Stewart would return to the office and say "I'm afraid I was unable to persuade my colleagues of the wisdom of our case." Whereas George Brown would come back with, "Those so and so's did not agree," and then followed, special abuse for his envied Oxbridge colleagues and orders to examine how the decision of the Cabinet could be revised or even circumvented. But, beneath the bluster occasionally it was apparent how highly strung he was. I went with him to

New York where he was to address the General Assembly for the first time in September 1966. We went down early to the UN building and paced up and down the garden. I tried to calm him down by saying that he had an excellent speech, it was not the first time he had addressed a large gathering and so on. This did not prevent him rushing into the cloakroom and being heartily sick before he took his place in the hall. Harold Macmillan's biographer tells the same story of his subject. George Brown had an almost uncanny intuition in identifying the vulnerable aspects of the personalities with whom he was dealing. Having identified the weak spot he hit it, if he was so minded, again and again. It was painful to watch and particularly so with such people as Lord Caradon who so often unintentionally provoked him and whose justifiable vanities irritated him.

On one occasion, George Brown arrived in new York on his way to a United Nations meeting. It was late in the afternoon and he expected to be met by Lord Caradon. In the event, he was met by Roger Jackling, his deputy. "Where is the Lord?" demanded the Secretary of State, with evident annoyance. It was explained that he was attending the Annual Dinner given by the Secretary General to the Heads of all Delegations - an event of importance in the United Nations calendar. "I shall go to the dinner," said Brown. We pointed out how unsuitable his sudden uninvited appearance would be. He brushed this aside, as well as other objections. Finally, in desperation, Jackling played his imagined trump card knowing the Secretary of State would have brought no evening clothes.

"It is a black tie affair," he pointed out.

"In that case, I shall certainly go," came the reply.

He duly interrupted the dinner, took Caradon by the shoulders and lifted him from his seat. He could hardly have done anything more damaging to Caradon's dignity and was never forgiven.

On another occasion in New York, the Secretary of State was invited to an elaborate dinner given by Princess Ashraf, the Shah's sister. I went with him. We arrived late at the entrance of her apartment building as a score of press photographers was leaving. Finally, we got into the hallway, where we were alone. The Secretary of State said he wanted to relieve himself before going up to the Princess's apartment. He disappeared and was gone some long time and returned with a worried expression. His trouser zip had stuck. Together we struggled with it, jumping up and down in our efforts to jerk it up. Had any of the press photographers looked back, we would have been forever embarrassed. It was a narrow escape. Later, during the dinner, Brown left the table, giving me an apprehensive glance. I waited on tenterhooks. He soon reappeared, smiling, and gave a 'thumbs up' sign.

I was present at several clashes between Brown and Gromyko, who must have had unrivalled experience with dealing with vodka inspired abuse from Soviet leaders like Khrushchev. Nevertheless he had a soft spot for George Brown, as I learned in 1970. After the fall of the Labour Government Gromyko was invited as the guest of Alec Home in London. I found myself alone with Gromyko (at the Soviet Embassy) before going into dinner. He had come from a reception at Lancaster House where I knew George Brown had been present. I asked Gromyko if he had seen him. He looked at me with a twinkle in his eye and said thoughtfully,

"Yes, I saw him, and then paused and added "Sometimes I think Mr. Brown has inside him powerful motor - possibly nuclear!"

Many of us thought the same. Nevertheless he made cruel and unforgivable errors of judgement with senior officials of the Foreign Office notably (Sir) Con O'Neill and (Sir) Patrick Reilly. Both were abominably treated. It would be charitable to conclude that these cruelties arose in part from jealousy and envy dating back to his childhood in Peabody Buildings and his conviction that given the educational advantages of others he could have succeeded in the leadership of his party and the country. Nevertheless these events left a bad taste.

His first visit to Moscow was a memorable episode which further revealed his underlying character. He was greatly excited at the prospect. Unhappily it coincided with appalling weather in the USSR. Day after day the flight was postponed and the Secretary of State clearly believed there was some conspiracy to prevent the visit on the excuse of fog at Moscow. Finally I was sent to see the Soviet Ambassador - Smirnovsky - with whom I was on good terms. I was instructed to say that the Secretary of State knew that there were airfields in East Germany which had special fog dispersal resources and that he proposed to take off on the assumption that one of these airfields would be made available to receive our plane. He asked that Moscow be informed accordingly. I knew this was mission impossible but I duly saw the Ambassador. He looked me knowingly in the eye and said

"Very bad line to Moscow." In due course we did take off without any response but with Copenhagen rather than East Germany as the intermediate stop. George Brown was less than satisfied and became fascinated by the information about the fact that there was "a point of no return" on the journey at which we had to turn back if Moscow remained closed. He somehow thought this navigational decision was up to him. However, as we got on the plane, Murray Maclehose, Brown's trusted private secretary, said firmly to the Captain of the plane that under no circumstances was he to take any notice of anything the Secretary of State said. The reply from the Captain was that he had not the slightest intention of doing so. Both Maclehose and Lord Hood had a special ability to handle Brown and he had great respect for them.

Moscow airport remained closed and we were diverted to Leningrad where the airport was crowded with thwarted aircraft including the plane of the Deputy to the Egyptian President Nasser with whom we were not in diplomatic relationship. With remarkable skill the Russians not only kept us apart but moved us by car with great rapidity to the only large hotel in the city from which guests were bundled out to make room for us to bath and dine. I was put in the first car with the Secretary of State. At the last moment an English speaking Russian jumped in and started to bombard the Secretary of State with statistics about Leningrad. At one point he mentioned the number of churches. This immediately aroused George Brown who asked how many were open and why were people prevented from worship. An ugly argument looked like developing but was terminated by our arrival at the hotel. In the event Brown brushed aside diplomatic protocol and succeeded in making contact with the Egyptian with later beneficial results.

Towards midnight that evening we were all put on a special sleeper train to Moscow. It was an administrative tour de force by the Russians. But there was a final scare. Shortly after the train was under way I was summoned to the Secretary of State's compartment. His wallet had gone. Not only money but other documents. The worst seemed to have happened. Everything was turned upside down and suspicion fell upon an extremely ugly samovar lady who sat sphinx-like at the end of our corridor. One final search produced the wallet and the train continued at little more than walking pace towards Moscow. There was one further touch of comedy. His Private Secretary announced to a colleague that he had, as instructed, given the Secretary of State 'his sleeping pill.' "So have I," the other replied. There was no problem however in the morning. The visit was as successful as could be expected.

With the exception of Michael Stewart, senior members of the Labour Party often seemed ill at ease meeting Soviet leaders. It was as if they were nonconformists meeting the Pope. They showed signs of an inferiority complex in the face of the high priests of socialism. George Brown was no exception, although he had got into a sharp quarrel with Khrushchev on his visit to London. The Labour Government, and in particular, Harold Wilson, had the very laudable objective of trying to act as intermediaries between the Americans and the Soviet Union over the Vietnam War. At that stage in their history the Americans did not like to admit the need for such help from the UK and simultaneously used other channels. They were quite prepared to string the British Government along whilst being suspicious of its motives and doubtful of its ability to help. George Brown tried his hand over Vietnam, but was more interested and more effective in dealing with the Middle East and with Europe. In both these areas he moved the government's policies in a beneficial direction into Europe and away from the Labour movement's traditional support of Israel. Distrust and jealousy marred the communication between Brown and Wilson. On one occasion when I accompanied the Prime Minister to Moscow without the Secretary of State, Brown forbad me to disclose to Wilson, certain important information we had just received from Washington. In the event, I was compelled to do so, to prevent the Prime Minister making a fool of himself by sending a misguided telegram to President Johnson. On my return he sent for me and said,

"Did you have to tell him?"

I answered, "Yes". The matter was not mentioned again.

Other times when I was in the Prime Minister's party to Moscow there were moments of light relief. One had to admire the determination and skill with which the Prime Minister pursued his attempts to reconcile the Soviet and U.S. positions on Vietnam. These are recorded in his book *The Labour Government 1964-70* but in retrospect it is questionable whether the British efforts could ever have succeeded. On the first visit the Prime Minister and members of the party were allowed to equip themselves (it was February) with full winter clothing from Moss Bros. The fur coats and hats evoked jeers from the British Press. On a second occasion it was forbidden by No. 10 and a small allowance was made to purchase linings for our normal overcoats. For the Prime Minister himself, Lord Kagan produced a special super Gannex coat. Another problem was the choice of a present for Kosygin. The usual Foreign Office policy was antique silver or valuable prints of Westminster and so on. The Prime Minister, rather sensibly, insisted on a product of British high technology. The choice was a very up-to-date 'walkie-talkie.' At the first meeting in the Kremlin the Prime Minister tried to hand it over to Kosygin but the instrument never got more than half way across the table before it was intercepted by a large security man. It was fairly certain that Kosygin never saw it again. In the evening there was a dinner at the Kremlin. The principals sat at a top table well out of earshot. Michael Palliser, the Prime Minister's private secretary, myself and Andrei Gromyko, at that time still only an official and not a member of the Politburo, were put well below the salt. Suddenly the Prime Minister rose to his feet and called upon the British guests to stand and sing "Happy birthday, dear Andrei, happy birthday to you." We all joined in with some embarrassment.

Kosygin and his colleagues were completely mystified but Gromyko, who was the only Russian who understood what was happening was not displeased. As he seemed in a mellow mood, Palliser and I encouraged him to tell us some of his early experiences. He had been obviously greatly amused by the incongruity of his joint appearances as Soviet Ambassador to the U.S., with our immensely tall aristocratic ambassador Lord Halifax at fund raising meetings in the U.S. during the war. He also told of how his small daughter and a friend vanished on their way home from school in Washington in 1941 only to be discovered with some elderly American couple in their home nearby, where they had called to enquire where they could find a ship to take them to the Soviet Union 'to fight the Fascist invader.' He then recalled a visit to see U.S. troops with Lord Halifax at Fort Worth in Texas. He found the Ambassador towering above a circle of GI's to whom he was speaking. Gromyko hurried up to ask one of the GI's what the Ambassador was saying, only to be told "I guess that guy doesn't speak English." Gromyko's usual glum exterior concealed a keen sense of the ridiculous. He suffered greatly, so rumour said, at the hands of his bosses, particularly Khrushchev, who bullied and abused him. When he became later a member of the Politburo and ultimately President of the USSR, most of those of us who had dealt with him drew a certain satisfaction.

When travelling abroad officially, the Prime Minister usually took with him his 'kitchen cabinet' consisting of Marcia Williams (later Lady Falkender), Joe Haines ex-lobby correspondent and Gerald Kaufman, whose talent was not then as visible as it has become. Marcia's political gifts were always evident, but more than once there was an incident arising out of some imagined or accidental insult on a protocol matter. Included in the group was the Prime Minister's devoted driver, listed always as 'Baggage Master,' but who in reality acted as his valet and an unfailing guide to a bargain in a foreign city. The Prime Minister's conduct of his official business was always skilful and much to be admired. But he did not always command the respect among his own people which most of us would have wished to see accorded to a Prime Minister. For example, there were shouting matches between him and his personal staff on board HMS Fearless within sight and earshot of wide-eyed crew members. The lobby correspondents, no doubt old friends, who on one occasion accompanied him to Moscow, addressed him with a casual and disrespectful familiarity which came as a shock to those unaccustomed to House of Commons lobby ways. In the U.S. the President is never addressed on official occasions by his christian name. Many of us would prefer the same formality to be followed with a Prime Minister.

During one visit the Foreign Ministry had agreed to the Prime Minister making a short speech on Soviet T.V. This caused great excitement amongst the members of his personal staff and led to a ridiculous incident. One of them said to the Prime Minister

"You can speak some Russian." The Prime Minister modestly demurred.

"Imagine the headlines,' the three continued,

"Prime Minister addresses Russian people in their own language." This led to the suggestion that Tom Brimelow of the Embassy staff, who spoke perfect Russian, should translate the speech and then type out a phonetical version of it for the Prime Minister to read. Brimelow protested that it was not possible, but great pressure was put on him to try. He sat up all night putting the idea into practice and typing it himself. In the morning it was handed to the Prime Minister who attempted a dummy run. The result was a fiasco. Brimelow said curtly that he was going home and was not seen again that day.

It is difficult to know what impression British Ministers made in Moscow. The visit of Wedgwood Benn as Minister of Technology was not a success but I was not witness to it myself. He told the Embassy that he wished to give a lecture to the Soviet Academy of Sciences. The Ambassador ꞓed him that if he did so he would have to say something that would ꞓ sophisticated audience. This advice was ignored and he ꞓ a kind more suited to a school children's Christmas ꞓ Russians later expressed to the Embassy their ꞓ ment. The impression created did us no good. ꞓ the impression of being more at home in ꞓ Washington. He had paid several visits ꞓ was at the Board of Trade and had ꞓ n to which he often referred. ꞓ nd thoughtful face could ꞓ ꞓe. On one occasion we were ꞓ ꞓrters by Brezhnev. He was an ꞓ ꞓ natural bully. There seemed to be a lot ꞓ ꞓis person. Wilson kept his end up well in ꞓ ꞓnine. In his writings he claims to have hit it off with ꞓ ꞓd was on especially good terms with Senator Humphrey ꞓ ꞓour Government's hope for a future President. In my short ꞓservations, Wilson and Johnson gave no clue of any special liking for each other. Indeed, they had little or nothing in common. On one visit to the White House the President was particularly unattractive. We arrived mid morning but, in spite of all the Embassy's efforts, it was not clear whether an invitation for luncheon was intended. The President did not discuss much business but showed off his parlour tricks by singing to his famous mongrel, who sang in return seated together on a sofa. It was becoming distinctly embarrassing until the President sent for his wife. On her arrival he asked if she had 'some lunch for these nice people.' She thought so and in a few minutes we were each facing an enormous steak. Throughout lunch the President recounted unceasingly, highly amusing anecdotes of his childhood, political career and of famous Texan characters. Hardly anyone else had a word to say. After lunch the meeting broke up - a wasted morning. In contrast Wilson got on excellently with Nixon in later years.

CHAPTER 15

NEW APPOINTMENT IN THE FOREIGN OFFICE

During 1968 George Brown told me in confidence that he wanted me to succeed Paul Gore-Booth as Permanent Under Secretary when the latter was due to retire early in the following year. I had learned a great deal from Gore-Booth both in Washington and in Whitehall. Michael Stewart described him as 'wise and urbane'. This was indeed correct. In manners and intellect he was in the best Balliol and Foreign Office tradition. Unlike some of his predecessors he had a wide knowledge of the world outside the U.S. and Europe. This fact suited the merged Foreign and Commonwealth Office. George Brown's proposal came as a complete surprise to me. It was something that I had never envisaged, never coveted and had not been rumoured. He explains his reasons in his autobiography *In My Way*.. I imagine also that he enjoyed making a surprise choice. I was embarrassed somewhat as I knew that it would not have been the wish of some of my seniors and others. I suspect that some pressure was put on him to change his mind as he also tempted me with an alternative very senior appointment in the intelligence world. For this I knew I was unsuited and I stuck to his first offer. According to Crossman's diary, Brown had explained to him that one of my recommendations was that my father had been an engine driver!

Whilst I was trying privately to accustom myself to the idea, I heard late one night that George Brown had suddenly resigned from the Government. Angela and I decided that as we had never expected the promotion there was no need to be disappointed. Indeed, in some ways, I was relieved. No doubt in the fullness of time, Michael Stewart, his successor, would make his own decision. Some months later I was in the men's washroom in No. 10 prior to a meeting when the Prime Minister came in. As we stood side by side he remarked

"I am very glad Michael Stewart is going to appoint you Permanent Under Secretary."

Stewart says in his autobiography that George Brown had earlier told him of his decision and "this was very much to my liking."

I would have preferred the news had been broken to me in more dignified surroundings.

Michael Stewart was always good to work for and was unusually high minded. One day I had to explain to him the British Government's interest in a certain disarmament question. When I had finished he turned to me and said, "You have told me very well what is the interest of the British

Government; what is the interest of mankind?" I cannot imagine any other Minister I have known who would have put the same question to me with such obvious sincerity. He incurred the hostility of his own colleagues over his famous defence, at the Oxford Union, of American policy in Vietnam and of our policy on the Nigerian Civil War in the House of Commons, which was greatly resented by the left wing of the party. It was soon being rumoured that he would no longer be Foreign Secretary if Labour won the next Election. Its defeat in 1970 spared him the public humiliation of being excluded from a new Labour Government.

I had greatly enjoyed my role as Deputy Under Secretary in charge of defence and intelligence. This dated from October 1966. I had many friends in the defence establishment arising, not only from my own war service, but from my year at the Imperial Defence College in 1954 and from my close contact with the military in Singapore (1956-8) and the large defence groups at our Embassy in Washington (1959-64). The relationship between the Foreign Office and Ministry of Defence was good, due often to the fact that the two Ministers were, during the Labour administration, frequently on the defensive together against other cabinet colleagues. Although Denis Healey at the Ministry of Defence would, I believe, have preferred to have been Secretary of State at the Foreign Office, his knowledge and experience ensured mutual understanding between the two offices. Our paths had crossed during the war, as he points out in his autobiography, when he was a major at the Headquarters of the Allied Armies in Italy. I shared his contempt for his then commanding officer whose identity he conceals by referring to him as 'Basil the Bastard' and with whom I had previously served in Cairo.

As for intelligence work, I knew, by virtue of Angela's employment in Cairo, several members of the services. These contacts had been multiplied by my appointment as Chairman of the Joint Intelligence Committee (Far East) in Singapore and by being the Foreign Office liaison officer in London with S.I.S. in 1959. The senior joint intelligence committee in Whitehall, consisting of the important departments with the exception of the Treasury, dated back to war time when the chairman had been a Foreign Office official, Bill Cavendish-Bentinck (later Duke of Portland) who had made a considerable reputation as a result of which the chair had traditionally been held by the Foreign Office. This tradition continued until the post mortem on the Falklands war when Lord Franks' committee had questioned the desirability of this. As a result, the Prime Minister, Mrs. Thatcher, removed one Foreign Office chairman only to replace him by another from the same source.

During my chairmanship, initially the committee dealt primarily with intelligence gathered by covert means and forecasts on a very restricted distribution were based on this. Insufficient attention was paid to information obtained from all sources. I discussed the problem with Burke Trend the Cabinet Secretary and eventually an assessment staff was established in the Cabinet Office. Its responsibility was to make forecasts and assessments on foreign affairs using all information, covert and overt at the Government's disposal. It was inevitable that the biggest input came from the Foreign Office and the first head of the group was from the Foreign Office, John Thomson, the son and grandson of Nobel Prize winners and a suitably gifted man himself and who had been with me in Washington. After initial hesitation the Treasury cooperated thanks to Frank Figgures - an unusual Treasury official. The Bank of England which, of course, had considerable intelligence staff of their own were ready to use Thomson's information but were unwilling to pool theirs. We found the American Departments in addition to the CIA were helpful. I believe the problem still remains of how best to assess the future for the purpose of government planning. Obviously overt and covert intelligence from Foreign Office sources is essential, but so also are global economic forecasts and the input from the increasing number of highly skilled academic groups, which must also be consulted. The opinions of trusted allies must be evaluated and views exchanged. How all this can be brought together for government advice deserves attention in the current changing international conditions. Should a truly common defence and foreign policy emerge from the development of the European union, new methods of sharing forward estimates will have to be evolved. This will not be easy. Our government will have to insist on a major role.

During the period, in which as Deputy Under Secretary I was supervising defence security and intelligence matters were three unusual cases of special concern to me. I have kept no personal records, but I have a vivid recollection of them. Sometimes this recollection differs from those who have already written about them, but where I differ, I feel reasonably certain of my version. The three cases were:

1. The exchange of the highly professional KGB husband and wife spies, the Krogers, for Gerald Brooke, a British prisoner held in the Soviet Union,
2. The D Notice affair and,
3. The Sunday Times and Kim Philby's memoirs.

In the first case Gerald Brooke was a young, religious, married man who had come into contact in this country with refugees from the USSR. He was persuaded by friends to try to smuggle bibles into the Soviet Union together with some elementary spying equipment. The refugee group had been penetrated by Soviet agents in the U.K. and Brooke was arrested on arrival in Moscow. A well publicised trial took place and he was sentenced to a period of detention in prison and a longer sentence in a Labour camp. The purpose of this charade soon became clear. The Russians proposed a swap between the naive and foolish Brooke for two of their most experienced agents, the Krogers, of Polish origin, who were serving a 25 year sentence in the U.K., having previously been imprisoned for other espionage offences in North America. The Soviets have made it a point of principle that they never abandon those who have served them well. They were determined to get the Krogers back as they had successfully rescued for example, their agents Philby, Maclean, Blake from the U.K. and Col. Abel from the U.S. This did not deter the Prime Minister and the Foreign Secretary from making strong representations on behalf of the innocent Brooke.

On one particular occasion in Moscow, George Brown had a violent exchange on this subject with Gromyko. It was a humiliating experience to see an impassive Soviet Minister, justifiably looking with contempt at his British counterpart, whose sincere emotions had been raised above acceptable limits by a modest amount of drink. By 1969 the Krogers had served nine years of their sentence in this country and matters were at an impasse. I had recently taken over as Permanent Under Secretary (February 1969) and I suggested to Michael Stewart, who was back as Secretary of State again after Brown's resignation, that the case for an exchange had become stronger and should be looked at anew. He agreed that I should meet with the Soviet Ambassador in London. After several meetings, the Russians tried a new ploy. They 'regretted' that Brooke was making trouble in the labour camp, which was indeed partly true. There was likely to be a new trial on new charges, the outcome of which could be 'very serious.' This was outrageous blackmail and our Security Service and others, fearful of setting precedents, resisted any change in our position. But in my view, the case for an exchange rested on three points:

First, the Krogers had been in jail for nine years - a significant part of their middle life together had been blanked out.

Second, Brooke was young and undeniably foolish, but his wife was behaving with dignity and patience. Were their lives to be blighted by an unjust sentence?

Finally, to settle the case could perhaps remove one obstacle to a small improvement in Anglo-Soviet relations which HMG was seeking.

In October 1969, the Prime Minister accepted the Secretary of State's recommendation for the exchange. Brooke was released and the Soviets made certain other concessions of a minor nature. Amongst our professional security staff the decision was thought a typically 'soft' Foreign Office move. I must admit that the photograph of a defiant Mrs. Kroger at the top of the steps of a homeward bound Aeroflot plane at Heathrow made me wonder, for a few moments, whether we had not let our hearts run away with our heads. I believe the Brookes eventually separated, but better by choice in freedom, than the consequence of an injustice in prison. A recent interview (1991) with the Krogers on T.V. did not give me the impression they were enjoying a luxurious life in retirement.

The so called 'D' notice affair was an entirely different matter of domestic political importance. Harold Wilson refers to it in personal terms as 'One of my costliest mistakes of our near six years of office.' From a party political point of view it may have been. Indeed, Lord Rawlinson in his autobiography says 'From that moment on the glitter began to fall away from Harold Wilson.'

From the departmental angle, the Foreign Office was right in trying to prevent the publication in the Daily Express of highly classified information about cable vetting, which for many years had been protected by the 'D' notice system. This system was a voluntary agreement between the Press and the Government, operated by an Advisory Committee under the chairmanship of the Ministry of Defence. The Foreign Office was satisfied that the newspaper was aware that the publication would be in breach of the 'D' notice procedure. Their legal advisers agreed. Indeed, one newspaper already was willing to withhold publication. But in the case of the Express, the matter had been confused by ambiguous guidance given over an expensive lunch meeting between the Secretary of the committee, an unsuitable man, and a notorious journalist who had a reputation for damaging disclosures. In spite of the appeal by the Secretary of the Cabinet, Sir Burke Trend, the Prime Minister made a provocative statement in the House in answer to a question on the publication.

In his book, *The Labour Government, 1964-70*, the Prime Minister denies that any contrary advice was given to him by his colleague Colonel Wigg. This is not my clear recollection of the discussion on the morning of the statement. I was shocked by the vindictive way in which Wigg spoke of the journalist and his wish to humiliate him.. A serious Parliamentary row broke out in which the Press closed ranks and joined in the defence of their colleague on the Express. The Prime Minister finally agreed to set up a Tribunal of Privy Councillors to review the matter. The chairman was Lord Radcliffe, assisted by Selwyn Lloyd and Emanuel Shinwell. Lord Radcliffe had an impeccable reputation and was persuaded to serve by the Cabinet Secretary only with great difficulty as his wife was seriously ill. During my examination by the Tribunal, Lloyd showed not the slightest interest. Shinwell was particularly offensive claiming that civil servants always concealed the truth from their ministerial superiors and other observations in the same vein. Lord Radcliffe obviously wished to get the matter over as quickly as possible. It would be an impertinence, and perhaps unjust, for me to suggest that he came to the Tribunal with a clear idea of the conclusion he wished to reach. He certainly gave me that impression. The conclusion of the Tribunal, critical of the Government, can best be described as 'fuzzy' and the Prime Minister took the highly unusual step of rejecting it. Whilst the Press employed the formidable Sir Peter (Lord) Rawlinson, the shadow Attorney General to make their case, the Government did not try to match him in their own defence. The rejection led to a further Parliamentary row which I witnessed from the official box in the House and saw the Prime Minister defend himself with great dexterity. The matter then fizzled out. But widespread damage had been done.

Many years later followed a tragic consequence. My good friend and Foreign Office colleague, Christopher Ewart-Biggs, who also appeared before the Tribunal, received a good deal of publicity, which underlined his connection with intelligence matters at that particular time. In 1976 he was appointed Ambassador in Dublin and was picked out for assassination by the IRA, by reason, it is said, that they thought he would have a special intelligence function in Dublin. This was, of course, quite untrue. His widow Jane has been particularly courageous and has carved out a successful and enterprising political career on the Labour front benches in the House of Lords.

The Sunday Times and the Philby articles in 1967 were the beginning of a whole stream of writing on this evil man which have often been designed to represent him as an idealistic anti-establishment hero. They set a fashion for investigative journalism not only about Philby. The articles were sometimes the work of Australian journalists and culminated in Knightley's book based on interviews with him in Moscow a few months before his death in 1988. I am sorry he did not live to see the failure of the system which he had made his life's work and for which he had mercilessly betrayed his friends. Indeed I wonder if he would have cared as he had been amply rewarded for his sins. Such idealism as he had once had no doubt withered. When the Foreign Office heard of the proposal to publish in the Sunday Times we were in touch with Harold Evans, the highly effective new editor of the paper. Our discussions ranged from an initial request not to publish, to an agreement that I would be allowed to see the articles before publication. But the circumstances in which I was to see the articles threw a revealing light on the relations between the Editor and his investigative 'Insight' team who prepared the material. Evans agreed to come on Friday afternoons to a small Bloomsbury hotel where I was allowed to read the following Sunday's instalment and make comment, which would not necessarily be acted upon. The meetings were to be secret and under no circumstances be known to the Insight team. Throughout the meetings, Evans can only be described as jumpy, constantly looking over his shoulder for his colleagues. He makes no mention of these meetings in his book *Good Times Bad Times*.

A problem arose over whether any payment was to be made to Philby. I maintained payment would be rewarding treason - a phrase for which Evans seemed to claim authorship. A suggestion was then made that money should be given to Philby's son who lived in England and was causing his father anxiety. I pointed out that this anxiety was perhaps a proper reward for treachery. In his book, Evans implies he was against any payments. This is not my recollection. Finally, Lord Thomson, the paper's proprietor forbade them, after being publicly rebuked by George Brown. Times have moved on and in retrospect it is hard to assess how serious was the damage done to the national interest by the memoirs. At the time, and in a totally different atmosphere, it was important and set a fashion for a certain kind of journalism.

I record these matters here because of my close personal involvement. They were not matters of vital foreign policy. Between 1966 and the defeat of the Labour Government in June 1970, there were other much more important events of foreign policy in which I was involved as a Deputy Under Secretary and after February 1969 as Permanent Under Secretary. These included our attempted entry to the European Community, the Nigerian Civil war, the Vietnamese conflict and relations with the U.S., Middle Eastern crises, the British position in the Persian Gulf and far reaching decisions on Defence and Commonwealth matters. All these questions were debated against a background of economic decline and industrial unrest. They have been, or will be dealt with, by historians, politicians with access to private state papers and diaries and all official documents. I have no intention of writing my history of these events, but wish to record some incidents involving personalities which will give an idea of the atmosphere in which Whitehall and particularly the Foreign Office were compelled to conduct its business during the Labour and later Governments.

CHAPTER 16

THE FOREIGN OFFICE AND THE DIPLOMATIC SERVICE

When Stewart had returned to the Foreign Office in March 1968, the Foreign and Commonwealth offices were, as had long been expected, amalgamated. The initiative for this came from the Prime Minister, but the Foreign Secretary certainly decided on the name for the new office, which happily differed from 'External Affairs,' which is the usual Commonwealth country practice. If Gordon-Walker had been able to stay as Foreign Secretary in 1964 it would probably have come earlier.

An amalgamation necessarily involved a slimming down of staff, primarily at senior level. The task of selecting victims was made more difficult by the fact that promotion within the Commonwealth office was, in terms of age, rather more advanced than in the Foreign Office. Officers of a comparable age, generally speaking, were graded higher in the Commonwealth Office than in the Foreign Office. The cynical believed that Gilbert Lathwaite, the highly experienced Permanent Under Secretary of the Commonwealth Office had, in anticipation of an amalgamation, sought to safeguard his people by these early promotions. I doubt it.

Another factor was that recruitment to the Diplomatic Service pre-war, had been extremely competitive. Those officers who had entered after the most intense pre-war selection process had found themselves swamped by the post-war recruits, taken in large numbers, straight from the armed services. It was natural that in some cases this caused jealousy. Moreover, several of those serving in the Commonwealth Office had initially been members of the Home Civil Service. Paul Gore-Booth, the Permanent Under Secretary who was on the point of retirement, took charge of the selection process, together with the senior members of both offices, of which I was one. It was not an easy task, but on the whole, it was fairly done. Inevitably, some worthy people found that the prospects that they had envisaged at the time of their pre-war recruitment, were disappointed. When, at a later date, appointments were more directly my responsibility, I tried to give careful consideration to those capable pre-war recruits who had been overwhelmed by the post-war intake, some of whose members would not have survived the selection process at that earlier time, including myself.

George Brown and Michael Stewart have given their views on the Diplomatic Service in their respective autobiographies. The views of the Service on those two chiefs have been less frequently recorded. (Sir) Nicko Henderson in particular, has paid tribute to Stewart, as I have indicated earlier and few would quarrel with his assessment. In contrast to the thoughtful and stable regime of Stewart, who, however, first approached the Service with some suspicion, the advent of George Brown was a new experience. Stories, of course, had reached the office from his Department of Economic Affairs, including exchanges of missiles with civil servants. But those who worked closely with him at the Foreign Office found they could sometimes forgive his instability, intolerance and cruelty in face of his undoubted brilliance and the rightness of many of his policy aims. Admirable too was his loyalty to the Labour movement in which he and his wife had grown up. One can only imagine the depth of his feeling when he finally broke with the party and moved to the cross benches in the House of Lords. When he spoke there in bitter and often justifiable criticism of his former colleagues, many of them felt compelled ostentatiously to leave the Chamber. His defection was not forgiven and at his Memorial Service in St. Margaret's there were present no more than two Labour members currently serving in the Commons. The address was given by Lord Shawcross in carefully chosen words. 'The Times' report of the Service was an appalling breach of taste, drawing special attention to the presence of his wife and the lady with whom he latterly lived.

Michael Stewart seldom gave the impression that he was enjoying his official life. Indeed he once wryly remarked that its only recompense seemed to have been that he got to know Joseph Luns the highly entertaining, boisterous and long serving Netherlands Foreign Minister and Secretary General of N.A.T.O. But Stewart enjoyed debate with his colleagues and officials. I was present when Barbara Castle came to see him and made a strong bid to take over the British Council and include it in her Department of Overseas Development. He demolished her arguments with great skill and courtesy and admitted after she had left that he had greatly enjoyed the encounter. Indicative of his attitude to his ministerial life was a conversation with me one evening when, about 7 p.m. he was about to leave the office for a constituency 'surgery' in Fulham. He had had a hard morning in the office and a very rough time in the Commons in the afternoon. I suggested he gave the surgery a miss. He looked sharply at me and said, "Certainly not, that is why I am here as Member of Parliament for Fulham."

In contrast, George Brown clearly relished some of the aspects of his job and on those occasions it was fun to work with him. But his disruptive manners put a strain on the Service, who liked to admire their Minister and were saddened when the Press made the most of some of his public antics. He found it hard to conceal his likes and dislikes. He wanted to be seen to exercise the Secretary of State's undoubted right to play a decisive role in the choice of Ambassadors. He wrongly believed that the Service disliked the appointment of outsiders. It is only unsuitable outsiders that the Service resists. For example the appointment of Oliver Franks to Washington by an earlier Labour Government was highly successful and popular with the Service. Lord Cromer and Lord Harlech (Ormsby-Gore) were 'outsiders' but very much liked and admired by the regular Foreign Office professionals.

The choice of John Freeman, former Labour MP as Ambassador in Washington was an error in one respect, not because he was not fitted for the job, but because the choice was made on the Labour Party's assumption that a Democrat, Senator Humphrey, would be the next American President. This view was not based on professional advice. Freeman had been a success as High Commissioner in India and his clever wife was particularly popular everywhere. In practice, as Henry Kissinger strongly asserts, Freeman did extremely well with Republican President Nixon for the short time he continued at his post. On the other hand, George Brown's choice of Soames for Paris, which surprised many, was an unqualified success. The success was due in part to the enthusiasm with which Soames inspired selected members of his Diplomatic Service staff in Paris and the fact that, unlike Freeman, he knew how to make the best of the Foreign Office system. However, working in Whitehall from 1964-70, one became conscious of the divisions amongst personalities in the Cabinet and the mutual suspicions amongst them. Every civil servant prays for a strong Minister and a united Cabinet. Bad relations between No. 10 and the Foreign Office have a sad history, as Prime Ministers must necessarily frequently play a dominant role in foreign policy and, such a role, conflicts sometimes with a strong Foreign Secretary. There must, in the national interest, be confidence between them.

CHAPTER 17

PERMANENT UNDER SECRETARY AND CHANGE OF GOVERNMENT

Shortly before I took up my new appointment there was an opportunity to go to Cairo very briefly. I was glad to do so for two reasons. First to see what changes had occurred since I had left in 1943 and secondly for a chance to meet President Nasser. Our Ambassador (Sir) Harold Beeley had come into the Foreign Office during the war from academic life. He later established himself as a trusted adviser to Ernest Bevin on Middle East affairs. At the time he was often criticised for favouring the Arab cause and for being in part responsible for Bevin's unpopularity with Israel and the Americans and his hostility to Richard Crossman. But times had moved on and by the late nineteen sixties he was an obvious choice for the Embassy in Cairo and where he would have good access to Nasser.

Together we called on the Egyptian leader in his surprisingly modest residence. A well built and good looking man, his most striking feature was his remarkably penetrating eyes which he fixed steadily on you. He was the embodiment of a national hero and it was easy to understand his appeal throughout the Arab world, which he came nearer to unifying than any before or after him. Our talk was informal and the atmosphere relaxed. But whatever he had achieved internationally, he had done little for his capital city whose centre looked much as I had last seen it, 25 years earlier. But at our meeting at least, he fitted ill into Eden's conception of him as a latter day Hitler.

When the time came in February 1969 to take over from Paul Gore-Booth, I had been more than four years in Whitehall since our return from Washington. Throughout this time Harold Wilson's Government had been in power and I had come to know many Ministers and Members of both Houses of Parliament. I was also on familiar terms with most of the chief people in the Ministries and the organisations with which the Foreign Office had to work. I especially valued the friendship of (Sir) Antony Part. I felt myself amongst pleasant acquaintances, many friends, and comparatively at home with my new responsibilities. This was an undoubted advantage over an individual brought to the appointment straight from a long overseas posting.

But there were two very senior civil servants I had not met. Philip Allen at the Home Office and Otto Clarke at the Ministry of Technology. I thought it right to call on them and phoned them for appointments. Both seemed rather surprised but I insisted that I went to them. Philip said it had not been done before but promised to unlock a private door leading directly to his office from the Foreign Office courtyard. On arrival I noticed a copy of Private Eye in his waiting room and realised he was not in the usual Home Office tradition. He is now a good friend and undoubtedly amongst the best Cross Bench Life Peers in the House of Lords. Otto Clarke was said to be the cleverest Civil Servant in Whitehall. Sadly he died in 1975. Fifteen years later his wife introduced herself to me on a social occasion. She said she remembered me because her husband had said I was the only Foreign Office official who had ever taken the trouble to call on him in his office. These meetings suggested to me that the Foreign Office had perhaps been neglecting some potential allies.

There was a full and difficult international agenda ahead. Barring accidents I would have to be ready for the next election and possibly a government of a different complexion. At the time this seemed unlikely but by no means impossible as the Wilson Government had serious difficulties with its own trade union supporters. I remember thinking that except for a most exceptional person in No. 10, five years was about the limit the health of a 'hands on' Prime Minister, like Harold Wilson, could sustain. Such an exceptional person was to come to Downing Street ten years later.

Trouble was not long delayed. The negotiations for entry into the Common Market were proving to be heavy going, with General de Gaulle leading the obstruction. Prime Minister Wilson was due to meet the German Government in Bonn and was hoping to secure their active cooperation. The next U.S. President was coming to Europe for an introductory visit shortly afterwards. I was to be in the party for Bonn. On the eve of our departure the unexpected happened. Christopher Soames secured a meeting with the General who, over lunch, outlined his views on the future shape of Europe, which were in direct conflict with the plans for the Community which were currently under discussion and advocated by his own people.

He proposed a loose association of the type originally advocated by the U.K. - a free trade area, not a Community - under the direction of the main European Powers. The General proposed that the U.K. should take the initiative in this and there should be secret discussions between us. It was a tempting bait. But his plans also included the eventual elimination of the U.S. from Europe and the demise of N.A.T.O. Those in the Foreign Office who had been engaged in the negotiations with the members of the Community immediately smelled a rat. The timing of the proposal coming on the eve of the Bonn visit and its apparent reversal of the constant hostility of the General to important aspects of current U.K. policy aroused their suspicions. The urgent departmental recommendation to Michael Stewart, who basically shared these suspicions, was that the Prime Minister would have to disclose the General's approach to us to the Germans during this visit to Bonn and to the other Europeans simultaneously if we were to retain their confidence.

After a short meeting in his office, Michael Stewart crossed the road at once to No. 10 by himself with this recommendation. It was not at all to the Prime Minister's liking. The party left for Bonn with the matter undecided and the Prime Minister resentful of the pressure being put upon him. In the event the Prime Minister made a half-hearted revelation to the Germans, but the Foreign Office, to his great annoyance, let the cat completely out of the bag in the capitals of the Community.

The General was furious. The French Government made an official protest and made public a dishonest account of events. Christopher Soames felt, with some reason, that his position had been undermined. Sensibly he did not resign. In later years when we were both in the House of Lords, he diminished his criticism of the Foreign Office and never reproached me personally. He must have realised that this was the General's last fling and that the federalist elements in the French Establishment would never have tolerated his plan if indeed it was sincere. They were determined to keep the U.K. at arms length from the Community until they were ready. Nevertheless it was not a happy start for me and the relations between No. 10 and our Office were soured. In his autobiography, Michael Stewart argues that our suspicions of the General were justified. Kissinger shared his views. Before the Soames lunch there was no doubt of the General's hostility towards us. Subsequent events confirmed it.

The meetings in Bonn were not enjoyable. There was little rapport between Wilson and Dr. Kiesinger. They were not well known to each other and not politically sympathetic. The Labour Government was more comfortable with Willy Brandt, whose government was soon to follow.

On this visit, I was interested incidentally, to see how a capital for West Germany was being made out of the quiet town of Bonn. Thirty five years earlier I had been there on a tandem bicycle with a fellow undergraduate, stayed at the youth hostel and seen Nazis marching in its modest streets. Good progress was being made but it fell far short of pre-war Berlin. I was certainly not surprised by the choice of Berlin again by the unified Germany in 1991.

Later in February, recently elected President Nixon came to London in the course of an introductory tour of European capitals. He was accompanied by Henry Kissinger at the start of his international career.

Nixon was entertained by the Prime Minister at Chequers and No. 10. The visit was a considerable success and was skilfully orchestrated by Harold Wilson at his best. It is noteworthy to read in Henry Kissinger's, *The White House Years*, how effectively the Americans were entertained and impressed and how the visit laid the "basis for fruitful collaboration later." Under the Governments of both Wilson and Heath I was privileged to see Nixon many times in action across the conference table. It has not surprised me how he has regained influence and grudging admiration in the years after the disaster of the Watergate Scandal.

There was a small incident after the Chequers dinner that gave a revealing glimpse of how Ministers in this country were expected to do their work. Barbara Castle, the Minister of Labour was in the middle of her unsuccessful battle for Trade Union reform. Her White Paper, 'In Place of Strife' was the centre of a bitter Party struggle. As we were getting into our cars I saw her standing, ministerial box in hand, talking to her Government chauffeuse. She turned to me and said, "My car won't start." The look on the driver's face gave me the clear impression that she had made other arrangements for the late evening. Angela and I offered the Minister a lift to London which she accepted at once and sank exhausted into the rear seat and in a few minutes was fast asleep. She roused herself as we got to London and directed us to her Islington flat. She explained that her husband was in hospital and asked me to escort her in. The access stairs and the empty flat were in complete darkness. After she had switched on the lights, I left her and her box of official papers to a solitary night's work before a bleak day of political conflict. So much for the fruits of office.

In addition to the problems of entry into the European Community, the Government was in difficulties over its policy towards the Nigerian Civil War. There were international and domestic complications. There were real dangers of increased Russian influence in Nigeria and the French Colonial 'mafia' were deliberately obstructing British policy. On the domestic front, some on the right and far left were opposing the supply of arms to the Federal Government. Well organised Biafran propaganda was strongly supported by a vocal Catholic lobby. Opposition to the Government's policy reached a peak when the bombing of Biafra by Federal planes increased and a report by Winston Churchill M.P. after a visit to Nigeria, roused further criticism of the Federal Government. The Prime Minister, understandably, wanted to visit Lagos to discuss the problem face to face with the Federal Head of State General Gowon who was little known here, although he had trained at Sandhurst. However Wilson feared a snub, which would increase his problems in the House. Michael Stewart was also deeply involved emotionally and shared the Prime Minister's anxiety.

It was decided that I should go to Lagos to see Gowon and try to secure from him, an invitation to the Prime Minister. (Sir) David Hunt, our neighbour from Maunsel Street, the experienced and wise High Commissioner arranged for me to see the General. On arrival I went as soon as possible to his residence. This was a medium sized building but the driveway was blocked by a large military tank. I was shown into an austere room and after a short delay, the General came in. I was struck at once by his good looks, his quiet voice and modest bearing. I explained my purpose. I emphasised how the bombing was arousing much hostility at home which could, inter alia, threaten the supply of arms. I urged him to receive the Prime Minister and discuss their common problems. He readily agreed. As I was leaving, he said about a certain commitment, "I give you my word as a Sandhurst man."

I reported to the Prime Minister and quoted the General's words. This raised a rather cynical laugh when I tried to convey the type of man the General was. He clearly visualised him as a brutal African leader. After surviving a debate in the Commons, the Prime Minister visited Lagos at the end of March, which held the position for the time being. On his return, he typically apologised to me for his disbelief of my account and for mocking at the General's quaint assurance. The War continued until the end of the year when it suddenly ended one weekend in victory for the Federal Government and Gowon's remarkable 'magnanimity in victory.' Michael Stewart's relief at the outcome made him temporarily incapable of work. So much so that, after discussion with John Graham his Private Secretary, I consulted his doctor. Fortunately the Secretary of State recovered his balance after a little delay.

Gowon continued in power long enough to visit this country and be the guest at a State Banquet at Buckingham Palace at which we were present. Not long afterwards he was deposed and sought exile here. I have met him from time to time over the years. He told me how he took the decision, quite alone, to offer reconciliation to the rebels after their surrender and spent a night of anxiety uncertainly awaiting the national reception of his dramatic offer. He spoke with great modesty of his action which is almost unique in history. Happily he is now reconciled with the Nigerian Government. He spent some of his exile in studying for degrees at Warwick University and his children have been educated at famous English schools.

The Nigerian problem involved me in one further interesting journey. The Vatican is often supposed, through its worldwide network, to have a unique knowledge of many foreign countries. The Biafrans were largely

Christian. The majority of missionaries living there were Irish Catholic priests. These, no doubt sincere men were the source of anti-British and anti-central federal government propaganda.

Our Diplomatic Mission to the Vatican arranged for me to visit Rome and meet my opposite number in the Pope's foreign affairs department - Monseigneur (now Cardinal) Caseroli. Before I left for Rome I asked my colleague Donald Maitland, who later became an outstanding Press Secretary at No. 10 under Mr. Heath, what I should say to Caseroli. He replied, "That's easy, Monseigneur Caseroli, what's cooking?"

I was fascinated to see the beautiful interior of the Vatican and to discuss our conflicting impressions of the civil war. I tried to convince him that his views of the war were unbalanced. For the Irish priests, it was the ancient conflict between the heathens of Northern Nigeria and the Christians of the South and the news that they were receiving from Ulster no doubt influenced their hostility towards us. It was an interesting discussion. Afterwards I was led through gorgeous corridors to a very elderly American Cardinal. He spoke to me earnestly about the need for younger cardinals but he clearly excluded himself from any stricture.

The extent of Vatican misjudgment was the Pope's prediction that genocide would follow the end of hostilities, although he might be forgiven for not foreseeing Gowon's surprising Christian gesture of reconciliation.

The whole year of 1969 was very busy. In February the Defence Secretary, Denis Healey had issued a White Paper signalling our withdrawal from the Persian Gulf and posing diplomatic problems with Iran and the Sheikdoms for which we had been responsible since the days of the British Raj. There were continuous Four Power talks on the Middle East, the Vietnam War rolled on, the break with Rhodesia became wider and the revolution in Libya brought military and commercial difficulties for the U.K. At the other end of the scale was a mini-revolt in the Caribbean island of Anguilla, for which members of the Metropolitan police had to be sent abroad for the first time. This little incident gave the Press a field day at the expense of the Foreign Office, but reminded us how much remained to be done to help the small territories left over from Imperial days. The year ended with a Foreign affairs debate on Vietnam when a significant number of Labour MP's voted against the Government, or abstained. Michael Stewart bore the full force of their disapproval and he was let down during the debate by the criticism of two members of the Cabinet, (Barbara Castle and Dick Crossman), who had approved his speech at their morning meeting. One bright light at least was agreement of the EEC to open negotiations in June for British entry.

Early in 1970 a Gallup Poll had shown a small lead for the Conservative Party and speculation on the date of the election increased. October was the expected date. Earlier in the year Michael Stewart and his wife visited Tokyo for Expo 70 and I accompanied them with others. The Exhibition was a triumph for the Japanese and established them in the eyes of the world in the top class of economic powers. The British Pavilion seemed to me designed more to try to eclipse its European rivals rather than to impress the Japanese visitors. All day long the Exhibition was thronged with neatly dressed crocodiles of Japanese school children led by flag carrying guides. They could hardly be moved by clever British tableaux based on literature, with which they were unfamiliar. One of the centre pieces of both the French and British Pavilions were dummies of the Concorde airliner. In the British Pavilion it was accurately described as the Anglo-French Concorde. The 'Anglo' was entirely absent from the French exhibit. France, Germany and the U.K. all claimed pioneer work in the circulation of blood in the human body. It was an exhausting day for the Secretary of State and his party, but the greatest praise was due to the elderly Japanese Ambassador in London who hobbled around as our guide.

The decision on the British election came in May and the polling day was fixed for June 18th. I had had experience of working for both parties. For the office staff it meant the preparation of 'neutral' briefs on the world situation throughout the responsibilities of the Foreign and Commonwealth Office. These were to be handed at once, unamended, to whatsoever party emerged victorious. Morale in the Office was much better and had survived the recommendations of the Duncan Report on its organisation. We were happy working with Michael Stewart, but were saddened by criticisms of him by his party colleagues.

It was not only his party colleagues who criticised him. Soon after I had become his Permanent Under Secretary, I received an invitation from Cecil King of the Daily Mirror to lunch in his rooms in Albany. I was a little surprised to find myself the only guest. Very soon, I found the reason why. He began to try to put derogatory words into my mouth about Michael Stewart. I did not cooperate and ultimately he changed the subject. He took his revenge later by maligning me as 'futile' in his memoirs in which he later betrayed the confidences he has extracted from many others. My 'futility' was based on my lack of enthusiasm for stationing tanks in industrial cities to curb the power of the unions - a proposal he put forward at a dinner party given by his son and included Jo Grimond as the principal guest.

We all admired the Prime Minister's energy in Foreign affairs and his willingness to examine the advice offered to him. From time to time secret information reaches the Foreign Office, which it is desirable to pass also to the Opposition. The Prime Minister's approval has of course to be obtained. Harold Wilson was always reasonable. More often than not he prefaced his approval with, "Tell only Alec Home."

But it was natural that we should sometimes wonder whether the international stature of H.M.G. was adequate to negotiate our entry into the Common Market on acceptable terms. The status of the United Kingdom had unquestionably and inevitably declined and it was more than ever important that the impression should be given internationally that our Government was united and had the capacity to meet the challenges of our new situation in the world.

Prestige is a significant element in the conduct of international relations as the earlier years of the Thatcher administration were later to show. But our prestige had declined under the Labour Government and disputes within the Party were making the Prime Minister's task doubly difficult.

Personally, the prospect of a possible Conservative Government did not disturb me. Facts would have to be faced. If elected, Edward Heath might well want to pick his own Permanent Under Secretary. I had met him only once when he came to Washington to discuss European Affairs with the State Department. He and his group had called me in to talk to them. As a result, I had then been a little worried by his apparent distrust of Americans. But this distrust had, from time to time, been evident in Prime Minister Macmillan and is never far below the surface of some Conservative politicians. It seemed fairly certain that Alec Home would be the choice for Foreign Secretary in a Conservative Government and this gave comfort to many of us. As for the result of the coming election, nobody seemed certain. We should have listened to one of our Ambassadors in the Far East who reported two weeks before Polling Day that a local soothsayer had predicted Heath would win. He came very close indeed to predicting exactly Heath's eventual majority.

Harold Wilson claims that he was one of the few of his colleagues who had doubts about the issue. Michael Stewart, rather modestly and uncharacteristically, told us that he was confident that his party would win. Immediately before Polling Day, there was a late night meeting in No. 10 about the Persian Gulf. When the Prime Minister came in I was struck by his appearance of fatigue. I put this down to the strain of the campaign. But others in closer daily contact with him, had remarked that he had recently slowed down noticeably. I doubt whether he could, in fact, have sustained a further long period of office without the break that his defeat permitted.

I have wondered how many of the embassies in London accurately forecast the result to their governments. Any self respecting ambassador should have made the attempt. London must be the easiest capital in the world for foreign diplomats to have unobstructed access to every source of opinion and information. It was interesting in those days to see how few of them took advantage of the opportunities. Not more than half a dozen were diligent in this respect. The best Heads of Mission in my experience were the American David Bruce, Herman van Roijen of the Netherlands, Zeki Kuneralp of Turkey and Charles Ritchie of Canada. Very occasionally a representative of a small country excelled, like Nadim Dimechkié of Lebanon and Lakhdar Brahimi of Algeria. The composition of the attendance of British guests at the parties given by Missions on their national days were good evidence of their effectiveness. Although costly in time and effort, Angela and I made a point of attending all such parties. A lot could be learned at them.

CHAPTER 18

A NEW GOVERNMENT

The new Conservative Government was quickly in place. Few had reservations about the Ministers appointed to our department. A new departure was giving Anthony Barber, the Chancellor of the Duchy of Lancaster, special responsibility for the negotiations for entry into Europe. Unhappily he had only time for one effective appearance in Brussels before the tragic death of Iain Macleod caused him to be moved to the Treasury. He was replaced in the European negotiations by Geoffrey Rippon, who instantly made his mark. Crispin Tickell (Sir) now Warden of Green College Oxford and environmentalist was his effective and ambitious private secretary. He did not disguise that he was keeping a diary and in the fullness of time no doubt will publish it.

The return of Alec Douglas-Home to our Department was most welcome. The greatest blessing the Foreign Office can have is an experienced Secretary of State, admired in his own country, respected abroad by friend and foe and gifted with an instinct for foreign affairs. Alec Home fitted all these requirements and combined them with politeness, charm and humour in the daily conduct of business. Ruff's Guide to the Turf always lay on his desk within reach of his right hand and gave an assurance of interests beyond affairs of state. Lady Home was most understanding of the problems of Foreign Office wives and families. In the three years that followed, my role as his Permanent Under Secretary was to be full of excitement and enjoyment. At the outset he told me he wanted to bring some style into the conduct of foreign affairs. He clearly had the unhappy example of George Brown in mind. Amongst the many qualities of Michael Stewart, I do not think he himself would have claimed stylishness.

Early in the life of the new Government its competence was put on trial. There occurred simultaneous incidents of hijacking of planes off the English East Coast and in Jordan where a civil war was raging. Both were of great potential danger and political consequence. An attempt was made in mid air by two terrorists, one male and one female, to take over an El Al plane en route from Amsterdam to the U.S. The male terrorist was shot dead and the girl Leila Khaled overpowered. A forced landing was made at Heathrow, the body removed and the girl arrested. The plane then took off. At the same time, two planes were seized by Palestinians on a Jordanian airfield. The planes and their passengers were threatened with destruction. One British plane contained several British children returning to school in England after holidays with their parents in India and in the Persian Gulf. The safety of the passengers, including the children, were at once linked with the fate of the girl terrorist being held in Ealing police station. The Prime Minister, Edward Heath, immediately called a meeting in Downing Street, which met on and off for nearly a week. It soon became clear that a difficult problem was created by the uncertainty of the precise position of the El Al plane when the crime was committed. Its position would determine which country would have jurisdiction - Israel or the U.K. During the debate in our meetings, the Attorney General, Peter Rawlinson, rightly defended his independent position in face of pressure from the Lord Chancellor, Lord Hailsham, who clearly enjoyed teasing him on legal points. For myself, it gave an opportunity to know better and to understand the Prime Minister. He was calm and decisive throughout. At one point tension was somewhat relaxed when a message came from Jordan to say that the British school children had endeared themselves to the hijackers and were marching round the trapped planes in good natured imitation of their guards. The message said it was difficult to imagine that the guards would bring themselves to harm their new young friends. But other passengers continued to be in danger and it looked very much as if our Embassy in Amman would be attacked. In the face of all evidence of the plane's position, or lack of it, the Attorney General ruled that there was no legal basis to continue to detain the girl Leila Khaled in Ealing. She was accordingly released and for a time was an acclaimed heroine amongst her people. The two planes in Jordan, were blown up on the ground, but no passengers were harmed. Leila Khaled herself later perished in a Palestinian feud. The decision of the Cabinet was criticised in the House of Commons by Enoch Powell and Duncan Sandys, but there was general relief at the outcome. Whether, in the light of subsequent history of terrorism the same decisions would have been taken by the Thatcher Government is debatable.

There was one small incident in one of the Prime Minister's meetings which gave a foretaste of developments several years later. One evening about 7 p.m. the Minister of Education, Mrs. Margaret Thatcher was shown into the Cabinet Room. She was in full evening dress and made a striking figure, inviting deserved compliments. The meeting remained seated. She addressed the Prime Minister saying that she would return at once from her dinner engagement if he wanted her help. His one word answer was a firm "No." There were no compliments and she withdrew.

The era of kidnappings and hijackings was about to begin. Jasper Cross, the British Trade Commissioner in Montreal was kidnapped by Quebec terrorists and was in mortal danger for several weeks. A Quebec

Minister was murdered. The Canadian authorities did well to rescue Cross, but he was considerably shaken. He felt dissatisfied with the treatment he had received at the hands of the Foreign Office to the extent of wishing to refuse the decoration offered to him on the recommendation of our office. In the end, he thought better of it.

A month later the British Ambassador to Uruguay, Geoffrey Jackson, was seized by Tupomaro guerillas who tried to use his seizure to bring pressure on their own government. Jackson had come to see me in my office just before returning from leave to his post. He told me that he fully expected to be kidnapped and had carefully prepared himself on how best to behave in such an event. He was a devout Catholic, having been converted in Beirut by the brother of Cardinal Heenan, who was at this time Archbishop at Westminster Cathedral. During nine months of captivity in poor conditions and often in solitary confinement, he conducted himself in an exemplary way. His behaviour greatly enhanced the reputation of the Diplomatic Service. On his release, we sent a plane to Spain with his wife and family to pick him up and bring him to Gatwick, where he was met by the Secretary of State. Faced with a barrage of Press and cameras he behaved with dignity and composure. A little later he gave a highly successful press conference in London. Thereafter, until his death in 1989, be became a great favourite with the media and lectured widely to the Services, police and other groups. Understandably he decided not to serve abroad again, but was once persuaded to lecture in Sweden, where his fears were confirmed when he narrowly escaped being on a plane which was hijacked. He retired from the Service, compensated financially and knighted, but not entirely satisfied by the way in which he had been rewarded. In the course of discussions with me about his future, I asked him what job in the Service he would be prepared to accept. To which he replied, "Yours." These events set in motion a process, still in progress, to protect our staffs from terrorists, which has greatly circumscribed their lives in certain posts.

Although the new Prime Minister set up a 'Think Tank' in the Cabinet office, it did not detract substantially from the central position in Foreign Affairs of the Cabinet Secretary, Sir Burke Trend, who had held the post since 1963. He was the official in Downing Street with whom I had the closest contact. A wiser man it would be hard to imagine and his sense of humour belied his ascetic appearance. Henry Kissinger noted in his autobiography that "his erudition and advice were among the benefit to us of the 'special relationship.'" He was a good friend to me and we retired from the public service about the same time in 1973.

Walter Annenberg, the immensely wealthy U.S. Ambassador, gave us a joint farewell party surrounded by his priceless pictures in the American Embassy residence in Regents Park. We were, for some time, at a loss to know how to show our appreciation to a man who had everything. The problem was solved by my former colleague, (Sir) Bernard Burrows, who suggested a half sized replica of the scarlet leather ministerial security box, normally carried by British Ministers. We agreed at once. It was specially made at the official Government workshop and a silver plate suitably inscribed, was fixed inside. With Trend's agreement I handed it to the Ambassador in his office in Grosvenor Square. For a short time he was too moved to speak. It is now at his mansion in Palm Springs in a room reserved for his 'memorabilia' and is used to keep all the letters he has received from the Royal Family.

William (Lord) Armstrong, the Head of the Civil Service, proved another good friend. Soon after the 1970 election he told me that as long as he held his position there would be no question of amalgamating the Diplomatic Service with the Home Service. This possibility had, from time to time, been canvassed and had caused anxiety in the Foreign Office. It was partially prompted by jealousy.

An appointment by the new Government, which attracted attention was that of Lord Cromer to be Ambassador in Washington in place of John Freeman, the former Labour M.P. and who had political and personal reasons for wishing to leave. These reasons he did not disclose to us, but when they became public, explained his persistent refusal to accept the Honours to which he would have normally been entitled. It is often alleged that Cromer's appointment was resented by the Foreign Office. This was far from the truth. Those, like myself, who had served with him when he was Economic Minister in Washington in the 1960s, greatly welcomed it. He proved highly successful, particularly with the secretive Kissinger whose close confidence he secured. This was especially useful in view of the Prime Minister's periodic suspicions of U.S. intentions.

Foreign Policy under the new Government soon took on a new complexion. Europe came first, but there were changes of course in Africa and the Middle East. The first formal negotiation for entry into Europe was opened by Geoffrey Rippon in October. It was on this question the Prime Minister's closest interest was centred. In view of likely developments I invited M. Alphand, the Secretary General of the French Foreign Ministry and my opposite number over to London for two days of talks in September. He brought his beautiful wife and step-daughter with him. We had overlapped in Washington where they had been a controversial social couple during the Kennedy Presidency. Such a visit to London would have been unheard of in the days of de Gaulle. It was a success in every way rather to my surprise as in Washington he had been noticeably distant from me. We took them to see David Storey's play 'The Contractor,' the novelty of which appealed greatly to him. It is a play in which a marquee is erected and dismantled on the stage in preparation for a wedding. The dialogue between those involved is entertaining and at times profound.

I later similarly invited his German counterpart - Dr. Paul Frank, a very different and grave person. He gave me a surprising insight into how differently our two governments then worked. He asked me how soon after a Cabinet Meeting did I learn of its decisions relevant to my Department. I told him that the Cabinet met in the mornings and, if the decision was important, I would know before lunch. He was astounded. In Bonn it might take one or two weeks. The next question involved the distribution of incoming Foreign Office telegrams. When did other Departments of the Government learn the contents that affected them? I said that unless there was a special restriction, copies of the telegrams would be automatically passed to them. We would then discuss before action was taken. In Bonn he said, his Department kept its sources of information to itself.

The Conservative Party Conference in October was more than usually occupied with foreign affairs including Southern Africa and the Middle East. Mrs. Golda Meir, the Israeli Prime Minister, came hot foot to London disturbed by an apparent shift away from the Labour Party's bias towards her country. She arrived late for her meeting with Heath in the Cabinet Room. Sweeping into the room she took her place at the table and announced in her gravelly Brooklyn accent, "Mr. Prime Minister, Israel lives in a bad neighbourhood and we ain't gonna move."

Alec Home had spoken often in opposition on arms for South Africa and on Rhodesia. It was soon obvious that he intended to tackle these problems in Government. In spite of strong opposition in Parliament the Government stuck to its plans to supply weapons for maritime defence basing itself on the Simonstown Agreement. Strong objections were voiced in black Africa, especially by Kaunda and Nyerere and the familiar threats of 'breaking up' the Commonwealth, used effectively against Labour, were repeated. But in October 1970 after a meeting with fellow Africans, Kenneth Kaunda came to London and it was decided that the Prime Minister, Lord Carrington the British High Commissioner in Zambia, and myself should try to explain British policy at a small dinner party in Downing Street. The President made a serious mistake on arrival by telling the press at London airport that he was going to appeal to the British people over the head of their Prime Minister. Not always a genial host, Heath received the President coolly and was obviously in no mood for compromise, having rightly resented the airport remarks. As he took his place at the dining table Kaunda looked down at the elegant table setting and remarked quietly "I had never seen a knife and fork until I went as a child to the Mission School." Carrington was at his most charming and carried the conversation along genially whilst the Prime Minister sat in silence. However, at an appropriate moment the Prime Minister explained quietly and logically why in the United Kingdom we found it necessary to do business with South Africa. Without warning Kaunda sprang up and crying again and again "My God, my God, I never expected to hear a British Minister speak to me like that!" He then rushed from the room defying all British and Zambian efforts to retrieve him. We could only await developments at the Commonwealth Conference due early in 1971.

About this time I accompanied the Prime Minister on a visit to the United Nations General Assembly in New York. I have little recollection of it except a call made by Heath on the Ethiopian Emperor Haile Selassie in his hotel. We were shown into his apartment and found him in an elaborate military uniform seated on a sofa, holding on his lap a minute chihuahua. At the sight of the Prime Minister the dog burst into a fury of puny barking which made conversation impossible. After a short delay the Emperor rang and a uniformed dwarf rushed into the room and snatched the animal from his master's arms. It took a few moments before a second attempt at conversation was made.

CHAPTER 19

RHODESIA

More difficult was the question of Rhodesia. There had been no movement since the terms proposed by Harold Wilson at the time of the Fearless Conference had been finally turned down by Ian Smith. Alec Home had long concerned himself both in government in 1963 and subsequently in opposition with this question. He was ready to try to succeed where Harold Wilson had failed. Whereas there was no love lost between Wilson and Smith, there was no clash of personality between Alec Home and the Rhodesian Prime Minister in 1971. Wilson might have settled on Fearless terms but the feeling in his party was too strong to risk it and in any case Smith turned the proposals down. Valuable time had been lost and black opposition to Smith within Rhodesia was growing. The Secretary of State therefore decided to test the feeling in Salisbury. Lord Goodman and others, including Philip Adams from the Foreign Office and Max Aitkin, were sent on a private reconnaissance. Goodman was a good choice as nobody who knew him could possibly accuse him of bias in favour of Smith and he had personal experience of South Africa. His unique appearance made it impossible for the visit to be made in secret. The reports brought back were sufficiently encouraging for the British government to prepare for negotiations. In November matters had progressed far enough for Lord Home to decide to go to Salisbury himself. The party included, in addition to Elizabeth Home, the Attorney General Peter Rawlinson, Goodman, Martin Le Quesne from the Foreign Office and myself, together with a Foreign Office legal expert and other appropriate officials. A more genial party was hard to imagine. Our plane was not permitted to overfly certain black African countries so the outward journey was longer than usual.

In Salisbury our party was split between the British High Commissioner's house, which had been standing empty for some time under the watchful eye of an English lady, and Meikle's Hotel in down town Salisbury. This and later experience, taught me its standards were as high as anywhere in the world. Our welcome by the Rhodesians was not unfriendly, but cautious. The Secretary of State was reluctantly allowed to have discussions with Joshua N'Komo the massive Matabele leader who was brought out of prison for the purpose. These discussions were unpromising but the preparatory talk we had with the Rhodesians and some blacks justified proceeding to full negotiations. On paper the two delegations facing each other across the table might have appeared a little unevenly matched. But Smith held his own with some help from his own Attorney General. His senior ministers made no helpful contribution. Eventually a draft agreement was reached which was compatible with the five principles which the Secretary of State had enumerated as early as 1964 and which included the submission of any agreement in due course for the approval of the Rhodesian people.

Some of the discussions took place in Smith's modest own office which was characteristic of him. On the walls hung coloured pictures of RAF fighter aircraft in which Smith had flown. Other war time emblems were visible. The whole had the air of the room of a successful undergraduate athlete. It had nevertheless been an exhausting week of argument but an agreement had been achieved. In the words of one participant, "The end of a bitter six year quarrel concluded in a typically unemotional way with the collecting up of papers, the closing of despatch boxes and we went out into a damp and deserted Salisbury Square with only the usual good nights." We left next day after group photographs in which Smith included the maximum number of his Ministers. There was little sign in the city that anything of importance was happening. On the way to the airport were only a few small groups of whites who waved a friendly goodbye. The flight home again avoided disapproving black countries but included Luanda in Portuguese Angola, a much more handsome city than I had imagined. We refuelled on Sal, an island off Guinea which was used by South African Airways and other less legitimate aircraft. The airfield was built on a flat dried out salt lake of incomparable barrenness. An unhappy Governor in an unusual uniform was hastily produced to greet the Secretary of State. Goodman remarked that the spot, "Could not be called God forsaken, because God had clearly never been there."

Alec Home in his autobiography describes Smith as a man of courage and he believed he would have honoured any agreement reached. Sadly others did not. After its eventual breakdown, I was subsequently sent to see Smith on several occasions. He constantly refused to face facts and put his faith in the U.S. and his South African neighbours. He was justifiably proud of the achievement of the post war whites in Rhodesia and despised the failure of the independent Africans in Zambia, Tanzania and Uganda. In 1976, after I had retired from the Foreign Office, James Callaghan sent me to see him once again and explore the possibility of reopening negotiations. Smith then went as far as to say that he would accept 'one man, one vote' and would split his party if necessary to reach an agreement. At last he was more realistic but neither the Prime Minister nor the Foreign Office officials trusted him by that time and a further year passed before Kissinger intervened and South

Africa withdrew support. Had it been possible for Smith to travel earlier and widely outside Rhodesia he might have come to see reason before the guerilla movement had grown. But in his isolation his vision remained tragically narrow. A contented multi-racial Rhodesia was, I believe, at one time possible. The rejection of the 1961 draft Constitution by N'komo was a turning point but even in 1971 it would not, in my view, have been beyond the reach of a more experienced and internationally experienced Rhodesian leader. It was one of history's missed opportunities.

In the event it was not easy to set up the Commission proposed in the draft agreement of 1971 to ascertain the views of the Rhodesian people. A suitable head was found in Lord Pearce, an Appeal Court Judge. But to assemble quickly a group of people experienced in Africa to take soundings on the spot proved very difficult. Christmas was near and suitable candidates were not easily persuaded to drop everything and sacrifice their holiday. By the time the team was put together the black opposition within Rhodesia, especially the 'frighteners' had got to work. There are those who allege the delay was the deliberate policy of certain officials. To the best of my belief this was not so and I never saw any evidence to justify this allegation. But in retrospect, the planning of a Commission should have been put in hand before we left for Rhodesia, if not earlier. But the Secretary of State's verdict was, "I do not believe, as events turned out, Lord Pearce could have recorded any verdict other than that the Africans rejected the proposed settlement." Smith had certainly counted on the Commission getting to work quickly. But a 'snap' verdict, if favourable, would have been strongly criticised in our own country.

The rejection in the Pearce report of the Agreement reached with Smith was a disappointment to Secretary of State Home and indeed to all of us. It had not seemed like negotiating with foreigners. I thought that we ought to have been able to agree. It was depressing to discover how wide was the gap between black and white. Nevertheless there were signs that some of the Africans were rallying behind Bishop Muzorewa. In May 1972 I was sent back to Salisbury with Miles Hudson, Alec Home's political assistant and also with a member of the appropriate department of the Foreign Office. We were to hand over formally the Pearce report to Smith and to talk if possible to the Bishop. There seemed to be a chance that he and Smith could work together. We were driven from Salisbury in a Special Branch car to a small place where the Bishop was holding a Sunday service. My talk with him took place on two chairs in the middle of what might have been a cricket field. The Special Branch officers lounged on the boundary. The Bishop was clearly not a leader of men like N'Komo and the talk yielded nothing.

Mugabe was not yet prominent although Smith's cabinet secretary, Jack Gaylard, an uncompromising ex-headmaster, admitted to me that he was the black leader the they feared most. Our talks with Smith were cordial enough but almost ended in disaster. Our Foreign Office companion left his brief case with our instructions behind in the Prime Minister's office, but managed to retrieve it before it had been noticed.

Personal assistants like Miles Hudson have always existed to a greater or lesser extent, drawn often from the Party faithful. In 1964 the Labour party had extended the practice. After 1970 the Conservatives followed suit. Miles was an ideal choice. He argued with us but we always felt he was a member of the team and his political advice was a great help. When Gough Whitlam, the Australian Socialist leader became Prime Minister, he too employed such people. I asked one of them how they got on with their departmental civil servants. He replied, "We only deal with Ministers." A recipe, in my view, for failure.

When I went back again to Salisbury at the request of James Callaghan the Foreign Secretary in 1976 I was accompanied by Tom MacNally, his personal assistant, both a good companion and a sensible man who later regrettably left politics.

CHAPTER 20

THE FOREIGN OFFICE, PARLIAMENT AND THE PUBLIC

Before proceeding further it may be worthwhile to refer to the position in which the Foreign Office found itself at times, in relation to parliamentary and to a lesser extent, public opinion. During the Labour administration (1964-70) it was under a significant amount of criticism. The Duncan Committee Report had been called for by the Labour Government to see how far reforms in the Diplomatic Service were desirable. The criticisms concerned mostly the selection of recruits, its cost to the taxpayer, the priorities of its activities abroad and its remoteness from parliamentary scrutiny. The report did not in fact, achieve significant change and in the event the desirable reforms evolved naturally and without too much prompting. The report attached over much importance on the need for commercial and economic work and created, as a concession to Andrew Shonfield the academic member of the committee, the bogey of 'an inner and outer circle' of officers. It was alleged that the decision to set up the committee arose from an ill tempered question raised by Barbara Castle at a Cabinet meeting. She had been angered by seeing a classified newspaper advertisement for a 'nanny' inserted by a British diplomat being posted abroad, with a family of small children. As far as Mrs. Castle was concerned the days of nannies were over. All this led to a general 'hate' round the Cabinet table against the style in which diplomats abroad lived at British taxpayers' expense. The discussion of course, also involved the supposed Oxbridge bias in recruitment. Michael Stewart had characteristically taken this latter point seriously when he first came to the office. He had consulted with an assembly of Vice Chancellors invited to London for dinner. Their reply had been that Oxbridge, through its scholarship system, was bound to attract a majority of the best students. If Mr. Stewart wanted to insist on the best, they were most likely to come from Oxford or Cambridge. But alternative universities had increased in number and the basic problem was to get their students to turn their attention to the Diplomatic Service. Undergraduates are inclined to follow the example of admired colleagues who had recently gone before them. Once a member of the Diplomatic Service (or any other career) reported back favourably to his friends, then others would follow. This indeed is what has happened over the years. It explains the stream of graduates who followed each other into the City in the nineteen eighties. The influence of dons is also relevant. No longer did they say at red brick universities, as once they did, "You will never get into the Foreign Office with that accent." Even under the long established system the Service had included the sons of miners who in due time had become ambassadors.

The promotion system within the service was also the subject of criticism. In my period as Head of the Office, senior appointments were dealt with in three stages. First was the Senior Appointments Board. This consisted of the Permanent Under Secretary, the Chief Clerk (the head personnel officer) and about the top ten or so in the office. There was of course, a constant turnover in that latter group. A Minister of State also attended, but did not preside. He intervened to the extent that he felt necessary and warned the Board of possible political points. He did not associate himself with its recommendations. It was of course, unusual for a Minister to attend and not preside. Only one, Geoffrey Rippon, a Conservative, did not choose to do so. The Board made its recommendations to the Secretary of State. He consulted the Prime Minister, if he wished, but claimed he did not need to do so. However, such consultations increased in frequency between 1969-73 and are now, I believe, obligatory. The whole procedure could, in my view, be defended as well-informed, fair and democratic. The small Parliamentary majority of Labour in 1964 caused Harold Wilson to be more sensitive on appointments than his predecessors.

As for the remote relationship with Parliament, there was some justification for members' dissatisfaction. This has now been, to a large extent, remedied by the advent of Select Committees in the Commons and to a lesser extent in the Lords. It has enormously added to the burden of the Permanent Under Secretary who now has to deal not only with important foreign policy matters before these committees, but has himself to answer questions about the minutiae of administration in embassies and consulates world wide. He also has to appear before the Public Accounts Committee - a necessary ordeal, which I never had to undergo. It is of course right that the requirements of Parliament should have priority over the convenience of the officials. Interrogation by the committees does much to clear their minds. These duties naturally affect the extent to which the Permanent Under Secretary can travel abroad with the Prime Minister or Foreign Secretary or needs to stay at home to 'mind the shop' in Whitehall.

During the governments of Wilson and Heath, it was the accepted practice for Permanent Under Secretary to travel with Ministers. Whether he could be of assistance was, of course, for them to decide. It is, in my view, unwise for either the Prime Minister or the Foreign Secretary to build up a monopoly of knowledge by failure to share his experiences with some of his senior staff. From his point of view, he has a second opinion of experienced people. From the officials point of view, it is of great help. It enables the official to understand better the minds of his own ministers and of his foreign opposite numbers. He gets to know his own foreign counterparts and is able to judge the ability of his colleagues serving in posts abroad. This latter point was of great value in the promotion system, which I have described above. From the selfish point of view of the Permanent Under Secretary, it makes his job vastly more interesting and easier to perform. Lady Home usually accompanied her husband abroad and Angela was allowed to be with her in Peking.

CHAPTER 21

THE U.K. AND THE SOVIET UNION

Before he tackled the Rhodesian problem, Alec Home made a determined attempt to get on to better terms with the Soviet Union. He was encouraged to do so by his long experience of dealing with Gromyko. They had negotiated together in the past in times of great tension in South East Asia and exchanged views with unusual frankness. But they were also on friendly terms personally, shared a sense of humour and Home advised him for example on the choice of sporting guns when he came to London. In 1970 Gromyko was not at that time a member of the Politburo but was the accepted mouthpiece of Soviet Foreign Policy. When eventually, not long before his death in 1989, he became President of the Soviet Union, Alec Home lost no time in sending him a message of congratulation. His rise in status, and indeed his survival for nearly fifty years in the high ranks of the Soviet system was an amazing achievement. He carried in his head an encyclopedic knowledge of past history. No doubt this had long stifled new ideas in his Department. He lived long enough to see the unmistakable signs of the collapse of the system for which he had so long striven. What were his feelings I cannot guess. He is believed to have played a decisive part in assisting Gorbachev to reach the top.

Not long after he took office, Home invited Gromyko to London to renew their contacts. To my surprise he rather mischievously decided to take him to lunch one day at the Tory Carlton Club and asked me to accompany him. We arrived rather late and the dining room was crowded. Our entry created a perceptible stir, but more was to come. The conversation turned soon to their common interest in the shooting of game - referred to by Gromyko as 'hunting.' They identified between them the birds common to both countries but there were a small number which remained unidentified merely by verbal description. The Secretary of State and Gromyko fell back on imitating the various bird calls. It was loud enough to attract the attention of neighbouring tables - a bizarre but enjoyable occasion.

But later in 1971 there was serious concern over the excessive numbers of intelligence officers which the Soviet Government were introducing into their large official establishment in Kensington and Highgate. The Secretary of State gave Gromyko fair and private warning that the situation was becoming intolerable. No action was taken and he made an oblique reference to the matter in the House of Commons. In May I was invited with Angela to Moscow by the Foreign Ministry and entertained there and in

Leningrad, (St. Petersburg). There we saw the palaces being restored, with no expense spared by expert craftsmen from Italy. The Director of the Hermitage Museum organised a special tour. He was a tall aristocratic man who must have yearned for more space for his treasures, which had been saved from destruction and looting during the Revolution by the strict personal intervention of Lenin. At a luncheon in Moscow organised by our Embassy, my neighbour was the wife of a senior Russian diplomat. She mentioned to me that to sit next to a black man made her feel physically sick. Her husband informed us that their two daughters were married - one to a Russian, the other to a Jew. Neither seemed to think that their views might give offence.

During discussions with the Ministry, the Soviet officials made it clear that we would be well advised to do nothing hostile to their London Mission. They had noted our hints and did not like them. On my return, the Secretary of State nevertheless decided that an unusually large number of the personnel engaged in intelligence duties should be expelled. There was a considerable argument about the numbers. Some in the Foreign Office thought the proposals were unnecessarily provocative and excessive. The Security Services felt they were inadequate. I attended a meeting in No. 10 presided over by the Prime Minister at which the Secretary of State and the Home Secretary Reginald Maudling were the main participants. The latter felt strongly that after a mass expulsion, the Government would be the laughing stock of the British public and that we should all look very foolish. It was left very much to me first to argue the case at the meeting for mass expulsion, whilst the Secretary of State held his fire. Finally the Prime Minister approved the number of 105.

A list was drawn up and we tried to guess the extent of the inevitable reprisals. This was difficult as (Sir) John Killick was about to leave to take up his post as our new Ambassador in Moscow. Fortunately he was a tough customer and after discussions with him and Lynette his courageous South African wife, it was decided they should go ahead. It seemed more than likely that there was serious trouble to come. Their departure may have had the advantage of putting the Soviet Embassy off their guard. After a few weeks I was then instructed by the Secretary of State to call in the Soviet Chargé d'affaires, Ivan Ippolitov to give him the names of those we wished to go. This I duly did. The Chargé conducted himself well. He took the list and studied it carefully. His face betrayed no emotion of any kind whatsoever and after remarking it was "a serious matter," he quietly left. Our security people who were watching the Embassy reported his arrival back in Kensington Palace Gardens. He disappeared into his office building and within a minute or two a figure was seen running at high speed across from the KGB office which was on the other side of the road. The Russians were, of course, furious but their reprisals in the short term were much less than expected.

Other countries followed our example to a greater or lesser extent and the British press and public were delighted. Maudling was good enough to admit to his misjudgment at the decisive meeting with the Prime Minister. From the Labour side James Callaghan remarked to me that he thought we had overdone the numbers, but he was in a minority. The Killicks did a splendid job in Moscow in maintaining morale, where our Embassy had to endure being sent to whatever was the Soviet equivalent of Coventry. It took many months for the Soviets to cool down, but our relations were in fact put on a better and more realistic basis. My own dealings with them in London continued with few problems and have done so ever since.

CHAPTER 22

THE COMMONWEALTH

During the period 1970-1973 there were two Commonwealth Conferences, which can appropriately be considered together.

I had been away from London during the 1969 Commonwealth Conference held in Lancaster House. Prime Minister Wilson, had then come under strong criticism from the Africans about our policy on Rhodesia and South Africa. Nyerere was the most eloquent critic. There had been much talk of 'breaking up the Commonwealth,' but Wilson held his ground although the party over-estimated the political influence of the Commonwealth. He and the Labour Party were well liked by the Africans in particular and the links stood the strain. After the meeting it was decided that future Conferences should not be held only in London. This was a concession intended to equate the U.K. with the other members. After some discussion, the choice for 1971 suitably fell on Singapore.

The lead-up to the Singapore Conference was a bitter dispute between the Africans and the new Conservative Government about the supply of arms to South Africa. The Government's policy had been clear before the election, although there was some strong domestic opposition to it. Attempts to explain it to the front line states in Africa (neighbours of Rhodesia) had failed. Prime Minister Heath showed no sign of changing and it was certain that the Conference fixed for mid January 1971, would be a battleground on this point. The bulk of the British party flew out to Singapore in good time. The Prime Minister came separately via the Indian sub-continent. H.M. the Queen very reluctantly accepted official advice not to be present. Having lived in Singapore for two years until 1958 I was very keen to see the progress that Lee Kwan Yew's regime had reportedly achieved. But I was not prepared for the astonishing metamorphosis. Lee was determined to impress and enjoyed doing so. New skyscrapers, new roads and recently planted floral street decorations confused those who thought they knew their way about. Signs of poverty had been put out of sight. The taxi drivers had been lectured personally by their Prime Minister not to spit out of their cabs into the street and always to give way to the specially imported limousines of the delegates. Our delegation was housed in a brand new hotel only very recently opened. The service was impeccable. On the first morning I rang room service for an ample breakfast. The response was so immediate that I believe the waiter was already standing outside the door. But the atmosphere in the Conference Hall was a very different matter.

It was not long before the question of arms for South Africa came to the surface in a violent form. Presidents Obote of Uganda and Kaunda of Zambia attacked Heath in the most unrestrained way. They were backed up similarly by Mrs. Bandaranika of Sri Lanka. The Prime Minister remained impassive and unprovoked and the abuse washed off him. The Australian delegation was helpful led by Prime Minister Gorton, whose prize fighter appearance belied his intellect. Some attention was diverted from him by the gossip about his striking lady assistant. Trudeau of Canada left the conference for a day to visit Indonesia and seemed dissatisfied with his role. At one time it seemed highly unlikely that a communique could be agreed and that the split in the meeting would not be healed. The formula which eventually proved acceptable was produced largely by the Australians and pacified the more extreme Africans who had looked for the most part to Trudeau for advice and guidance. A Declaration of Principles was unanimously adopted but was of questionable importance and meaning. Heath's experience on this occasion no doubt confirmed his own conviction that the value of the Commonwealth was at its best questionable. His mind was on Europe.

At the end of the Conference, the British Admiral at the Royal Navy Base gave a reception for the Prime Minister. It was a perfect tropical evening. The floodlit warships and the Marine Band, beating retreat, besides being a spectacle in itself, combined to create a powerful feeling of imperial nostalgia. This was especially poignant in that it was all taking place within a mile or two of the scene of the surrender to the Japanese forces in 1941, which could be considered as sealing the fate of our Empire in the East.

During the week, Lee Kwan Yew gave a luncheon for Heath in his official residence, which was the Colonial Secretary's former house in the grounds of the massive Government House of pre-war days. I was sitting next to Heath who was on Lee's right. Throughout the meal Lee boasted of his achievements and criticised patronisingly the way in which affairs were being managed in the U.K. Once again the Prime Minister remained impassive and took not the slightest notice. If Lee intended to provoke an argument, he failed completely.

Those of us who had heard Obote's outburst at the Conference could not but welcome the news that he had been overthrown on his return to Uganda by a certain Col. Amin. But we then had reckoned without knowledge of the evil of the Colonel of whom the Ministry of Defence knew 'nothing to his discredit.' He quickly promoted himself to General and after a decent interval, was invited to London. His interview with Secretary of State Home gave alarming evidence of the type of man with which we were going to have to deal. In a voice resembling a dazed heavyweight boxer in an American film, he asked the Secretary of State two questions.

First, would the U.K. supply him with bombers which could fly from Entebbe to Dar es Salaam and back without refuelling? These were required to bomb Nyerere. Secondly, if the British saw the Chinese fleet sailing towards Mombasa, would they intercept it? Understandably the Secretary of State's brief had not anticipated these questions. He passed me a note saying, "This nightmare is getting worse and worse." Nothing of course, came of the meeting. The full horror of Amin's regime was yet to come. One had to admit that, in full uniform, as host at his reception at the Hyde Park Hotel, he made a striking figure.

The next Commonwealth Conference took place in Ottawa in 1973. It was a much happier affair. The Queen was visiting Canada with full ceremony. The only cloud on the horizon was the possibility that General Amin, by now an international ogre, would choose to attend. Fortunately he made it a condition that a special plane should be provided and a troop of Scottish pipers should be in attendance.

The Chairman of the Conference, Prime Minister Trudeau, made a successful attempt to introduce 'informality and free discussion.' He was very much at home and had clearly overcome the doubts about being a Prime Minister, which he had expressed to an astonished Harold Wilson when they had first met in Ottawa immediately after his election. The tone of the meeting bore no relation to quarrels at Singapore. Australia was represented by the new Socialist Prime Minister Gough Whitlam. He made an eloquent bid to secure the support for Australia of the under-developed members of the Commonwealth. He maintained that the Australian Government was changing its immigration laws and no longer pursued an 'all white' policy. Lee Kwan Yew was highly cynical in his reply. It was true, he admitted, that Chinese doctors from Singapore were being admitted to Australia, but the purpose was only to ensure that Australian doctors were free to play golf at weekends. Even Whitlam laughed.

Nyerere made much of the ill effects on the small countries of the super powers' mutual hostility.

"When elephants fight, the grass beneath their feet is crushed." Lee Kwan Yew interjected that when elephants made love, the result was much the same.

The effect of our Prime Minister's naturally distant manner at these meetings was minimised by the charm and friendliness of Alec Home. During the week I noticed he seemed to make a point of speaking personally to all the delegates, senior or junior.

Whilst we were in Ottawa we had a chance of looking over the new External Affairs building. An unusual feature was a mechanical means of transferring papers to all parts of the office building. It was admitted however that one secret file had disappeared into the bowels of the building and had yet to be recovered or even located. It was also, for me, surprising to learn that the majority of telegrams received from Canadian posts overseas, were in French.

CHAPTER 23

THE U.S. AND EUROPE

During 1971, there was a distinct cooling off in the Anglo/U.S. relationship. This arose from several causes. Our government's preoccupation with Europe, arguments over the India/Pakistan war and, importantly, a lack of consultation by the U.S. on economic and financial policy which was largely handled by Governor John Connolly, the U.S. Secretary of the Treasury. There was clearly need for a summit meeting and a date was fixed for December 20-21 in Bermuda. Apart from the climatic attraction, there was symbolic value in a venue in mid Atlantic. It was arranged that Anthony Barber, the Chancellor of the Exchequer should join the Prime Minister and Foreign Secretary in Bermuda. He did so after being roughly handled by Connolly at financial meetings in Washington.

The Governor of Bermuda Lord Martonmere was a veteran Conservative ex M.P., from a north country constituency, who was married to a wealthy American. The President's security men had been allowed to check over his residence. At the very end of the search, one of the men put his foot through the ceiling of the bedroom which had been allocated to the Prime Minister. The Governor insisted that it must be repaired at once, but the security men said that if workmen were allowed in, the whole building would have to be checked again. This invited and received the negative rebuke it deserved, delivered by the Governor in brutal terms that if any Secret Service man thought a governor was going to entertain his Prime Minister in his house with a hole in his bedroom ceiling, he would have to think again.

A dinner party for the Prime Minister was arranged in Government House for the evening before the President arrived. The scene set in the dining room was almost regal. Two uniformed footmen, one black and one white, stood behind each guest. The Prime Minister sat on the hostess's right. I was next to him. He was understandably preoccupied with the approaching meeting. Scarcely a word was exchanged before the sweet course. When it was due, there was a short delay and an air of tension seemed to grow amongst the staff.

Suddenly, a footman entered carrying a very large edible replica of the Prime Minister's famous yacht 'Morning Cloud.' It was carefully lowered before him and the hostess looked expectantly towards him for approval. She received murmured thanks and a wintry smile. I do not draw this picture in criticism of him, but only to illustrate how the burden of responsibility affected this naturally solitary man and to question the wisdom of such elaborate festivity before serious diplomacy.

In the private discussions which preceded the meeting with the Americans next day, the Chancellor of the Exchequer Barber made a great deal of how difficult Connolly had been in Washington and was likely to be in Bermuda. Lunch followed immediately after the President's arrival. Connolly was seated next to the Secretary of State. I looked across the room a little anxiously to see how they were getting on together. It was soon apparent that they were finding much enjoyment in each other's company. After lunch the Foreign Secretary said to me with characteristic modesty "I didn't find Connolly a difficult man to get on with." As usual charm had succeeded in disarming a possible opponent.

In the event, the conference passed off well. Harmony between the two countries was largely restored. On the last evening a dinner was held for the President and the Prime Minister in HMS Glamorgan, a sizeable warship moored alongside in the harbour. It was an occasion in the best Royal Navy style. It revealed to us an unexpected side to the President. He sensed the mood and putting aside his prepared speech, delivered an extempore address, which was both moving and graceful. In reply the Prime Minister was effectively matter of fact and acknowledged the necessary change in our relationship which our coming entry into the European Economic Community foreshadowed.

We returned home for Christmas in a satisfied frame of mind. I, for one, was anxious to return to Bermuda as soon as opportunity allowed. Such an opportunity did not occur until after I had retired. By then, Sir Peter Ramsbotham was Governor. He had foolishly been removed by the Secretary of State, Dr. David Owen, from the Embassy in Washington. Dr. Owen chose to make the surprise announcement of the appointment of Peter Jay as Ramsbotham's replacement at a London meeting of the diplomatic correspondents. One of them later told me that the news was greeted first with silent astonishment and then by roars of unsympathetic laughter. Dr. Owen furiously closed the meeting at once. We found Sir Peter and his wife happy in Government House, much sustained by the support they had received from the Washingtonians when they had to leave.

The island seemed to have recovered its calm after the sudden assassination in 1973 of the popular Governor, Sir Richard Sharples. But Sir Peter sent me, with a senior police officer, round a slum area where the drug trade stubbornly flourished. As the car turned into the street, the groups who were gathered on the front steps of the shabby houses, vanished in a moment into thin air.

CHAPTER 24

INTO EUROPE

The conclusion of the conference in Bermuda rounded off a successful year for the Prime Minister and the Secretary of State in international affairs. Six months earlier, a confrontation had taken place in Paris between Heath and the French President M. Pompidou. Only interpreters - M. Andronikov and Michael Palliser, from our Diplomatic Service - were present. After more than ten hours the meeting concluded with a press conference. With a nice sense of history and drama the two leaders took their place at the same table from which General de Gaulle had spoken of the impossibility of Britain's entry into the Community and had declared his veto. President Pompidou, without mentioning the General by name referred to the negative views then expressed and turning to the audience said,
"You see before you tonight, two men who are convinced to the contrary". Andronikov and Palliser wisely agreed their minutes of the meetings. The deadlock had been broken. Tough negotiations had to continue but our Treaty of Accession was signed in January 1972 and our entry to the Community took place in January 1973.

The full and detailed story of how this point was reached has yet to be made public. Before he retired in 1973, (Sir) Con O'Neill who was one of the principal Foreign Office participants in the negotiations, wrote a voluminous account of them. This will no doubt rightly pay tribute to Geoffrey Rippon, who was the Foreign Minister and the member of the Government who led the British Delegation. The organisation of the British team was a new experience which had a profound effect on Whitehall and not least on the Foreign Office. It was a unique negotiation in that it involved vital interests of the majority of the government departments, including the most powerful and also those who had not hitherto been much concerned with international matters. The monopoly of the Foreign Office was at an end. Their coordination was a problem of great complexity and the resolution of conflicting priorities required frequent cabinet decisions. It was right and inevitable that the coordination of these departments should be centred in the Cabinet Office. I was not involved personally in the detailed negotiations and saw my duty as Permanent Under Secretary to ensure that Foreign Office views were strongly presented and that our officials at home and in posts abroad were capable of doing this.

The Prime Minister established special links with Christopher Soames in Paris, mostly through Robert Armstrong, his Private Secretary, who dealt also directly with M. Jobert, the politically ambitious confidant of the French President. I had been largely responsible, in the time of Michael Stewart, of bringing back Con O'Neill, a habitual 'resigner' into the office after his row with George Brown over the decision not to appoint him as Ambassador in Bonn. His principal and most active assistant was John Robinson a talented Whitehall conspirator. I was particularly concerned to see that, when we joined the Community, the chief British representative in Brussels should come from the Diplomatic Service and not from a Home Department. It was logical, in my view, that he should do so. Others did not agree. I found an opportunity to speak to the Prime Minister alone to try to ensure that his choice would be Michael Palliser. He did not need any persuasion. My good friend, Douglas Allen, the Permanent Secretary in the Treasury was a little put out, but he would agree the choice was justified by subsequent history.

The Treaty of Accession was, for the Prime Minister, the culmination of his greatest personal ambition. The Commons debate on the European Communities Bill took place immediately after the signature. For the debate, I had a seat in the Chamber under the gallery. In the excitement, the temptation to intervene was almost irresistible. After a high level debate the dignity of the House was somewhat upset by some scuffles which followed a very close result. It was certainly the most dramatic occasion I have ever witnessed in Westminster.

Several months later in October, I was in the party which accompanied the Prime Minister and the Foreign Secretary to the first summit meeting in Paris of the enlarged Community. It concluded with a triumphant call for European Union by 1980, of which the text was leaked in advance by the French. At that time, certainly no one knew what that meant, but the Euro-enthusiasts were satisfied and have successfully built on it. Many of the problems which have since dogged the Community, already began to appear at this meeting but few in the U.K. anticipated how the debate in the Community would in fact develop during the next two decades. Those British who were interested misjudged the extent to which they would be able to shape the development of the Community whilst the 'founding fathers' were careful not to disclose their ultimate federal objectives. History will record how we were steadily outsmarted between 1972-1992.

My memories of the gathering include the sartorial contrast between the original representatives of the Community and the Irish new entrants. The former appeared to be dressed in beautifully cut mohair suits with Hermes ties. The Irish wore heavy weight suits and looked somewhat like visitors to a county fair. This is of course no longer so, but it was clear to me that the days of the British domination of men's tailoring style were over.

During 1972 it was not only the U.K. which was uncertainly debating the merits of joining the Community. There were problems in Denmark. The Prime Minister Mr. J.O. Krag had consented to submit the decision of the Danish people in a referendum. The outcome was in some doubt. He wanted to bring home to his people that he was acting in company with the U.K. and that they would not be left to the mercy of the Germans. He discussed his fears with the British Ambassador, Sir Andrew Stark, an experienced and cheerful Scot. Together they persuaded Heath to visit Copenhagen in June and to try to make his visit something of an event. It was well stage-managed on both sides. Heath's party included the Cabinet Secretary Burke Trend, myself, Douglas Hurd, the future Foreign Secretary, then personal assistant to the Prime Minister, Donald Maitland and Robert Armstrong. Patricia Trend and Angela were with us. Some of the delegation were entertained to lunch at the Fredensborg Palace by Her Majesty, Queen Margrethe, which reminded us that the U.K. did not have a monopoly of an attractive and intelligent woman as Head of State. Heath's and Robert Armstrong's musical interests were catered for by a visit to the chapel of the Frederiksborg Castle where the Prime Minister was allowed to play a short piece on the 17th Century Compenius organ. A Danish quartet played during dinner but this did not exclude witty speeches. The end of the evening was enlivened by the arrival of Mr. Krag's attractive wife, straight from the stage of a city theatre, where she was nightly performing. The visit was a congenial success. Mr. Krag won his referendum and immediately resigned leaving the future to others. If the Danish felt more comfortable with us in the Community, the feeling was certainly reciprocated.

CHAPTER 25

AUSTRALIA/NEW ZEALAND/CHINA

The year 1972 was probably the busiest time of the whole of my period as Permanent Under Secretary. I have already referred above to some of the events of that year. But there was a steady flow inward to the U.K. of Heads of State, royal and presidential, Prime Ministers and Foreign Ministers. Useful as some of these visits were, there was always a heavy burden of briefs and minutes for the office to prepare or execute. This additional demand on the staff added to the normal official business, which was never light. I was lucky to have over three years, extremely able private secretaries, Richard Baker, Timothy Daunt and Mark Elliot. Two out of the three have become senior Ambassadors and the third exercised his unusual talents at the Imperial Defence College and in art and writing. Jennifer Garrod who was the senior lady in my outer office was faultless. She worked with me for more than twelve years both in the U.S. and U.K. She is now happily married in America to a British ex naval officer and has surprised herself as a competent sailor in their seagoing yacht. As a surprise farewell present on my retirement, my private office secretly commissioned a delightful monochrome picture of the interior of my room by Jean Reddaway the well known artist wife of one of our most successful diplomats. Vital to our ability to carry out busy schedules were a corps of Foreign Office drivers who combined serving the Queen's Messengers to and from the airports and meeting, in great good humour, our official social engagements.

Breaking into this heavy schedule were two long and interesting overseas journeys with the Secretary of State. The first was to Australia and New Zealand (June/July) and the second to Peking in the People's Republic of China, (October/November).

Canberra was the scene of a SEATO Council Meeting and from there we went on to Wellington, New Zealand. The first stage of the journey to Australia seemed interminable with stops at Frankfurt, Tel Aviv, Teheran, New Delhi, Darwin and Sydney. In both countries there were many official and personal friends to see. As our plane swept in over Sydney, the view of the harbour and the sight of so many swimming pools and tennis courts in the gardens of suburban houses reminded me of a headline I had lately seen in the Economist, which read, 'Australia - the fifteen million luckiest people in the world.' It was also satisfying to think that some of the descendants of poor British people so cruelly and unjustly sentenced to transportation for some paltry theft, were now enjoying beautiful estates flanking the

Hawksworth River below us.

The Seato Council was held in the Australian Parliament building (now replaced) and the chamber and all its facilities made it a most convenient setting. An Australian Air Force Group Captain steered us towards the choicest Australian wines, not normally for export. But it was good to see how much more like a capital city Canberra had become since I had first visited it nearly fifteen years before. Most of the senior civil servants in Australia were well known to us and were of a high standard - in particular, Messrs. Bunting, Waller, Moodie, Hay and McNicol. The first named, a mixture of our own Cabinet secretaries Brook and Trend, had long been a stabilising influence as cabinet secretary in successive governments. Seato was always an unexciting organisation and the discussion on this occasion, reflected this.

The Australian Government of Billy MacMahon, who had been so helpful at the Singapore Commonwealth Conference, was losing ground and was shortly to be ousted by Gough Whitlam, the socialist leader.

After two days we moved on to Melbourne where the Premier of the State of Victoria, Sir Henry Bolte was host. He had been in office seventeen years. Sir Henry was a archetypical 'Aussie' with an irresistible directness of speech and a love of the turf. His hospitality went with a swing. In the course of conversation at dinner with Lady Bolte, I told her how after a banquet at the Mansion House in London I had to go back after lights out, to recover Angela's expensive evening gloves, which she had dropped during the meal. "Good God," she commented, "Henry wouldn't have gone back for my teeth."

As a great horse racing enthusiast, he came to London, often for Ascot week. There, on one occasion he gave me the statistical details of his betting experience of the day. I was considerably taken aback at the extent of his success.

Alec Home's reception in New Zealand was, of course friendly. John Marshall the Prime Minister was admired in the U.K. for his skilful and well mannered defence of New Zealand's interests in the European Community negotiations. But his Government had not many more months to run. The Foreign Secretary and I called on the Leader of the Opposition, Norman Kirk, soon to be Prime Minister for a short time before his untimely death. He was a likeable, tubby, self made and self taught man who had been, before he took up politics, a 'stationary engine driver.' In his study he was surrounded by well selected books that he had clearly read. Alec Home got on well with him. We were driven out to Marshall's lovely house and farm at Wai Kane surrounded by enormous trees of great antiquity. The Governor

General Sir Arthur (later Lord) Porritt, a doctor of distinction and an Oxford athletic blue, entertained us at lunch. We all felt very much at home. On the return journey we stopped briefly in Perth to lunch with General Kendrew, the Governor of Western Australia, who as a boy I had watched many times when he was playing rugby for Woodford Rugby Club, my birth place and for England. He was one of the last Englishmen to be a governor of an Australian state.

The Foreign Secretary's visit to Peking was fixed for late October. For most of us it was their first visit to the People's Republic of China. My own experience was very limited and arose from the many times I had looked at China across the well guarded border from Hong Kong. In March, full diplomatic relations at Ambassadorial level had at last been restored. The October visit was designed to mark this overdue and important development. John Addis, a contemporary of mine at Christ Church had been appointed ambassador after waiting in the wings for years. He was an expert on China, in language and art and his family had long connections with the Far East. He was unmarried. The responsibility for coping with the ladies in our party, including Elizabeth Home and Angela fell on the handsome wife of Michael Morgan, an orientalist then the number two at the Embassy and later to be Ambassador in the Philippines. She discharged it well.

From the point of view of British interests, the visit was timely. China had been let down by the Soviet Union, had recently renewed links with the U.S. and was ready to learn more about us and the developments taking place in Europe. Alec Home and Chou en Lai were old acquaintances, having negotiated with each other in Geneva, some years before. There was evident mutual respect between them. It was easy for the Foreign Secretary to speak frankly. This he did and he was carefully listened to. It was not the beginning of an untroubled relationship but it was at least the start of higher level exchanges.

In addition to the business meetings, an extensive programme had been arranged, including all the tourist spots, which in later years became familiar to the thousands of British and other visitors. Having been disappointed by my first sight of the Pyramids in 1940, I was delighted to have my expectations far exceeded by the Great Wall. It was a perfect day for our visit and we could see the wall rising and falling over the hills into the far distance. The only part of the programme which was unique was the playing of the Eton Boating Song by a Chinese band at the banquet in honour of Alec Home. In what terms this was explained to the Chinese guests we never learned and can only be imagined. One of the sights in Peking City which remains in my mind was the parking of thousands upon thousands of bicycles round a large sports stadium in which an important match was taking place. We left China by Hong Kong, having entered at Shanghai, where we had hurriedly breakfasted.

It was not until many years later that I had another chance to see that city which, in contrast to Peking has so many signs of past foreign occupation.

During our time in Peking, the Homes were in their best form. The Foreign Secretary recklessly tackled all Chinese dishes and Elizabeth Home charmed the ladies and the many children paraded before her. She was greeted often with the same song, the theme of which in translation was, "Welcome, welcome, foreign aunties."

Elizabeth Home was much helped by a charming girl interpreter who revealed to her that her child was in Shanghai and her husband at the Chinese Embassy in London. She did not expect to see him for three years. At an appropriate moment, Elizabeth directly asked one of the high Chinese officials why the girl was separated from her husband when, with her fluency in English, she could be of such help to the Embassy in London. Would it not be sensible to send her there? This suggestion was greeted stonily. Nevertheless, in a very few months it was acted upon. Several years later, by chance I came face to face with her at a hotel in Peking. She greeted me warmly. There was no doubt that a firm friend of the U.K. had been made by Elizabeth's thoughtful intervention.

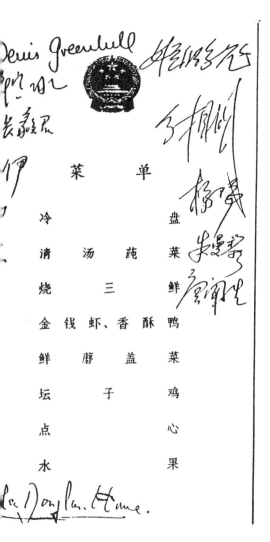

MENU

Cold Dishes

Consomme with West Lake Green

Stewed Three Delicacies

Prawn and Crisp Duck

Mushrooms and Mustard Green

Braised Chicken

Pastries

Fruits

SIGNED MENU ON THE OCCASION OF
SIR ALEC DOUGLAS-HOME'S
VISIT TO CHINA

CHAPTER 26

LAST MONTHS AT THE FOREIGN OFFICE

Time was passing quickly. In November of the year 1973 I would reach the age of retirement. H. V. Hodson editing the Annual Register described it as 'a year of tension and bitterness in which few problems were solved at home or abroad.' An oil crisis was looming world wide and in the U.K. there were continuing sharp quarrels between the Government and the unions. The economy was showing signs of severe strain. Against this unhappy background, foreign affairs were hard to manage. But entry to the European Community had been achieved and high hopes were pinned on it. For Angela and myself it was also to be a year of family sadness.

A summit meeting between the Prime Minister and President Nixon had been fixed for the end of January. The Prime Minister's party included, of course, the Foreign secretary, plus Burke Trend, Robert Armstrong and myself. Lord Cromer, our Ambassador in Washington joined it on our arrival. A new feature was that some of the discussions were to be overnight at Camp David. This was welcome. We all had had experience of such a meeting at the White House in December 1970 on the Prime Minister's first official visit to Nixon.

A roomy and quiet helicopter took us from the White House lawn up towards Camp David. It followed the rocky and fast flowing river gorge of the Potomac for most of the flight. Then fog halted the flight and we went the rest of the way by car. As soon as we arrived we were escorted to individual well furnished military type huts. On each comfortable bed was a collection of presents and souvenirs. These included two high quality U.S. naval jackets - one heavy and one lightweight. On the latter our names and titles were sewn. Unfortunately Burke's first name had been omitted and he had to be content for a short time with "Sir Trend." Dinner was served in a modest and unostentatious room in the main building. The President presided, sitting in the centre of the table, supported by his Secretary of State William Rogers, Ambassador Annenberg and Henry Kissinger. The Prime Minister seemed more relaxed than I had ever seen him on a comparable occasion. I was seated across the table from Kissinger. He was somewhat distracted by terrorist threats currently being made against his parents and his young son. He left the table from time to time to take messages about their safety. But the cordiality of the dinner concealed latent differences between our two governments.

Our new membership of the Community was at the root of the matter.

For the Prime Minister, Europe was the priority and he suspected with some reason that, with Vietnam out of the way, Kissinger was wishing to push America into the affairs of the Community and guide its development. In April, Kissinger made a major speech in New York without sufficient prior consultation. It included the fateful sentence 'nineteen seventy three, is the Year of Europe.' The use of this phrase fuelled the Prime Minister's suspicions and infuriated him. I recall an angry outburst about it in the Cabinet room. The intention of the speech was friendly, but the language was misjudged and it had the reverse effect, not only on our Prime Minister, but on the Germans and the French, who were always glad to keep the Americans at arms length. These developments set the scene for cooler Anglo/US relations which were unwelcome and unfamiliar to me and often to the Secretary of State. The shadow of Watergate was beginning to fall across Washington and in October disagreement over the Middle East made life more difficult.

The Israeli Ambassador in London for some years had been an aggressive man with strong South African connections. I was not sorry to learn in the summer that he was returning to Jerusalem but he had many admirers in this country. Terence Prittie, a Christ Church friend of mine had, after several years as a prisoner of war in Germany, become a highly successful Guardian Correspondent in Bonn. But he had latterly switched to an effective lobbyist on behalf of Israel. He invited me to a luncheon given in honour of the retiring Ambassador who took advantage of the occasion to make a speech on the relations of his country with its Arab neighbours. His theme was that the Arabs were completely at the mercy of the Israeli armed forces. They would not dare to make trouble. I doubt if anyone in the room disbelieved him.

Shortly afterwards, on October 6th Egypt and Syria made a carefully premeditated attack on Israel in the middle of Yom Kippur the Jewish festival. Complete surprise was achieved. It is not necessary for me to repeat the history of this brief and highly dangerous war. As far as our country was concerned it was essential that we should do nothing which would threaten our oil supplies from the Arab countries. Our insistence on neutrality angered the Americans who were very apprehensive of Russian reactions. I recall making anxious telephone calls to Lord Cromer in Washington whose closeness to Kissinger was of great value to us at this delicate moment. It was at this difficult time after the crisis was over that my responsibility at the Foreign Office came to an end in November.

Against this rather melancholy background, many pleasant things had happened to us before our great sadness on November 7th. During the year we had been the guest of Sir Duncan and Lady Wilson in Cambridge. A former Ambassador in Belgrade and Moscow he was a scholarly man himself and his wife was compiling a Russian dictionary. He had not long been elected Master of Corpus Christi College where an opening had occurred as a result of a split amongst the Fellows. One of those trying to persuade him to offer himself as a candidate had said,

" You know Sir Duncan, there is no need to meet the Students."

Not only was he meeting the students but, to the annoyance of some of the Fellows, his hospitality was becoming highly popular. But he was now finding out, as others before and after him, that being the head of a college is very different from being an ambassador running an obedient large embassy. Our visit made me reflect on what I might do after retirement and the need to look before one leapt. I knew very well that in any case, there was no possibility whatever of an academic life.

CHAPTER 27

RELAXATIONS

It is always difficult in a busy department to find the right time to go on leave. Whilst Parliament is sitting it is out of the question, but the long summer recess gives a reasonable time for choice. Our flat in Kensington to which we had moved from Westminster in 1967 was our only home. We had long decided that a second home in the country or at the sea, even if affordable, would be a mixed blessing. The business of the Foreign Office not infrequently required week end attendance. The best solution which we evolved was to go away for the whole month of August and to be for the rest of the year in comparatively easy distance from London. Angela's godmother generously allowed us to use in August a flat in her house in Salcombe Devon, which was large enough for us to meet also some family requirements. From there we were still accessible for any emergency.

But in May, my friend Sir Val Duncan, the Chairman of RTZ whom I had first met in wartime Algiers and who had written the Report on the Foreign and Commonwealth Office at the Wilson Government's request, invited us to join, for one week, a party which he annually assembled at his beautiful villa in Majorca. A regular guest was Harold Macmillan and others included Lord Carrington the Defence Secretary and Bill McFadzean, then chairman of BICC. It was immensely enjoyable and naturally focused on the ex Prime Minister who inevitably rose to the occasion. He used to appear first on the terrace each day about midday and reminisce indiscreetly until past midnight leading to discussions both serious and frivolous. Angela and I were once at the end of our week, left alone with him waiting for the car to take us to the airport. We thanked him for contributing so much to making the week such fun. He was silent for a moment or two and then said, "Yes, I always try to put on a good show." He certainly did. A high spot for him was if he was recognised in the street in small nearby town and a crowd of local people quickly gathered.

July 2nd was Alec Home's 70th birthday. The Prime Minister very kindly included us in a dinner he gave at No. 10. The company was interesting and, to my delight, included Sir John Masterman who had been tutor at Christ Church to both Alec Home and myself. The only guest about whom I had reservations was M. Jobert the ambitious adviser of President Pompidou who had played a significant part in our entry to the Community but whose friendship with this country was questionable.

In the Foreign Office we were in some doubt as how best to celebrate

the birthday. There were plenty of volunteers to subscribe for a present. But the choice of a gift was difficult. Antony Acland, his private secretary, now Provost of Eton, came up with the suggestion which seemed at once to be the right one. Knowing well his enthusiasm for gardens, Antony suggested that the Secretary of State should be given a plant or a tree associated with each of the countries he had visited in his career. With the assistance of the Director of Kew and Messrs. Hillers, the famous nursery firm of Winchester, a list was drawn up of plants which could be obtained. The secret was well kept. On his birthday the Secretary of State and his wife were invited to my office and with some of my colleagues I explained what we had done and handed over the list. He was clearly delighted and Antony's choice fully vindicated. I pointed out to him that the list included 'Magnolia Wilsoni' but this had no political significance. He replied at once,
"I know it well, it hangs upside down and is red at the centre."
Some years later Angela and I were invited to the Hirsel, the Home's Scottish home to see the plants and trees laid out in a special part of their beautiful garden. There were over ninety. Only one had died - Magnolia Wilsoni.

In July came the surprise invitation to Bulgaria to which I have referred on page 66. After the August holiday it was inevitable that farewell parties began, especially as we had for nine years been fairly prominent on the Whitehall stage and were known to a great many official and business people. Particularly memorable on October 4th was Ambassador Annenberg's party for the Trends and ourselves also mentioned earlier. If he was not the best professional diplomat, he was certainly the perfect host. On October 23rd, with characteristic generosity, the Prime Minister gave a dinner in our honour at No. 10. My elder son Nigel was included in the Prime Minister's invitation, my younger son Robin declined to come - something which in the light of later events, I should have thought about more carefully. My successor to be, (Sir) Thomas Brimelow and his wife Jean were, of course, also there with Alison, one of their two clever daughters.

Earlier in the year Alec Home had asked me who would be my recommendation for my successor as Permanent Under Secretary. I had no doubt in my own mind that it ought to be Thomas Brimelow for several decisive reasons. He was a highly experienced officer, having served several times in the Soviet Union, in Washington and been Ambassador in Ankara and Warsaw. He was an exceptional linguist with a professorial intellect. He did not 'learn' languages he 'absorbed' them. He was well known to Henry Kissinger and admired in the U.S. State Department and CIA as a Kremlinologist. A snag was that he was only two years younger than me and could not, if he retired at 60, serve for more than a comparatively short time.

I thought that at a time, when a General Election could not be far distant, it was highly desirable to have as Permanent Under Secretary, someone who was well known and trusted by both political parties, especially on questions relating to the Soviet Union. When I told him that I was going to put his name forward he demurred. He said that he preferred, as he had always done, to make decisions after study of original documents. For example he read all the Russian and Eastern European newspapers and so on. He would no longer be able to do this if he was Permanent Under Secretary. However, I insisted and in due time Alec Home made his selection. After his retirement Brimelow had the distinction of being nominated a Member of the European Parliament. In our House of Lords he sat on the Labour benches. It was most unusual for a former Civil Servant to associate himself with one party rather than joining the independents on the Cross Benches. This caused some comment but I did not join those who attempted to dissuade him.

The Prime Minister's dinner meant a great deal to us and was a light hearted affair. I wished my father had been there. In the course of speeches I was asked if I felt I would have been successful in the Diplomatic Service without Angela's help. Rather unguardedly I said that I thought I would, but it had been very pleasant to have her with me. This drew a good deal of laughter and general disagreement. Since then I have often regretted my unguarded observation and come to the irrefutable conclusion that practically every decisive decision in our lives has been taken at Angela's instigation. I tried to put the record straight in a short speech at our Golden Wedding Luncheon in 1991.

A week after the Prime Minister's dinner the Secretary of State took us to see his brother's play, *At the End of the Day*, which Elizabeth Home felt was in questionable taste and cruel to Harold Wilson. Afterwards we had supper at their flat in Carlton Gardens. They happily included Lord Hood who had been my predecessor as Minister in Washington and who, I always believed, played no small part in my advancement in the Diplomatic Service.

CHAPTER 28

THE LAST OVERSEAS VISIT AND A SAD ENDING

In the midst of this, Lord Carrington the Minister of Defence had invited me to join a delegation he was leading to visit the Shah of Iran. His main purpose was to discuss the further supply of arms and, in particular, to see what in the event, was an impressive demonstration of British tanks operated by the Iranian army. He was accompanied by General Sir David Fraser, who contributed significantly to the strength of the party. Happily our wives were included. The British Ambassador to Iran was (Sir) Peter Ramsbotham who was admired by us all and on excellent terms with the Shah. The Secretary of State asked me to sound him out during the visit on his willingness to leave Teheran and go to the Embassy in Washington, which was shortly to be vacant. For Teheran a very suitable successor was to hand in the person of Sir Anthony Parsons a Middle East expert who, in the years to come, played a vital part at the United Nations in New York during the Falklands War and, now living in Devonshire, may often to be heard in sensible contributions to BBC Radio 4.

The Shah granted an audience to Lord Carrington and some members of our group. It was in two stages. At first Lord Carrington, the General, the Ambassador and myself were admitted. I had met the Shah before but not at such close quarters. His detailed knowledge of weaponry was astonishing and he had clearly studied and memorised the capabilities of all competing types of planes and tanks. This knowledge, he was proud to display. After some time, the rest of our party was brought in. This included Sharpoor Reporter, very well known to the Shah, who had a British passport and whose father had originally come from India to Persia and had been of service both to the British Embassies and Persian Governments over many years. Sharpoor had recently helped the British Government in the negotiation of arms contracts. On entering the room he fell to his knees and hobbled across the floor to the side of the Shah and kissed his right hand, which hung at his side. At no time did the Shah acknowledge his presence by word or by glance, but left his hand hanging down as one might do to a favourite dog. It was uncomfortable to watch. Reporter escaped trouble when the Shah was overthrown. Some years later I came up on him one day quietly sitting on a Park Bench in Kensington Gardens. A casual passer by would never have guessed his controversial history.

Following the Shah's audience, we flew down to Kharg Island to see the tanker loading points, which later became a favourite target in the Iraq/

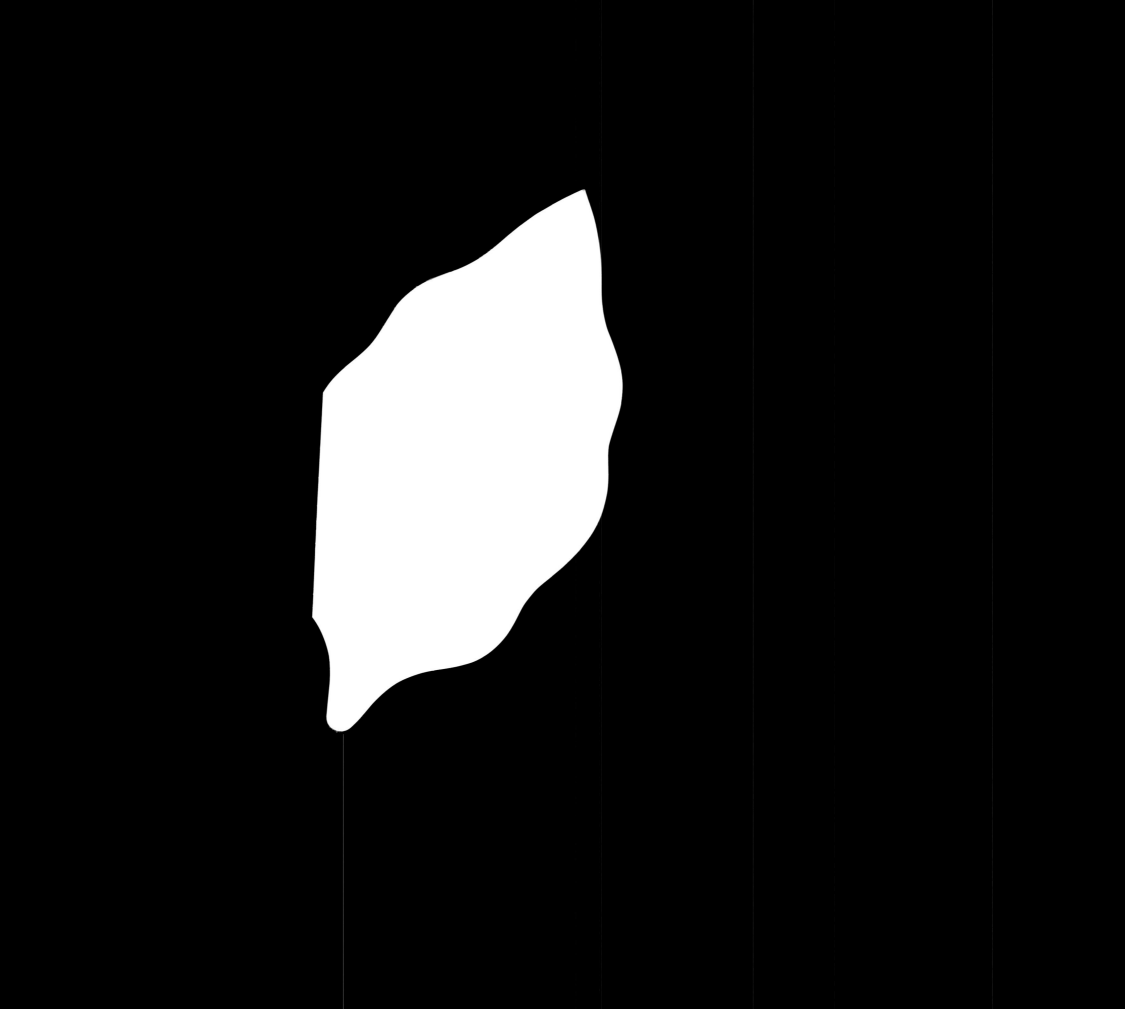

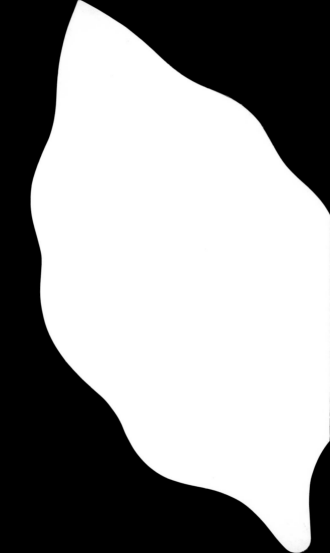

Iran war. I was, during the day, able to talk to Peter Ramsbotham about the Washington appointment. He was so much at home in Teheran where he had been for barely three years that he was reluctant to move, but ultimately consented to do so, if the Secretary of State wished it. At the time, he thought that the suggested move implied some criticism of his performance where he was. Nothing could have been further from the truth. He was to be a success in Washington until he was removed by Dr. Owen.

It had appeared to be a useful and encouraging visit. In fact there was to be an appalling failure of Western Intelligence. No signs of impending revolution were being identified which would soon sweep away the Shah and change the whole character of the country. More disturbing was the news of the domestic situation in the U.K. with continuing conflict between the Unions and the Government. On the way home in the plane, Carrington strongly expressed the urgent need for a General Election. Normally I would have avoided expressing any view, but as I was within weeks of retirement, I disagreed. In retrospect he was right.

In the first week of November 1973, final farewells had to be said. The Prime Minister asked me to see him. My admiration for him had steadily grown and I was sorry that our official contacts would be at an end. Inter alia he asked me how I thought Whitehall working could be improved. I suggested more regular meetings between Permanent Secretaries. He did not disagree. The Labour Governments had always frowned on such things as likely to be 'conspiracies' against them. Such meetings have now, I understand, taken place for many years.

On November 6th Angela and I went to take our leave of the Queen. It was a friendly talk. Privately I regretted our interesting audiences would cease. Later I was not displeased to learn from a reliable source that I was the only Permanent Secretary who did not make the Queen feel she was being lectured. In the evening the Secretary of State gave a reception at Lancaster House for members of the London Diplomatic Corps. My rather banal speech was saved by an appropriate anecdote which is too long to be reproduced, given to me at the last moment by my colleague Martin Le Quesne.

Very early in the morning of November 7th, my 60th birthday and my last day in the office - the telephone rang at my bedside. I was ill-prepared for a dreadful blow. It was the wife of our younger son Robin, to say that he had taken an overdose of Paracetamol and was in the Whittington Hospital in Highgate. Angela went straight there, whilst I went to handle matters from my office. She saw Robin who was very disorientated. The hospital people took her on one side to say that his liver might well be badly damaged and it would be thirty six hours or more before it would be known whether he would live or die. Angela sent a message back to me by the hand of one of our Foreign Office drivers, Mr. Emblen, who had rushed her there. I consulted our trusted Foreign Office medical adviser, Dr. V. C. Medvei. He decided to get in touch at once with Dr. Roger Williams, the Head of Kings College Hospital's world famous Liver Unit, who was probably the only man capable of saving the day. Dr. Williams agreed immediately to take Robin, and he and Angela were at once driven to King's College Hospital. He took many weeks to recover. It was thus with heavy hearts and on this note of foreboding that we left the Diplomatic Service, which we had both loved and enjoyed.

Robin was never well enough again to escape death by his own hand a few years later. This unforgettable tragedy still haunts us, not least because his gifted wife was the daughter of our very good friends Freda and Eric Roll.

CHAPTER 29

CEREMONIES AND STATE ENTERTAINMENT

Before leaving this account of our diplomatic life, I would like to refer to one other aspect of it. The post of Permanent Under Secretary and Head of the Diplomatic Service involved participation in a certain amount of ceremonial. The most frequent ceremony was the presentation to H.M. the Queen at Buckingham Palace by incoming Heads of Mission of their Letters of Credence. Without the acceptance of such a letter the Head of Mission could not take up his appointment. He/she comes to the Palace in a horse drawn carriage and returns to their residence in the same way. Incredibly, some not infrequently forget to bring their letters with them and a dummy is kept in readiness. If the Queen was away, the Queen Mother took over, assisted by one of the Princesses.

For this event the Permanent Under Secretary is required to wear full diplomatic uniform and decorations. He is expected to brief the Queen beforehand and stay for a short time with her after the Head of Mission has left. Sir Michael Adeane, her wise Private Secretary gave me valuable advice.

"Do not forget,' he said, "this lady has been doing her job for seventeen years." She had indeed been long studying Foreign Office telegrams and her Ambassadors' despatches. She had met almost every important person on the international scene except those behind the Iron Curtain. People were her speciality and she is a penetrating and accurate judge of character.

The ceremony itself is simple but sometimes moving. On one particular occasion the representative of a very small African country was delivering his letters. Her Majesty remarked that she had visited his country when, as Princess Elizabeth, she had gone there with her father on the way to South Africa, immediately after the war.

"Yes," he said, "I was one of the small boys lining your route with a Union Jack in my hand." He then paused, and, looking round his voice took on a strange and distant note, "Never" he said, as if talking to himself, "in my wildest dreams did I think I would ever be standing here in Buckingham Palace in the presence of the Queen." It was difficult not to be affected.

There was a different atmosphere when it was the turn of a certain Ambassador from a Central American Republic. He had spent little time in his own country and used his considerable wealth on many racehorses based usually in France. He had clearly decided to show off his racing knowledge by recalling to Her Majesty the results of many famous races, naming the first three horses in each race. In each case, Her Majesty quietly added the names of the fourth and fifth. The ambassador soon admitted defeat and the subject was quickly changed.

The first ever Mongolian Ambassador scored a considerable success. He asked to bring an interpreter, but acutely anticipated that the Queen at some stage would ask by what route he had come from Ulan Bator to London. She duly did so. With a sweep of his arm he brushed aside his interpreter and recited in passable English a carefully prepared account of his journey. He was justifiably delighted at the result and fortified by his success concluded the interview in English assisted by all of us who had shared his manifest pleasure.

The ceremony for Walter Annenberg, President Nixon's choice for London, achieved wide fame in this country and in the United States. It was later shown on an excellent BBC TV programme on the Queen's life and duties. It showed how the Ambassador, in the first of many achievements fixed, by his circumlocution, the word 'refurbishment' into current use in this country. In many such ceremonies I only saw one breach of etiquette. A Latin American diplomat brought with him a lady member of his staff. Before the ceremony in the outer room I noticed that she was wearing a long light coat over a dress. It did not seem quite appropriate for a royal audience but I gave it no further thought. However, when she was called in by the Ambassador to be presented, she slipped off her coat to reveal a mini skirt. It was highly unsuitable for a low cross-legged curtsey. The audience was brief.

There were many other public ceremonies in which Angela and I were fortunate to be included. I know she found them interesting and I was proud of her. Memorable were the investiture of the Prince of Wales, the funeral service of the Duke of Windsor and several banquets for visiting Heads of State at Windsor Castle. The investiture against the background of historic Caernarvon Castle was unforgettable. The tension was heightened by rumours of terrorist attacks. The first glimpse of a banquet table at Windsor, with the precious plate and banks of flowers, was breathtaking. As Henry Kissinger once observed, "Britain has raised understated pomp to a major art form."

The State visit of the Emperor of Japan in October 1971 was a memorable occasion of a particularly sensitive kind. It was to be an indication of post war reconciliation. Preceded by a certain amount of controversy, it was essential that the right note was struck. In the event official and public attitudes were correct, well mannered but cool. I was able to observe the Emperor at close range on several occasions. He was

BANQUET

IN HONOUR OF

THE QUEEN

AND

THE PRINCE PHILIP, DUKE OF EDINBURGH

Japanese Embassy

23 Kensington Palace Gardens, W.8

Thursday, 7th October, 1971

Sir Denis Greenhill	Sir John Pilcher
Marshal of the Royal Air Force Sir Thomas Pike	Lady Pike
Lady Douglas-Home	Lord Cobbold
Rear-Admiral Earl Cairns	Madame Clasen
Duchess of Abercorn	Prime Minister
Prince William of Gloucester	Duchess of Grafton
Duchess of Kent	H.E. Mr. T. Usami
H.E. Japanese Ambassador	Duchess of Gloucester
Queen Elizabeth The Queen Mother	THE PRINCE PHILIP, DUKE OF EDINBURGH
THE EMPEROR	THE EMPRESS
THE QUEEN	Earl of Snowdon
Minister for Foreign Affairs	Princess Anne
Princess Margaret, Countess of Snowdon	Prince Richard of Gloucester
Duke of Kent	Madame Yukawa
Madame Kitashirakawa	Right Hon. The Speaker
H.E. Luxembourg Ambassador	H.E. Mr. S. Irie
Lady Cobbold	Countess Cairns
Lieutenant-Colonel Rt.-Hon. Sir Michael Adeane	Secretary of State for Foreign and Commonwealth Affairs
Lady Greenhill	Lady Pilcher
H.E. Mr. S. Shima	

Table plan. Visit of Emperor Hirohito 1971

obviously under great strain and only once did I see him betray the slightest emotion. This was at the point when the very elderly Sir Frank Aston Gwatkin who had escorted him as a young prince on his first visit to this country, was presented to him. For the briefest moment a smile flickered on his impassive face. The Empress watched him carefully with affectionate anxiety.

Each year The Queen gives a reception at Buckingham Palace in November to all members of the Diplomatic Corps accredited to the Court of St. James. Each Ambassador or High Commissioner brings a selection of his staff with him or her. They are presented to Her Majesty and those members of the Royal Family who are with the Queen. It is clear that this gives great pleasure to the diplomatic staffs and the variety of national costumes and uniforms make it a spectacular pageant. The atmosphere, in my experience, is cordial and good humoured. A team of officers from the Foreign Office, who are normally in frequent contact with the guests, assist Her Majesty in the identifications and introductions. The evening ends with dancing in the Ballroom.

The skill of the Palace staff on these and other occasions is greatly to be admired as those will testify who have had the good fortune to be invested with an honour. The briefing in advance in my case by the elegant Col. (Sir) Eric Penn was both witty and reassuring and calculated to banish any incipient stage-fright. At my investiture, my elder son, working on a newspaper in Manchester, contrived to have his most suitable clothes shut in the cleaners and turned up in a civilian suit borrowed from his grandmother's hall porter. I was pleased that he persisted in coming.

The Lord Mayor of London is generous in the hospitality which the Corporation extends to distinguished foreign visitors both at the Guildhall and the Mansion House. This hospitality is also accompanied by spectacular ceremony which usually greatly impresses and sometimes, somewhat mystifies visitors. We, in the Foreign Office, naturally give what help we can and in return advise the Lord Mayor on his own overseas tour to which, I believe, each Lord Mayor is entitled during his year of office. Senior members of the Foreign Office are usually invited to these ceremonies and sometimes to banquets not involving foreign visitors. Such invitations were a privilege which Angela and I welcomed and valued.

Only once, in my experience was a disagreeably sour note struck by the City authorities. It was customary for guests to advance towards a formal introduction to the Lord Mayor up an aisle between seated members of the City authorities. During the advance, the names of the guests were called out and those seated clapped with a wide variety of enthusiasm. On this particular occasion, Lord and Lady Home, were loudly applauded. They were followed not long afterwards by the new Prime Minister and Mrs. Wilson. To the great embarrassment of many in the Hall, they were received with distinct hisses. As the future of the administration of the City was under some discussion and political criticism, this appalling breach of taste was an act of folly. What followed, I do not know, but I am certain there was no repetition and I know of no occasion when a Lord Mayor allowed such an error to be made again.

The country is fortunate in having a wide choice of historic and handsome buildings in which to entertain distinguished foreign visitors. Buckingham Palace and Windsor Castle are pre-eminent. The Library of the Castle holds many historic documents in the form of letters exchanged in the past with leaders of Europe and elsewhere. With the assistance of the Librarian of the Castle, some appropriate examples of these are usually selected by the Queen to be shown to visiting guests. I remember Willy Brandt being particularly fascinated by the documents set out for him.

Personally, I used to find the Painted Hall at Greenwich a most impressive venue for official dinners, except that on more than one occasion the kitchen staff, behind screens contrived to let fall in mid evening a tremendous clatter of metal trays and dishes. In suitable weather Hampton Court can also be made spectacular, but there is no doubt hospitality offered in No. 10 Downing Street has a special appeal.

Harold Wilson in his Premiership introduced a novel variation of the usual procedure. Apparently he was advised by his 'image makers' that the usual newspaper list of guests was becoming an object of criticism to certain members of the Labour Party. He therefore began to include in receptions held after dinner, guests with a popular appeal. Television personalities were favoured. Foreign visitors were often understandably baffled. However, on one occasion at the height of the success of the BBC Forsyte Saga series, a Yugoslav delegation were obviously delighted to recognise actors they had long been watching and appeared to find them even more interesting than their hosts.

CHAPTER 30

AFTER RETIREMENT

During the last few months in the Foreign Office, I naturally began to think about what to do in the future. Alec Home asked me if I "would like to throw my hat into the ring," for appointment as Ambassador in Washington. I was flattered and tempted, but Angela's great good sense prevailed and I knew she was right when she advised me to answer, "No." We both had had enough diplomatic life and I had doubts about my fitness for that particular job. It was true that I had never been an ambassador and it seemed a pity to give up the chance, but Lord Strang a former Permanent Under Secretary had done so before me. As I had been in Whitehall for nine continuous years it was not surprising that I began to be approached with offers of business appointments. Several were of interest, but the unwritten rule was, that no commitment could be made until after retirement.

In retrospect, I made the mistake of thinking that retirement had to be a period of reduced activity instead of preparing to make a new full time career which might, or might not, involve a course of training in unfamiliar subjects. I was inclined to think that the experience I had already gained would be enough and could be useful to potential employers in a variety of ways. Perhaps it was inevitable that my mind turned to continuing in some way to work for the Government. Lord Goodman asked me one day what I was going to do. I told him I wanted to do something 'useful.' He replied that I had 'done enough of that' and gave me a strong impression that I should be more self seeking. Later it was suggested to me that I should agree to being considered for Chairman of the Parole Board. This had an appeal until I found how limited his power was and how recommendations of the Board were made only by a study of prisoners' files and not by any personal interviews.

My problems were suddenly solved by two offers from the Government. First, to be a Governor of the BBC and second, to be one of the two government directors of British Petroleum. I readily agreed. The salary at the BBC turned out to be a modest £1,000 p.a. plus a T.V. set, a radio and free copies of the Radio Times and the Listener! I learned that the Director General of the BBC, Charles Curran was not best pleased with the idea. He had previously been Head of the Overseas Service, which had close contact with the Foreign Office and indeed was financed by it. But the Service claimed complete independence and resisted advice and direction although they had access to many Foreign Office telegrams. They justifiably rested on their war time laurels and believed their opposition to Anthony Eden over the Suez crisis had been a brave blow in the national interest. I had often crossed swords with Curran and he found it difficult to admit any fault. But it had been customary and sensible for many years to have an experienced ex Foreign Office official on the Board of Governors. Curran was over-ruled but continued to be a good but argumentative friend. I remained a Governor for five years but was not reappointed by Dr. David Owen.

The BBC is organisationally unique. In my opinion, the relationship between the Governors and the Executives has never been satisfactorily solved then or now. Much depends on the personality of the Chairman. In 1974 he was Sir Michael Swann an exceptional man of great quality who was much admired by the Prime Minister for his Vice Chancellorship during student troubles at Edinburgh University. But some of the Governors felt, as I did, that we were never really taken into the confidence of the executive staff. Much, for example, of future plans was kept concealed and governors were regarded more as opponents than colleagues. A golden rule was that the Governors should never see a programme in advance or hardly ever even know of its existence. Their wishes were not to be complied with, but to be circumvented. The two fellow-governors with whom I felt closest were the Trade Union leader, Vic Feather, who was often a thorn in the side of the executives and Roy Fuller, who at one time combined the Professorship of Poetry at Oxford with the post of Solicitor of the Woolwich Building Society. The BBC staff were justifiably proud of themselves and their products but carried their pride somewhat far and could not, at that time, admit to any error or accept any advice. There were delightfully gifted persons amongst them. Their hostility to commercial television was intense. Those who left to join the commercial television in search of higher salaries or for whatever reason, were looked upon at that time very much as 'political' defectors. The move of Lady Plowden, a governor much favoured by the BBC staff, to commercial television was never forgiven. Some of the shortcomings of the BBC were officially recognised. Lord Annan was commissioned to write a report. Its findings although elegantly written were for the most part evaded by the Corporation.

The choice of the two government directors of B.P. lay traditionally with the Treasury in agreement with the Foreign Office. Times were changing and after the Election in 1974, the Secretary of state for Energy was soon claiming, not without some reason, that he should share in the choice and indeed be the department primarily involved. Neither the Treasury nor the Foreign and Commonwealth Office accepted this and I was greatly pleased to be chosen. Throughout my diplomatic life I had had much to do with B.P. and knew and liked their people. When, after five years in 1978, the question of reappointment arose, Tony Wedgwood Benn, who was Secretary of State for Energy, rebelled against the wishes of the Treasury and Foreign Office and vetoed it. This was disappointing as the company wanted me to continue. Nobody was appointed until the Conservative Government came back into power in 1979.

My government colleague in 1973 was Tom Jackson the bewhiskered leader of the Post Office Trade Union. There was a fierce row about him between the Government and the T.U.C. who claimed that they should have made the choice. As a result Jackson thought it prudent not to accept the modest salary. When I talked to him before our first board meeting together, he said firmly, "I'm me own man!" His common sense proved valuable to the company and also his advice on trade union matters was listened to carefully.

An ex-member of the Diplomatic Service had always been a logical choice for B.P. whilst its main source of oil supply was oil concessions which lay in the Middle East. But the period 1973-8 was the time of the development of North Sea oil. The company's relations with the Government became very much a matter of domestic politics involving questions of taxation and of possible nationalisation. This greatly affected the status of the government directors and the confidence with which the company and government departments regarded them.

It was exciting to be party to the physical development of North Sea oil fields. Great credit must be given to the determination of Eric Drake, the Chairman, who had been in charge in Abadan during the Mossadeq years. He deserves greater recognition than he received. The engineering team responsible were predominantly young men. Their attitude to the novel problems was "it has never been done before, but we think we can do it," and they did. The cost was colossal but no funds came from the Government. I cannot pretend that I felt very much at home when visiting the off-shore rigs when they first went into production. Angela and I were both at the formal opening of the pioneer Forties field by Her Majesty the Queen. At the ceremonial luncheon Angela sat next to Jeremy Thorpe the Liberal leader, he was his usual entertaining self and expressed his confidence that he was eventually to take his place at No. 10 Downing Street. How different was the truth.

It was a proud day for the company and for private enterprise. The BBC reporter Michael Buerk contrived to introduce a sour note into the programme on the opening evening. I objected at the next BBC Governors' meeting and was supported by the chairman Michael Swann. Nevertheless it resulted in a certain amount of press coverage of the claim by BBC journalists about the alleged incompatibility of my being both a Governor and a Director of B.P.

Concurrently with the North sea work was the development in America of the Alaskan oil field and pipeline. I was able twice to visit the sites of this huge project. On the first occasion the climatic conditions in which the work was carried out were fearsome. Later the most imaginative improvements had been made which protected the men on the drilling rigs and accommodated and fed them in conditions of comfort especially adapted to minimise the physical and psychological health risks. The appetites which were generated by work in Alaska were an eye opener.

In April 1974 Angela was invited by Eric Drake to name a super tanker, 'British Renown,' then being completed in Nagasaki by Mitsubishi Heavy Industries. Japanese methods of construction had revolutionised, inter alia, the naming ceremonies. Unfinished ships no longer slid down slipways into the water with a huge rattle of chains after being blessed by a smashed bottle of champagne. 'British Renown' was lying offshore complete, like a new car in a showroom, due to sail on a commercial voyage on the day following the naming. The ceremony itself was both solemn and dignified. Single workers in special uniforms stood at strategic points facing towards the stern of the ship. From a platform, a representative of the builders called to each worker in turn asking him whether the ship fully met its specification in his department. One by one, a single arm was raised in assent. The builders' representative then turned to the B.P. representative, who handed him the cheque, which completed the vast payment. The ship was then named by Angela and a cloud of coloured balloons released. At dinner the previous evening I was seated next to the Mitsubishi Chairman Mr. Koga, who gave me a lecture in hull design, drawing on the menu card with great elegance. The evening concluded with the company song led on a stage by the Chairman with the gravity of a national anthem. I found my time with BP a fascinating education and was sorry that Tony Benn brought it to an end by a dispute between Ministers.

During the time I was with B.P. the question of the ineffectiveness of sanctions against Rhodesia came to the fore. After years of indifference, Parliament and especially the Labour Government, took up the issue. Like Mrs. Ramsbottom in Stanley Holloway's 'Albert and the Lion,' Parliament felt that 'someone had got to be summoned' and the oil companies were a popular target. I was especially interested both from my Foreign Office experience and from my official directorship of B.P. Dr. Owen, the Foreign Secretary called for a report 'on the supply of petroleum and petroleum products to Rhodesia.' The work was entrusted to (Sir) Thomas Bingham

QC and S. M. Gray an accountant. The inquiry caused a certain amount of concern in the Foreign and Commonwealth Office and in B.P. It was published in September 1978 and to the disappointment of the traditional critics of international oil companies, failed to reach the conclusions they hoped for. The authors shrewdly observed that 'any judgment upon this story does, in our opinion, require close attention to the context in which it occurred and such contemporaneous events are an important part of that context.' In other words, events which were acceptable in the nineteen sixties could not be fairly judged in the atmosphere of the late seventies.

The House of Commons was far from satisfied and after a fierce debate in February 1979, decided to set up a bi-party Commission of Inquiry. But the election in 1979 intervened and no legal action was taken against the oil companies. The tortuous tale of Rhodesian sanctions also featured in a Board of Trade enquiry into Lonhro plc, at which Burke Trend and I gave evidence. Neither Trend nor I were impressed by the Report's conclusions. How far it was, in the light of later events, from reality is revealed by its final smug sentence, which reads, 'We believe that Mr. Rowland's (Lonhro's chairman) achievements, will be all the greater if he will allow his enthusiasm to operate within the ordinary processes of company management.'

Offers of private business appointments for me continued. Secretly I would have welcomed an invitation to join the board of the National Westminster Bank in view of my late father's long and successful connection. This, however, was more deservedly later made to (Sir) Alan Campbell a most effective ambassadorial colleague who succeeded Lord Caccia on the board. It so happened that the role of non-executive directors was, rightly or wrongly, becoming more highly regarded and many companies were recruiting them. I was invited to join S.G. Warburg & Co., merchant bankers with uniquely high standards, where Eric (Lord) Roll was a senior executive and Sir Sigmund Warburg was Chairman. Eric had been a colleague in Paris and at the Embassy in Washington as Economic Minister. George Brown had chosen him as Permanent Secretary in the ill fated Economic Department he had set up in 1964 with the incoming Labour Government. Eric had played an important role in the Marshall Plan and in the team of British negotiators for membership of the European Community. He is a genuine European, not only by birth but by experience and has a truly international understanding. He is in many respects ahead of his time in international affairs. Subsequent association with this rapidly expanding bank was an inspiring experience under the impeccable guidance of Henry Grunfeld and of (Sir) David Scholey the star of the younger generation and a product of Christ Church. They both represented the best traditions on which the City once made its reputation. Both the British American Tobacco Company and the Wellcome Foundation recruited me as an outside director, the first in their history. In the case of the Wellcome Foundation, my appointment was owed to Lord Franks my former ambassador in Washington who was the Chairman of the Wellcome Trust, which drew its large charitable funds from the commercial success of the Foundation's pharmaceutical products. On arrival, I found the chairman of it was Andy Gray, one of the few science undergraduates at Christ Church and with whom I had frequently played rugby football. I remained connected with the Foundation when Gray was succeeded by Alfred Sheppard a keen businessman and a thoughtful employer of a large workforce. The Foundation's accelerated success under his leadership, made the Trust one of the largest benefactors of medical research in this country. I found it very satisfying to work for such a world wide company which combined commercial success with a humanitarian objective. He has become a very good friend.

The invitation to join the British American Tobacco Company came as a complete surprise. Sir Joe Thorley, an experienced industrialist, joined with me at the same time. He had survived horrors in a Japanese prisoner of war camp to become the moving spirit in Allied Breweries and British Sugar. We found this rich company embarking on a period of not always successful diversification. The Chairman was the scholarly (Sir) Richard Dobson, the son of a professor, who translated French poetry and quoted Latin to his puzzled colleagues. It was a friendly company which, like BP, made its outside directors feel welcome members of a team. On my appointment I was asked by a Daily Express reporter how a non-smoker could serve on such a company. I replied that the company had very wide cosmetic interests but I did not use those products either. He was content with that reply.

I was proud also to be recruited by Hawker Siddeley, whose aircraft I had heard about since a child. When I joined the company it was in the process, unwillingly, of changing its course. Its aircraft assets were on the point of nationalisation. The Chairman, Sir Arnold Hall, a brilliant scientist with wartime achievements and a dominating industrialist, was trying to maintain its earnings by moving to other activities. I had first had contact with him when he was taking a firm line on the supply of Trident airliners to communist China against the wishes of certain sections of the Foreign Office and the Defence Department. The sale went through, but was not, I believe in the long term profitable. The heart of the company had been in aviation. The transfer of loyalty to other industries was a great achievement of Sir Arnold. The first Hawker Siddeley Annual General Meeting at which I was present gave me a new impression of the Chairman and our shareholders. His speech was a thoughtful and clear account of the difficult situation in which the company found itself in the face of approaching nationalisation of its aviation activities. When the meeting was thrown open to questions, not a single shareholder spoke. Sir Arnold's speech had either satisfied them or been above their heads.

In contrast the shareholders of British American Tobacco were vociferous and, of course, included anti-smoking lobbyists with whom, over a period of time, with patience and courtesy a good natured relationship with the platform was established.

The shareholders of British Leyland were a very different story. I was delighted to accept Lord Stokes' invitation to join his board. There had been many arguments with him in the Foreign Office over the supply of buses to Cuba, strongly opposed by the United States. His view eventually prevailed but he had always been pleasant to do business with. On my first day Stokes explained that his Board had just appointed a new Chief Executive. It had been a particularly difficult choice. The unsuccessful candidate (Sir) George Turnbull soon left the company and made his fame and fortune in creating motor industries in Iran and Korea. There was then no outward sign of the disaster towards which the Leyland Company was moving. The final collapse has been fully documented and is well known. The initiative for its creation by a merger of the biggest British companies had sprung from the Labour Party leadership. I found myself party to the failure of the Company by its uncertain direction, poor workmanship, persistent and savage union sabotage, political meddling and distant city relationships. These shortcomings undermined the usually sound conception of their products and brought the company to its knees. The declining fortunes meant that Lord Stokes could not attend one of the meetings periodically held by the chief European Motor Manufacturers. I was sent as an inadequate substitute with one of the Leyland engineers. The meeting was held in the beautiful Roman home of Giovanni Agnelli, the head of Fiat. I could see from the assembled company that the European motor industry was in the hands of very different people from our own. For me it was a harsh lesson and a great disappointment. For the first time in my life, I was sacked along with the other board members. On its financial collapse the Board was called in by Tony Benn, who, wearing an expression of smugness and triumph, dismissed the whole lot. By his side was Lord Ryder, the Government's industrial adviser. The complete nationalisation of the company was immediate. After a week, Lord Ryder sent for me. In the meantime I had learned privately that Prime Minister Wilson had intervened successfully to question my dismissal. Ryder told me, with contrived sincerity, that he had been worrying all the week how I could be persuaded to stay with the company. I resisted making the reply he deserved.

I stayed with the company for a further period and saw the purge of the unions by the courage of Michael Edwardes, the new Chairman. It was his initiative to forge the link with the Japanese Honda company. I wrongly thought a European partner would have been preferable.

When the plight of Leyland had first become apparent, the largest city bankers had belatedly formed a committee to keep the situation under close review. Lord Stokes was in fact a member of the main board of one of these banks. He repeatedly said in answer to our questions that he believed that the crisis would be overcome with their help. Suddenly the Banks' Committee pulled the rug from under British Leyland and the nationalisation of the company - a prime political objective of Tony Benn - was certain. Some years later I asked one of the bankers who had taken part, if the main board of his bank had been consulted on the fateful decision, which was so politically charged. "Certainly not," he replied, "it was a purely commercial matter, which was the responsibility of the executives only." I am still astonished, if indeed, that was the truth.

During the decline of the company there were stormy shareholders' meetings. British Leyland had an unusually large number of small shareholders. It was a widespread practice for people of modest means, often on retirement, to buy a Leyland car and at the same time, invest some of their savings in the company. When they realised what was happening, their anger was alarming to see. At one meeting the platform came near to being rushed and we were only saved by some shareholders fighting amongst themselves and a defensive speech by Jim Slater a non executive director, who was at that time, a darling of the small investor. Whenever my own name came up for re-election as a director, I could not help noticing that I usually received significantly less votes than the others.

Looking back on my career in commerce and industry, I do not think that I would have made, as my tutor John Masterman said, a better business man than civil servant. Perhaps my Government Service diminished any talent that I might once have had to be an entrepreneur. I do not believe I could have developed a loyalty to a company as great as the loyalty I felt for the Foreign Office. Nor, from my limited observation do I believe that the atmosphere in commerce could have equalled the camaraderie of the Diplomatic Service.

Business for the companies of which I was a director, took me in my new capacity to several of the countries which I knew well as a diplomat. It took me also to countries which I had neglected when I was at the Foreign Office. For example, Brazil, Venezuela and the Caribbean Islands. I was however, occasionally asked by my old office to do official jobs. James

Callaghan sent me to Rhodesia in 1976 and in 1980 Mrs. Margaret Thatcher sent me with a special message for the Indian Prime Minister Indira Gandhi. I had not met Mrs. Gandhi before. She received me in her drab office, dominated by a single, large portrait of her father. She looked ill and talked a long time about being surrounded by enemies and contrived to blame it all on the Americans who were supporting them. It seemed incredible that this lonely old lady, for that is what she seemed to be, ruled over 600 or more million people. I felt great sympathy for her.

In pursuit of my original intention of doing something 'useful' in my retirement, I accepted some voluntary assignments.

I was asked to be Chairman of Kings College Hospital Medical Council. I was glad to try to repay what their Liver Unit had done for my son Robin in 1973. I was involved with the Royal Society of Asian Affairs, the School of Oriental and African Studies, BUPA and the Anglo-Finnish Society. I joined the governing body of Wellington College, whose Vice President was General John Cowley with whom I had served in the War Office and in Egypt and who had been the best man at our wedding in Cairo Cathedral. Another activity, which I still greatly value, is to be a Trustee of the Rayne Foundation, built on the fortune of Max (Lord) Rayne, one of the most generous and self-effacing philanthropists who has been of great help to the National Theatre, to medicine, education and the arts. For three years I was a member of the International Advisory Board of the First National Bank of Chicago, which enabled me to attend some meetings of the most blue blooded board of a Middle Western American Bank. These duties were, of course, spread over nearly ten years and did not always overlap. But I think I can honestly say that I took my responsibility towards them all seriously. Life had become more agreeable by the birth of our only grandchild Aster in 1978.

Free from duty at the Foreign Office, Angela and I were able to go further afield for holidays. The most enjoyable was a three week sea trip from Plymouth to Capetown in a modest Greek passenger ship, which had been chartered by the British Company whose regular ship had been requisitioned for the supply of the Falkland Islands. The ticket for the voyage was the surprise gift from our sons for my 70th birthday. One of the most interesting parts of the voyage was the call at the almost totally inaccessible, St. Helena - Napoleon's place of exile. The island has virtually no port and no airfield. At the Foreign Office I was much concerned for the well being of the island, left over from the break up of the British Empire, for which the Foreign Office was responsible with the inherited parsimony of the old Colonial Office. An airfield at St. Helena had been considered but was rejected as impossible for technical and financial reasons. But in my retirement I had become acquainted with an ex Royal Engineer Officer, Major Charlesworth, who specialised in 'alternative engineering' in under-developed countries. He had devised a plan for an airfield in St. Helena at the cost of about one tenth of the British Government estimates. Together with Lord Shackleton and Lord Buxton, we have for several years, canvassed this plan or some variation of it in the House of Lords and elsewhere.

I was particularly pleased to be able to visit this isolated island to see for myself. We also saw over 'Longwood' the estate of Napoleon's incarceration, which now flies the French flag and boasted, at the time of our visit, a historically minded French consul. As one might expect he was in constant conflict with the British Governor over trivialities.

It had been customary for many years for the retiring Permanent Under Secretary at the Foreign Office to be made a peer. The Life Peers Act of 1958 made such an honour far more appropriate than a hereditary title. Prime Minister Wilson had reduced the number of titles given to members of the Diplomatic Service. I thought rightly so. When the Conservative Government was elected in 1970, an attempt was made by well wishers to restore the number. I did not support them as I believed an excessive number harmed the reputation of the Service. My predecessor, Paul Gore-Booth, deservedly received a peerage, but I expected that he would be the last. I would not have been too downcast if it had proved to be so. However, I received the honour in 1974 and I cannot deny that it gave us both pleasure. Paul Gore-Booth and my Oxford friend, Stormont Mancroft, were the sponsors on my introduction. I have tried to make a contribution by concentrating my work there in many Select Committees as well as speaking from time to time in major debates.

Having told my story so far what is my conclusion? I did not consciously plan my career. Not many do so and achieve what they early aim for. When I finally took my place on the red leather of the cross-benches in the Chamber, I reminded myself that my position had been achieved, as the title of this memoir implies, more by accident than design.

INDEX

Index

Index

Index

Index

Index

Index

Index